POSH AND PERILOUS

BOOK THREE

THE DAVIA GLENN SERIES

LAURA AKERS

ISBN 979-8-9873832-1-6 eBook

ISBN 979-8-9873832-2-3 Paperbacks

ISBN 979-8-9873832-5-4

ISBN 979-8-9873832-6-1

ISBN 979-8-9873832-3-0 Hardback

ISBN 979-8-9873832-4-7 Audible

The Davia Glenn Series

DIOR OR DIE

KILLING WITH KINDNESS

Praise for The Davia Glenn Series

For those who do the right thing,
No matter how difficult

*If ignorant both of yourself and your enemy,
you are sure to be in peril.*
-Sun Tzu

*I don't have any cell service here,
and it's making me have a rash*
-Kris Jenner

ONE

Sherilyn peruses the menu. "What are you going to order, Davia?"

"I've never heard of Branzino, so I'll be adventurous for once and try some."

"That's ironic coming from you," my friend and interior designer says. "Now I know you're a deadly, top-secret, well, whatever you are, my curiosity's eating me alive. I understand you can't share anything, but, like, why didn't I figure it out sooner? I thought you were a nerdy tomboy raised in a commune."

"A commune? Where'd you get that idea?"

"Well, first, you have no clue about anything to do with luxury living. You should see your face when you have to put on designer clothes or when I discuss a unique art piece of furniture that lasts a life-time. Most people would die to have your wardrobe or what I bought for your home, but all I get from you is a blank stare. When I told you the modular sectional I ordered for your living room was $30,000, you didn't blink. I swear you never pay attention to what I say."

"Thirty-thousand, what?"

"Don't worry; I threw in a crazy high number just now as a test. I've suspected for a while that you tune me out when I discuss subjects that don't interest you."

We sit in a booth upholstered with rich, dark leather at a five-star French restaurant in the exclusive community of Rancho Suprema, California. Around us, the jet-set crowd tucks into their meals. Patrons pretend not to notice each other, but hands with sparkling diamonds cover mouths to whisper gossip. Candlelight and relaxing music add to the atmosphere, perhaps to soothe customers before they receive bills totaling as much as a monthly car payment.

I put down the menu. "I'm glad you convinced me to come out. A broken sprinkler in my yard's been the only excitement since last week's fashion show."

"You shouldn't complain—" Sherilyn begins, but a raven-haired woman at a table near us rises so fast her chair falls over.

"You're not going to divorce your wife?" she shrieks. "Did you think informing me in public would keep me quiet?"

"Erica, you need to sit down," her companion hisses. He's at least three decades older than his thirtyish mistress, and his face is a mask of pinched disapproval.

"Or what, Ray? I've had enough of your lies."

"My children—"

"Your 'children' are adults and have nothing to do with this."

"Erica, you're embarrassing me."

"You're embarrassed? *Embarrassed*?" With lightning speed, she pulls her knit top over her head and undoes the clasp of a black brassiere.

Her creamy, perfect breasts spring out.

The man's eyes widen as gasps and titters fill the room.

"Take a long look, Ray, because this is the last time you'll see these." To punctuate her words, Erica picks up her glass of red wine and tosses the contents into his face. The drops stain his white shirt like blood.

Ray sputters and grabs a napkin while Erica gathers her garments and marches away, not bothering to cover herself, back straight and head high.

"Good for you," Sherilyn calls, and the woman's lips curve into a satisfied smile. Ray, red-faced from more than the wine, stumbles after her to a buzz of excited conversation and laughter.

When they're gone, I say, "Should I be shocked or applaud?"

Sherilyn laughs. "The story of their altercation will spread like wildfire. When we hear the tale again, they'll have removed all their clothes, smashed up the place, or run away together."

"Ah, the wealthy and their problems."

We order, and it isn't long before the waiter arrives with our meals. Onions and cherry tomatoes smother my fish, and after taking a bite, I say, "This has a mild and sweet flavor. I'm a fan."

Sherilyn cuts her grilled salmon with the side of her fork. "This is perfect. Chef Paul's food is so impressive. Anyway, can you believe it's May already, and summer fun's around the corner? Are you going to Virginia to see Warden? I bet spending time with him naked would outweigh the heat and humidity."

A flash image of my operative team leader in my bed makes me reach for my wine and take a long drink.

Nothing is easy.

"Can we talk about something else? Wondering how to solve our long-distance relationship woes plague me enough."

"Fine. We can return to discussing luxury furniture."

"Stop tormenting me."

Our conversation becomes general, we finish our meals, and a server presents us with dessert menus. I sit back, relaxed. "Are you full?"

"Life's too short to be anything but happy, and dessert makes me happy."

"It's my treat, so order away."

"I'm taking you up on that since I know you can afford it. How much money did your aunt leave you again?"

"Almost ninety million, but with conditions."

"Even with conditions, you have way more reasons than the dessert menu to be happy."

Scanning the offerings, I wonder what a pear poached in red wine with a chamomile flower would taste like and speculate on the meaning of *Crèmeux*. My aunt didn't provide an instruction manual on the intricacies of life with the rich when she left me her fortune. Perplexed, I order a lemon tart while Sherilyn decides on a deconstructed strawberry shortcake, another menu mystery.

When our hot tea and desserts arrive, Sherilyn's plate is an artful arrangement of cream-covered strawberries and small pieces of cake. She takes a mouthful and sighs with pleasure.

"This is yum! And speaking of yum, what's going on with Adair?"

"You're determined to remain on challenging subjects, aren't you? He's in Europe right now because of a business emergency. He left after the fashion show."

Sherilyn waves her fork at me. "I'm sure you're relieved. Almost any woman would love to be courted by a hot British billionaire, but you? You don't have a problem taking on armed assassins, but when the subject of Adair Monroe comes up, you're ready to bolt."

"You're not wrong."

Perhaps I won't have dreams about him if he stays on another continent.

Wanting off this topic, I ask, "What about Detective Montoya?"

Sherilyn squirms with excitement. "As long as Ric doesn't get a call about a homicide case, we have a date this weekend. We're going to Old Town for a Cinco de Mayo celebration. We'll drink margaritas, enjoy Mexican food, and become better acquainted. We haven't kissed yet, but I almost melted into a puddle when we hugged, so I can't wait."

"San Diego Sherlock's my nickname for him," I say.

"He's smart, isn't he? When we went to the Ladies' League Fashion Show, he said, 'You have a cat,' and picked a small piece of cat hair from my hem. He's like a guided missile."

"Which is why he's so skilled at catching criminals."

"I hope he's as skilled with other things," Sherilyn says with a wink.

After our meal, we go to the front, where an auburn-haired hostess named Sarah is at her station. "Did you enjoy your meals?" she inquires.

"I didn't know you included theater with dinner," I joke.

"I've worked here for over twenty years, and tonight's drama was minor, believe me. I meant to ask when you came in, but are you two sisters?"

We both have fair complexions and blonde hair, but at 5'9", I tower over my petite friend.

Sherilyn loops her arm through mine. "We're not blood-related, but she's my soul sister."

"Chosen sisters are the best kind," Sarah says with a smile. "Did you have umbrellas or coats? It's raining."

We shake our heads.

"I can lend you some," she offers.

"Thanks, but a little rain won't hurt me. You?" Sherilyn says.

"I'm good."

When we step outside, drops pelt a tiered fountain in the courtyard, and high winds cause the branches of a mature pepper tree to wave in an erratic dance. We huddle back into the entryway.

"At least I'm not in heels and a dress," I say, grateful to be in slacks and loafers.

"Right? Since when do we have rain, Southern California?" Sherilyn gripes. "The weather app's forty-percent-chance prediction seemed unlikely, so I didn't bring a coat. Now it's late, and I'll have to watch for drunk drivers *and* idiots who lose their minds when it rains. I mean, it's only water, people."

"You can stay with me if you want," I offer. My home is less than a mile away.

"I'll be fine."

"Where'd you park?"

Sherilyn points. "On the side street."

"I'm the other way. Stay safe."

We exchange a quick hug, and Sherilyn dashes into the storm. Placing my hands above my forehead to shield my face, I hurry across the Spanish-style courtyard and emerge onto the main street's sidewalk. It's nearing eleven p.m., so downtown is quiet, and most businesses are closed.

Crash!

Men in hoodies and black face coverings swarm before a storefront a block away. Several hold crowbars while others go back and forth carrying items to a waiting SUV.

Don't get involved, Wonder Woman. Remember what occurred the last time you rushed headlong into a crime scene.

My still-healing broken ribs are a palpable reminder of the fallout from my involvement in a homicide case. Stepping under the roofline of a real estate office, I call 911.

"911. What's your emergency?"

"Four men are breaking into a business down the block from me in downtown Rancho Suprema." A heavy downpour kills visibility, so I can't read the license on their getaway vehicle.

"Do you know the business's name?" the operator asks.

"I think it's Jenson's Jewelry."

By the time flashing emergency lights appear, the SUV is long gone, the whole operation lasting no more than five minutes. A deputy drives alongside me and rolls down her passenger-side window, rain blasting through the opening and soaking the seat.

"Did you report this?"

"Yes, they went that way about ten minutes ago." I gesture to the empty road.

She accelerates away.

The turbulent wind whips my long hair, strands plaster my face and neck, and my soaked clothing clings to me. I look in both directions and jog across the street. Entering a jasmine-vine trellised walkway leading to a back lot, I fear the latticework will fall apart as the gale buffets it back and forth. I rush along the path, which ends at Bryce's Boutique, a favorite upscale clothing store.

I stop.

The door to the business is open, and shattered glass lies on the ground. Ahead, a different knot of men carries bundles toward a cargo van, the rear open and the interior half-filled.

If this is a coordinated string of thefts, were they off schedule?

Did they wait for the sheriffs to chase the other vehicle so they'd have more time?

What should I do?

Bryce is my friend, but my still-healing injuries remind me again this is not my fight. I back away, intent on retracing my steps to a safe location and redialing emergency services.

Before I can retreat, a lookout carrying a pipe catapults from his hiding place in the shadows. I lash out with a kick, and the blow connects with his knee. He collapses, dropping his weapon.

The pipe crashes to the sidewalk with a loud clang that reverberates above the storm's noise like a clarion call.

The thieves freeze.

Mask-covered faces turn in my direction. Two men charge toward me. I deliver a spinning roundhouse kick to the first man, but my back foot slips on the wet ground. My foot connects with his chin instead of the side of his head, but he staggers back. I punch the second man in the throat, and he bends over, choking.

Stolen goods drop into the back of the van.

Two more men rush forward, one carrying a crowbar.

I go for the firearm concealed in my purse.

Before I raise my gun, the fallen lookout leaps up with his reacquired pipe. I dodge, but the weapon strikes my head, the force slamming me to the wet sidewalk.

"You weren't supposed to hurt anyone," a man yells.

"She's got a gun," my assailant says.

His booted feet jump over me as the surroundings grow hazy.

Everything goes dark.

Two

Strong arms lift me. A man clutches me against his chest and, in reassuring tones, says, "I'm taking you to a hospital. Hang in there."

A car speeds along, bright fluorescent lights in a ceiling blur as medics wheel me on a stretcher, strange, pinging noises sound in a confined space, and a needle jabs the central vein of my arm.

These brief recollections are my only recent memories when I open my eyes. I'm in a hospital bed, the curtains drawn around me.

"You're awake." A man leans over the bed. He's familiar, but I can't come up with a name.

"Lights," I cover my eyes with an arm.

Footsteps sound, and the room grows dim.

"Better?" he asks, and I nod, causing bolts of pain to shoot through my head.

A whimper escapes me.

"I'm going to find a nurse."

A woman in scrubs fusses with the IV drip, and I fall asleep.

"You have a concussion," a doctor informs me, her bright red hair a vibrant contrast to her ebony skin. "We did an MRI, and your brain isn't bleeding. However, you do have a hairline fracture to your skull."

She shines a light into my pupils, and I move around the room without dizziness or nausea overwhelming me.

"When can I leave?"

"You arrived near midnight, and it's not yet seven a.m. It would be prudent for you to stay for observation until tomorrow."

"Bring me the release form."

The doctor's face fills with the same disapproval as the medics before her whose orders I've ignored. "A blow to the head is serious."

So is being shot, breaking bones, or other injuries I've endured.

"The form, please," I repeat.

Spinning on her heel, she leaves without another word.

A man is beside my bed. "What did you say to the doc?"

I blink. Alex Gordon's the last person I expect to be in my room.

"Alex? Why are you here?"

"At least you aren't calling me Jax anymore."

"Jax?"

"I found you last night in downtown Rancho, lying on the ground, soaked from the storm. At first, I thought you were drunk and passed out, but then I saw someone had broken into Bryce's Boutique. When I pushed the hair back from your face, I recognized you. You stared at me and said, 'Jax?' then lapsed into unconsciousness. I didn't want to wait in the pouring rain for an ambulance, so I wrapped my jacket around you, put you in my car, and came here."

"That was kind of you." I sit up while he drags a chair next to the bed.

"Who's Jax, by the way? An old boyfriend?"

My face heats with embarrassment. "I obsessed over *Sons of Anarchy* in middle school, and you resemble the lead actor, Charlie Hunnam. His character's name was Jax."

"So, you like bad boys, do you? I knew you were a troublemaker."

Alex is six feet of lean, toned muscle, with blond-red hair and a closely cropped mustache and beard. Silver and diamond studs dot his left ear, a black arm-band tattoo in an intricate design wraps his right bicep, and the edge of a colorful tattoo peeks out from his collar. In contrast to his edgy appearance, he's a successful ultra-high-net-worth wealth advisor and handles my investments. When we first met, he bluntly complimented my physical assets, and I thought I might have to hurt him.

He sits forward. "What happened? Was it part of the burglaries?"

"The last thing I remember was calling 911 about men breaking into Jenson's Jewelry." I pause. "I have an unrelated question, though. Why are you still here?"

"I wasn't sure who to call since we barely know each other, but my nature isn't to dump and run. I did put your gun back in your bag, though."

"My gun?"

"It was in your hand when I found you. Good thing I've already seen you in action. Most Rancho men would've thought you were involved in the break-in and called the cops."

If I went for my weapon, how did I fail?

A nurse bustles in with a clipboard, and I sign the release.

"Your clothes are in that cupboard, and here are your prescriptions for pain."

I take the paperwork, not intending to fill them.

"While you dress, I'll find a wheelchair," Alex says.

"I can order an Uber."

"You can, but are you sure you're up to life right now? I'm happy to drive you."

A wave of wooziness makes me clutch my stomach. Did I have the stamina to wait outside and identify a car and driver? Should I call Sherilyn? I reject the ideas, unwilling to stay here any longer.

"I appreciate it."

I locate my damp garments in a plastic bag, and putting them on is unpleasant.

I've been through much worse.

When Alex pushes a wheelchair toward me, I say, "Can't I walk out of here?"

"You can try, but why? You're already foolish for leaving early, but you won't be released if you crash face-first to the floor."

I sit, and Alex wheels me to the front of the hospital. "Be back in a sec," he says after securing the brakes.

Southern California's usual blue skies have returned, so he puts on sunglasses and goes toward a parking structure. In minutes, Alex drives up in a sleek silver-gray car and comes around to assist me.

"Stylish wheels," I comment.

"At least the judgment portion of your brain is unaffected. This is a Mercedes AMG One, meant to be similar to Formula One racecars. You have plenty of funds to buy one. They're less than three million."

Three million? For a car?

"I bought a Maserati MC20 and a Land Rover since moving here, which is plenty," I say. "Darn, my car's still in the lot near Bryce's."

"I would normally say car thieves don't plague Rancho Suprema, but now I'm not sure. Do you want to go by before I take you home?"

Extreme fatigue causes me to sag back in the seat. "No, I'll go later."

The other cars on the freeway appear at a standstill as we speed past, and I appreciate Alex's skilled driving. Once on the side road to Rancho Suprema, he slows to avoid debris littering the streets and yanks the wheel to miss a fallen tree branch. "We might find Dorothy and her red slippers," he says.

"Has there ever been a tornado in San Diego County?"

"Not since I moved here from New York, so not in the past four years."

"They were common where I grew up, but I pray they didn't follow me."

"Me, too. What's your address?"

I give directions to my home and provide Alex with the gate code. José Valenzuela Macías, my young property manager, is beside the court-yard entry. A ball cap covers his dark hair, and he holds a rake next to a bin full of refuse from the yard. He leans the rake against a wall, squinting with confusion at my return home in the early morning hours in the company of a stranger.

"I've been in the hospital," I tell José when I get out of the car.

He hurries toward me. "Are you okay?"

"I'm fine."

When Alex joins us, I make introductions and say, "José can help me from here."

Alex puts a hand on his open car door. "You okay for me to leave, LT?"

I ignore his reference to the "Little Troublemaker" nickname he labeled me with at our first meeting. "Yes. Thanks for what you did."

"Make an appointment with me when you're better."

Alex drives away, and José says, "How do you know him?"

"I met him a few weeks ago and have since learned he was Aunt Lilah's money manager and now handles my trust. He found me unconscious on the pavement near Bryce's Boutique last night, which someone burglarized, and took me to the hospital."

"What happened?"

I shrug as I unlock the front door. "I have a hairline fracture to my skull."

José takes my arm. "You can't keep getting hurt. You're still—"

"Recovering from my last fight, I know." Once inside, my knees buckle. José lifts me, carries me to my bedroom, and lays me on the bed.

"What do you want me to do?"

"Give me a second."

"Where's your phone?"

"In my purse."

José retrieves it and places it on my nightstand. "What else do you need?"

"When the room stops spinning, I'll shower and change. If I don't text you in fifteen, come back."

His lifted eyebrows convey he doesn't like my plan. "Last night's storm made a huge mess and will take most of today to clear, so I'll be nearby if you need anything. I'll bring you a glass of water from the kitchen first, though."

After José brings the water and leaves, I peel off my sodden attire and shower. Toweling, I notice the bruises from my last fight are almost gone.

Injuries teach us to be better.

With all the injuries I sustained throughout my career, few people should be better than me. How did I get hurt? While I dress, I think about one of the pre-team tests I endured at age seventeen.

————

"Today's going to be the beginning of testing some of the tactics you've learned," Kyle Kavanagh, my mentor, said.

We were in a wooded location on private property owned by one of his Delta Force friends. I wore a ghillie suit crafted out of strips of canvas painted camouflage colors to look like heavy foliage and secured to canvas netting. When we arrived, I collected local leaves to add from my knees to the ground. My sniper rifle was tied with olive-colored material and bits of canvas to break up the shape.

Kyle and I spent weekends playing invisibility games in war paint and our ghillie suits, seeing who could spot the other first. Now, the test was real. My goal was an "assassination" at a distant location, with Kyle's buddies acting as "enemies."

"What are the rules of a successful stalk?" Kyle asked.

"The closer I get to the target, the slower I go. Each twig, blade of grass, or anything else that makes noise or moves is a giveaway."

"Don't let an enemy catch you. Remember your training." Kyle instructed.

I slipped through the wooded terrain from cover point to cover point. For the last half mile, I crawled with my butt as low as manageable, each hand or foot creeping forward at around thirty seconds per movement. I was aware men with binoculars scanned the area to detect a bush or branch movement, trying to gain a fix on me.

When I obtained a position to attempt a shot at the "target," a dummy figure, I knew the flash of my muzzle might give me away if the concussion moved any of the surrounding flora. After dialing in, I slowed my breathing and made a deliberate trigger pull.

Shot one was a success, and no one came for me. I double-checked for any foliage interference, squeezed off another round, and exfiltrated back the way I came.

Kyle's big grin at the finish conveyed I had passed.

————

"You bested highly-trained operators and joined the most elite team in existence, but a low-level crook took you out," I grouse. Sinking onto the bed, I wrap myself in the thick comforter. Wracking my brain but finding only fragments, I begin to fall asleep.

My phone vibrates on the nightstand, and I bring the device to eye level.

Unknown caller.

Is it Warden? Will I have to pretend I'm okay?

"Hi, Davia! It's Francis. How are you?"

Francis Downs serves with me on the Ladies' League board, the community's most iconic non-profit.

"You never call me. What's going on?"

"Since you're our new Vice President, I wanted to make sure you knew about your responsibilities for putting together the Spring Home and Garden Tour."

I sit up. "The what?"

"Spring Home and Garden Tour. Didn't you read the rule book? It's on our website now."

"Not yet."

"I didn't want Beatrice to ask about your progress at the next board meeting and have her blindside you, so I thought I should call. She can be demanding sometimes."

Sometimes? Beatrice Gibbs, President of the Ladies' League, holds a master's degree in prickly perversity.

"What will I have to do?"

"Three homeowners have offered their properties for the tour. You'll need to go to each location and note which features to highlight."

I want to scream, 'I have zero qualifications, and my interest is even less,' but say, "Can you either text or email me the details?"

"I'll email you. The tour's three weeks away, so I suggest you schedule times with each homeowner now. Our board meeting is next week, and Beatrice will demand an update."

I'm sure she will, and the sacrifice of a goat.

After we disconnect, I text José I'm taking a nap, silence my phone, and fall asleep.

THREE

In the early evening, I wake much restored and request a ride to my car from José. When I get in his truck, he studies me. "How are you?"

"I'm upright and breathing, so it's a win."

He puts the truck in drive. "Since you moved here, you've been through a lot."

"I can't disagree, but you got injured, too. You might quit."

"I won't. I have to live up to the macho stereotype."

The trip is short, but we pass multiple crews of gardeners working to clean flower beds along the road. Spanish-style buildings make up the downtown area, and more laborers sweep fallen leaves into piles and dispose of large branches.

My car is where I left it.

José says, "Are you sure you can drive?"

"The earth hasn't tilted since my nap. I'm going to make a grocery store and mail run. If I have any issues, I'll text."

When he leaves, I retrace my steps to the path near Bryce's Boutique, but nothing about the location helps me remember what happened the night I was injured. The store's front door is open, and a temporary steel barrier covers its shattered frame. Once packed with designer clothing, bags, shoes, and accessories, the store now contains only empty racks, fallen shelves, and broken fixtures like a desiccated skeleton. Bryce and his partner, Ramon, are intent on cleaning the mess, so I knock on the door frame.

Ramon doesn't turn from where he fixes brackets for a shelf. "We're closed."

Bryce also faces away from me and sweeps broken glass near a shattered display cabinet.

"I don't want to interrupt, but I was here last night when the burglary happened."

Bryce turns. "*Quelle?* Davia, do you know who did this?"

"No. It's a long story."

They invite me in. Bryce's dark hair is uncombed, and he's paler than usual.

"We should take a break." Ramon puts an arm around Bryce. He owns Salon Divine, is Black, and is larger than a linebacker, yet both men appear diminished today.

We go to a room containing a table, refrigerator, microwave, and sink.

"Water, okay?" Ramon retrieves three bottles from a case on the counter.

"Sure," I say, and we all sit. Ramon twists the cap off Bryce's bottle and urges him to drink.

"Whoever did this took most of our beverages, " Ramon says. "It's like when the Grinch stole Christmas down to the last can of Who hash. Bryce has insurance, but replacing unique clothing and accessories will be challenging."

"I'm astonished by how much they took," I say.

"Us, too," Bryce says. "Tell us what happened."

"Last night, I went to Château Rouge. Around 11 p.m., I emerged from the courtyard onto the main street and saw men burglarizing Jenson's Jewelry. I called 911, but they were gone when the sheriff arrived. The last thing I remember is approaching your store. Someone knocked me unconscious, which has affected my memory."

"*Je suis choquée!*" Bryce exclaims.

"I suffered no significant damage." I don't mention the fracture.

"Did you go to the hospital?" Ramon says.

"Alex Gordon found me. He drove me to the hospital, hung around, and took me home this morning."

"Alex Gordon? He's always struck me as, how you say, arrogant?" Bryce says.

I nod my agreement. "A fair assessment, at least on the surface."

"This whole incident's been a nightmare, but your injury makes it worse," Ramon says.

"'I wish I could remember."

Bryce covers my hands with his. "Focus on getting better."

"I will. I should let you get back to what you were doing."

As we return to the store's front, Ramon says, "Have you talked to the police?"

"Not yet."

Bryce retrieves a business card from a leather folder on a counter. "This is the detective handling the case."

I photograph the card with my phone and hand it back. "I'll call, but I'm unsure what to add."

"An assault charge might give the thieves a lengthier sentence," Ramon says.

Bryce sighs. "If the police catch them. They disarmed our cameras somehow, so there's no footage."

Saddened by how the crime has changed Bryce from dynamic to despondent, I hug him. "My dad taught me to use a hammer, paintbrush, and screwdriver if you need help."

"*Merci,* but we're almost done."

Ramon says, "This is completely off-topic, but be sure to call Bambi and make an appointment for your hair extensions. You're pushing the time limits for replacement."

Heists, hospitals, and hair extensions.

My life's a catastrophe.

———

Unretrieved mail clogs my post office box, and I take the stack to a table at the front of the building to sort junk into a nearby recycle bin. *The*

Suprema Gazette, a local newspaper, features a front-page photo of me with fashion designer Kincaid Foxx at last month's Ladies' League fashion show. We're on the catwalk, me in his hideous haute-couture creation.

More unwanted publicity, although it fulfills another of Aunt Lilah's requirements to appear on the society pages.

Beneath the paper is a pile of high-quality envelopes with my name and address in fancy calligraphy. Since I haven't given my mailing address to anyone except my parents and Kyle Kavanagh, I'm surprised. Opening one, I remove a heavy piece of stationery embossed with gold lettering.

Please Join Us. The Huntly-Hart Family is hosting an event on....
Who are the Huntley-Harts?

Alex Gordon's sister, Ava, had predicted my appearance on last month's entertainment magazine cover alongside Adair Monroe would result in a deluge of invitations. Now that my noteworthy performance on the catwalk is public knowledge, I surmise these two occurrences are responsible for the surge in unwelcome attention.

"Davia?" Amelia Meadows sorts through a stack of mail beside me. When I moved to Rancho Suprema, she served on the Ladies' League board.

"Amelia, how are you? I haven't seen you since the Ladies' League Gala in March."

She wears her trademark vivid red lipstick, but her black hair is in a softer style than before. When we met, her long-time partner Willie Weston had been murdered, and everything about her was unyielding. Now she appears refreshed.

"I took time off from society but am ready to resurface. I missed the fashion show but heard you wowed the crowd," Amelia says, her Southern roots evident in her voice.

"Say, have you heard of the Huntly-Harts?"

She wrinkles her nose. "High society climbers of the first order, attempting to be part of the 'in' crowd. Why do you ask?"

"Got an invite from them to some party, along with a stack of more from who knows, but I'll decline them all."

"You should go to the Huntly-Hart event."

"You can't be serious. Why?"

"You might loathe the idea, but if you don't accept at least one invitation, you'll only receive more and more."

"Won't people give up?"

"No. They'll think you're so exclusive that everyone will keep after you until you go mad."

That won't take long.

"Are you sure?"

"Davia, what's the worst that can happen?"

Given my experience, a lot.

After placing the mail in the passenger seat of my car, I hesitate. Did I want to go into the Suprema Market? Since I moved here, each trip has been a trial.

A crook defeated me, and now I hesitate to shop for groceries. What's wrong with me?

Entering the market, I pick up a basket and focus on finding supplies for at least a week. In the first aisle, a woman's cart is skewed sideways in the center, and she talks on her cell phone.

"I wanted eighteen-karat gold paint for the trim in my bedroom, but what did they do? They used *fourteen*-karat," she says, voice shrill. "Can you believe it? They ruined the whole effect."

I inch past her and remind myself to hurry.

While I hunt through various packaged pasta in the fourth aisle, a person sidles up beside me. An unremarkable male shopper shoots me an insolent grin and spreads his Burberry raincoat wide.

He wears nothing underneath.

FOUR

Am I hallucinating? I place my fingers on my temples and concentrate. Concluding the naughty nudist's real, I reach for his arm, but he closes his coat and darts away.

Placing my basket on the floor, I go after him, but he's not in any aisle. Rounding the final corner near the meat and deli department, the store manager is before me. A nametag on his broad chest reads, 'Matt.'

"Did a man in a raincoat go past you a moment ago?" I say.

"No. Are you looking for someone in particular?"

I keep my voice low. "A man in his forties flashed me in Aisle Four."

"He what?"

I mime the opening and closing of a garment.

"What did he look like?"

Small and shriveled?

"Five-ten, brown hair, brown eyes, medium build, in a khaki-colored raincoat with black loafers."

The manager makes for the front of the store, and I check the aisles on my way to retrieve my basket, but only shoppers fill them.

Matt comes to find me. "He's gone."

"Do you have security cameras?"

"Yes, but they're on the fritz this morning, and the repair service can't fix them until tomorrow."

"Has anyone complained about conduct like this before?"

Matt makes a face. "No, but nothing shocks me."

"I believe you. How long have you worked here?"

"Too long."

Fatigue replaces the jolt from Rancho Reality. When I pay for my items, I admonish myself for the millionth time to find another place to shop.

———

Once home and done unpacking the groceries, I pour myself a glass of iced tea and sit in a padded chair on the back patio to await the sunset. Scrolling through my phone, I find the email from Francis Downs containing the names of the home tour property owners. Stacey Templeton, Bradford and Hazel Kensington, and...Adair Monroe.

"Why?" The word comes out in a plaintive wail. Adair hasn't contacted me for about a week, and the chance another woman caught his eye relieves me and...what?

He's out of the country.

Forcing myself to terminate needless thoughts, I read on. The pre-contact tour person listed for Adair's estate is Jason McCall. It figures. The former MI6 agent might kill and bury me somewhere on the thirty-two-acre property since he's made no secret he's labeled me a threat to Adair's safety. While I contemplate how to approach the problem, a video call from Warden chimes.

"Hi, gorgeous." He sits before his laptop, dark hair damp from a shower and a towel slung low around his hips. His handsome face and sculpted body make me want to walk right through the phone and into his arms.

Pushing away the longing, I force cheer into my voice. "Did you dress up for me?"

A corner of his mouth lifts as he reaches toward the knot holding everything in place. "I can drop this if you want."

"No."

"No? Why not? Nothing you haven't seen before." He gives me a wicked grin.

"I miss you enough already."

His grass-green eyes gleam. "As long as we're on the same page."

"We are, James Warden, and you know it.

"At least I don't have to take cold showers like I did when you worked with us."

"You took cold showers?"

"How else could I appear disinterested? It would've been obvious otherwise."

The image of him toweling his wet hair in the team's locker room and my first full view of his nude, impressive physique flashes through my mind. "So, besides calling me up to be a major tease, how are you?"

He leans nearer to the screen and frowns. "You don't look so good."

"Uh—"

"What happened?"

"It's embarrassing to talk about."

"What is?"

"Last night, Sherilyn and I had dinner in downtown Rancho Suprema, and I interrupted a burglary." I relay what happened after that.

Warden sits up straighter. "Someone knocked you unconscious?"

"Yes, but I got released early this morning."

"You mean you released yourself."

"You'd do the same, so don't be a hypocrite."

"Any after-effects?"

"I was a little unsteady but came home and slept. When I woke, José took me to my car, and I ran errands and chased some weirdo who flashed me at the grocery store."

"I hope you caught him. Wait, maybe I don't."

"By the time I went after him, he disappeared."

"Back to the burglary. How did someone get past your skillset?"

"Not sure, but the person who found me said I held a gun. It had to be more than one person or an armed robber to make me go for a weapon."

"You might have done something you shouldn't have."

Remembering our recent heated exchange when I chose to insert myself into a dangerous situation, I say, "Are you assuming I did something wrong?"

"I'm not saying that."

"That's how you make it sound."

Warden crosses his arms, exposing the side scar gained when an enemy combatant attempted to gut him with a knife. "Since you left the team, you've gotten injured more than when you worked with us. Either you're becoming careless or—"

"I'm not. Kyle Kavanagh recently scolded me about my lessened effectiveness, and I'm cautious."

A few seconds slide by before Warden says, "Fine. Let's drop it. How's your leg?" He refers to the gunshot wound I received in Africa on my last mission with the team.

"It's giving me less trouble, but I haven't pushed myself. Kyle advised me to rest and let the nerve damage heal."

"Are you telling me the truth?"

"Warden," I pause. "We should agree to be honest with each other. We pretend to be okay for work, but we're a couple now."

"We are, but—"

"No buts. I think we shouldn't hide anything. We fought when I kept quiet about going to the homicide scene."

"What exactly do you mean by not hiding anything?"

"We should open up about what's happening in our lives."

"If I share the daily weight of my job, when you come back..." His hesitant words trail off.

"If we were only teammates like before, sure, but what will happen if we can't share our feelings now?"

"Are you saying this because of that other guy?"

"I realize you don't like to say Adair's name, but yes."

"Yes?" His voice is as sharp as a gunshot.

"Since I met Adair, I think about his advice because—"

"Because he's a cover model billionaire who can't keep his hands off you," Warden interrupts.

"I'm trying to have a serious conversation."

"So am I. Davia, we worked together for three years, and I fought my attraction to you the entire time. Now I have to compete for your affection."

"It's not a competition."

"It isn't? That Brit said otherwise, and he was damned plain with his words."

"All I'm saying is Adair encourages me not to stuff my feelings, and I think you and I should be more open."

Warden's forehead creases. "What do you mean?"

"We lock ourselves down to deal with our missions and never admit how wrecked we are. Adair doesn't think that's a healthy way to live."

"He doesn't, does he?" Warden says. "Has he ever done our jobs? No. Should I call you and whine because a mission demolished my body, a bullet made me spring a leak, or I woke up soaked with sweat from nightmares?"

"Yes."

"Yes? Why would you want to hear stuff like that?"

"Why not?"

"Davia, we're warriors. We don't run off course due to injuries and emotions."

When I don't say anything, Warden says, "I think you need to get away from Rancho Suprema. I have some vacation time coming up soon. Do you want to fly out to Colorado? I'm going home and would love for you to meet my parents."

"Your parents? Um, I—"

"Don't freak out. I'm not proposing or anything."

"You're not?" I give him an exaggerated pout. "You sent me a text saying you love me, so it's the next logical step."

Warden scowls. "I told you Ned sent that text when he somehow unlocked my phone. If there's a way to cause trouble, he'll find it."

Ned's our team prankster and I believe Warden, but I fight to keep from laughing at his discomfort.

"So, you don't feel that way?" I press.

"You're enjoying this way too much. Besides, I need to say those words in person."

"I'm pretty sure you're employing a delaying tactic."

Warden's face softens. "I plan to make my feelings clear when I tell you. Since that Brit said he intends to steal you from me and plans to explore your deepest secrets, I don't want you to think I'm making a casual declaration to beat his game."

The timbre of his low voice, coupled with the intensity of his gaze, makes me turn my head as I blink back tears.

Stop hiding your emotions after asking him to share.

"Are you crying?" Warden's eyes are huge.

I swallow and nod. "I said we should be honest. It's difficult to be away from you."

"Come to Colorado, babe." His voice is gentle. "It'll give us time to relax, fish, or do nothing."

I give him a shaky smile. "Nothing?"

"Well, nothing we don't want to do."

"I have an obligation this month," I say. "Are you on a vacation deadline?"

"No. What is it this time? Another fashion show?"

"Worse. I'm responsible for coordinating a Home and Garden Tour."

Warden can't disguise his amusement. "You'll need to brief the team so we can use your new skills in the field."

"Stop. It's bad enough."

"Text me the dates, and we can make plans."

———

When the sun goes down, I go in to fix dinner. While I wait for the oven to preheat, I replay my conversation with Warden. What did I expect from him when I mentioned opening up to each other? We were in different places in more than a literal sense.

My voice is in my sword—a quote from Shakespeare's Macbeth and how my team dealt with our missions. Our training and effectiveness spoke for us; our mindset was on success, not consequences. Was it wrong to expect him to remove his invisible armor?

Bringing myself back to the present, I take in the details of my opulent kitchen. The granite counters gleam golden brown with white swirls, the Viking range features six burners, the upright refrigerator and freezer are Sub-Zero, and the cabinets are custom wood. The lush beauty of my surroundings, contrasted with my previous life, causes my head to hurt.

Will the after-effects of the concussion cause more than short-term memory loss?

The sting of my defeat by an unknown person remains, and I don't want further problems, so I decide to play Kim's Game, a daily routine during my training to improve my recall of details. I shut the pantry door and center my concentration.

Twelve objects. Ten seconds.

Go.

When I open the door, I use a basic strategy, studying the objects to my left for the prescribed time. I shut the door and write what I recall on my phone.

A case of bottled water, crackers, cereal, oatmeal, peanut butter, spaghetti, pasta sauce, flour, protein bars, chicken broth, soup cans....

What type of soup? How many cans? My peak skills would've allowed me to remember colors, contents, and manufacturer names. Now...soup.

The oven beeps, and I retrieve a chicken pot pie, put it on a baking sheet, and pop it in. I perform additional pantry drills but struggle to recall all the items accurately.

"From a daily exercise to can't remember when. Less than three months in Rancho, and you've gone soft," I say aloud.

To stop my spiral of self-flagellation, I inspect the home tour list again.

Think of the tour as a mission. Gather facts and allies, and prepare.

Who's an ally in Rancho Suprema besides Sherilyn? I didn't want to bother her because her booming interior design business ran her ragged. After weighing options, I think of Bob Brooks, the realtor who sold me my property. He's in his sixties, a long-time resident of the area, and a member of the Ladies' League with his wife, Alexandra.

"Davia! It's so lovely to hear from you," he says when I call. "How's Kyle?"

"Every time we talk, he mentions coming back to play golf with you."

"I hope he does."

"I called because I'm coordinating the Ladies' League Home and Garden Tour this year. Francis Downs sent me the property owner names, and I wanted some insight."

Bob laughs. "Prudent of you."

I read him the names, omitting Adair.

"Stacey Templeton's the only person who might be odd."

"In what way?"

Bob hesitates. "She's eccentric, is all. Nothing you can't handle, I'm sure."

"And the rest?"

"Some people in Rancho Suprema are ultra-rich, and the Kensingtons are among them."

"Are they unfriendly?"

"They're in a different stratosphere from most of us because of their immense wealth, but I never found them off-putting."

"I'm relieved. I won't be as unnerved. What have you been up to?"

"I have a couple of new listings, but our daughter's getting married at the end of June. We love the young man who'll be our son-in-law, and Alexandra spends all her time helping with the wedding planning."

"Congratulations."

"We're beyond excited. Say, when you schedule an appointment with the Kensingtons, would you mind if I tag along?"

"No, why?"

"They've never opened their property to tours, held parties, or at least any they invited me to. I've heard astonishing rumors about their place, so I'm curious."

"I'll appreciate the backup."

My concerns ease after we conclude our call, and my mood lightens. The oven dings, indicating my comfort food is ready, and I resolve to eat, go to bed early, and schedule tours first thing the following day.

FIVE

White wooden gates emblazoned with the initials S and T greet me when I arrive at Stacey Templeton's property. That morning, she invited me to come over immediately. When I touch the monitor buzzer, the gates open, and I drive past mature trees, manicured lawns, and beds of flowers bordering the gravel driveway, ending at an immense residence.

Parking before the home, I open my car door and stop. Peering up at me is a white male turkey with a red head wearing a—hat. The creation has four cherry blossom branches jutting from a pink fabric flower. A hot pink band tied under the bird's chin secures the piece.

"Hello," I say to the turkey, wondering if I might get hurt by friendly fowl.

A brunette woman in her fifties bustles out the front door. She's in a cream knit outfit and a hat matching the turkey's, but in a larger size.

"Hello, hello! I'm Stacey Templeton, and I see Tiberius Torston Templeton IV has welcomed you. He doesn't like too many people, so you must be an old soul with a high vibration and clear aura."

"Uh—"

"Relax, he doesn't bite."

Tiberius totters beside me like an escort to where Stacey waits beside her front lawn, which features a fifteen-foot-tall brass sculpture of three turkeys in flight. "Each of these winged beings lived with me, and I memorialized them when they moved on to the Great Wilds in the Sky."

Does my poker face still work?

"Do you mind if I take notes? I need to put together descriptions."

"Go ahead, dear," Stacey says, and I take down the artist's name and wonder what other information would be pertinent. Cost? How the sculptor ensured the turkeys were life-like replicas? Did I want to know?

When I finish typing on my phone, we go inside. The home is three stories in the center, with two-story sections on either side. Stacey leaves the front door open, and the turkey enters.

"Is he allowed in the house?" I say.

"Of course. He's my shadow."

Ahead is an open space with black-and-white marble patterned floors and a crystal chandelier suspended thirty feet above us. "The chandelier is a replica of an antique piece I tried to buy at a Sotheby's auction. The original sold for over $800,000," Stacey says.

"Mm," I murmur.

Barely three months of luxury living and ridiculous prices don't faze me.

The chandelier has a central column of gold from which ornate, draped crystals hang like teardrops. Eighteen electric candles sit on gold bases, and their reflected light cause the crystals to glitter.

"The original, made by one of St. Petersburg's most celebrated neo-classical craftsmen, came from Russia's Pavlovsk Palace and Empress Maria Feodorovna's bedroom."

I attempt to spell the empress's surname but am sure I'm dead wrong. "Who made it?"

"You'll be able to find the information online."

"What else would you like featured?"

"The house is 18,000 square feet with eight bedrooms, eleven bathrooms, a theater, a kitchen, a servant's kitchen, formal and informal dining rooms, an office, a gym, an outdoor kitchen—the usual. I'm proudest of my closet."

"Oh?"

"It's two-and-a-half stories high and around 3,500 square feet. Would you like to see it?"

"Sure."

To our right is a sloping staircase with ornate wrought-iron railings. The turkey heads in a different direction when we go up the stairs. When we reach the second level, he struts toward us.

"How did he beat us here?"

"He took his elevator."

"His elevator?" I repeat, unable to stop myself.

"I clip his wings to ensure he doesn't take flight, and stairs are too much for his little legs." Stacey indicates a turkey-sized door with a button. "I trained him to use it. Turkeys are clever. They can recognize faces and voices and remember the details of a big area. They also have keen hearing and sight."

Stacey continues along the hall, and Tiberius trails after us.

"How long do turkeys live?"

"Up to ten years. As a teen, I began keeping turkeys as companions and named the first one after my favorite grandfather. Triple T, as I called him for short, was brought home by my dad to be served as our Thanksgiving meal. When he began to purr and rub against me, I stopped the notion of eating him."

"Turkeys purr?"

"Yes. Triple T4 is house-trained, too. He responds to voice commands, loves to sing along to music, and plays hide-and-seek. Here we are."

Glass doors glide open at our approach, and we enter. Ahead is a wall of at least one-hundred cubby holes with matched hats on stands, one for humans, one for turkeys. Stacey flicks a switch, and spotlights come on inside each case.

"I keep them in glass to prevent the hats from getting dusty," she explains.

We ascend a central spiral staircase to three levels filled with more outfits, gowns, shoes, bags, and cabinets for jewelry than Bryce's Boutique at its fullest. I recognize the red-soled Christian Louboutin shoes and Chanel handbags but lump the other items into a catch-all "will break the bank" category.

Stacey gestures to a wet bar. "Would you like some champagne? I know it's not noon, but having some bubbly when I dress is fun, so I keep this fully stocked. I also use this space for parties and fundraisers."

"I'm not much of a drinker, but thank you. Do you want to include the closet in the tour?"

"Of course, it and the turkey playroom are my favorite places."

Turkey playroom? If it's like the BDSM room from *Fifty Shades of Grey*, I'm out.

"We'll have to add extra security if you let people in here."

Stacey waves off my words. "They're Ladies' League members. Rich people don't steal."

"That's not true."

"I love you're cautious, but I'm not worried."

The turkey playroom possesses a sandbox similar to the boxes cats use for waste, miniature chairs, sofas, and a four-poster bed. Picture windows frame the backyard, with a nest of straw in a box so Triple T4 can enjoy the view.

"Is there a downside to having a turkey for a—companion?" I almost said pet but caught myself.

"Well, they're rather clumsy. They crash into things and trip over slippers, stuff like that. When T4's angry, he becomes destructive. I had to replace a lot of furniture when he went on a rampage."

While Stacey shares this, T4 hops onto the bed and shuts his eyes. Stacey lowers her voice. "Time for Tiberius's nap. Turkeys sleep often, so if we're quiet, we can meander through the gardens before he wakes."

When the tour concludes, my energy wanes, and an uncomfortable pain in my head makes me rub my brow as I drive home, irritated by my vulnerability. I hadn't fast-roped from a helicopter, been on surveillance in a building with rats as giant as dogs, or had a bullet from my sniper rifle pierce my target. My biggest challenge was not reacting to Stacey Templeton and Triple T4.

The stack of mail I discarded on the kitchen table draws my eye. Amelia Meadow's advice comes back to me, and I decide to respond to the only invitation I've opened. Locating the contact information for the Huntly-Hart family, I input the listed number.

After several rings, the call goes to voicemail.

This. Is. The. Huntly-Harts!

Four different children's voices announce the words.

If. You're. Coming. To. Our. Party…Leave your name!

Others say the remaining words, and I want to disconnect but recite my name and number.

"Weirdest RSVP message ever." My headache intensifies, and I go toward my bedroom to lie down when the front doorbell rings.

"Hi, Davia! I wasn't sure you'd be home," Sherilyn chirps, beaming at me. "I finally got the window treatments for the guest house, and I don't have time to install them today, but I dropped them off. You're all dressed up. Are you going somewhere?"

"Been out and back already. Do you have time to come in?"

We pour ourselves glasses of lemonade in the kitchen and sit on a couch.

"You have on some of your despised designer clothes, but your complexion is full-on ghost. Are you still having problems from what happened last month?"

"No, this is new."

"New?"

I relate what occurred after we parted company at Château Rouge, and Sherilyn's face is a mix of anger and disbelief. "Why didn't you call me?"

"I didn't want to bother you."

"Davia," Sherilyn places her glass on the coffee table more forcefully than necessary. "I'm becoming used to your 'the world might be ending, but I'm fine' attitude, but you need to call me. You might have memory issues, but you must remember our friendship discussion."

"I do."

"You do? Why didn't you at least text?"

"It's not a habit I have."

"Before you moved here, what did you do when things went wrong?"

"Relied on iciness and sarcasm?"

Sherilyn lets out a huff. "Did you tell Warden?"

"He video-called me and, of course, spotted I was unwell."

"Is he able to fly out to be with you?"

"No, but he wants me to vacation with him in Colorado soon."

"Though a statue has more emotion than you most of the time, you clearly miss him." Sherilyn picks up her lemonade again. "I heard about the burglaries but never thought you'd get involved, although I'm not surprised, given how you run toward danger. Alex Gordon taking you to the hospital is more difficult to believe than the rest."

"Perhaps there's more to him than we realize."

"Perhaps. On another subject, have you cleaned this place since you moved here?"

I frown. "I dust and vacuum."

"I'm not saying it's messy or anything, far from, but you should hire a housekeeper or use some service. This residence is a lot for one person to manage."

"I don't want random people in and out of my property."

"You should ask José if he knows anyone." Sherilyn stands and picks up our empty glasses.

"I'll take those."

"What you'll do is go lie down. I swear, Davia, I'll have to move in here as your full-time nurse if you don't take better care of yourself."

"I'll go rest, I promise. Hey, are you free on Friday evening? I'm going to a party and—"

Sherilyn's face falls. "Sorry, but a friend from college will be in town. A party? You never like those. Why are you going?"

I fill her in on the stack of invitations, Amelia's advice, and the RSVP message for the Huntly-Harts.

"I've never heard of them, and that's a good thing from the sounds of it."

"Do you have a second to help me choose an outfit? I'm still a failure at making those decisions."

"What are the party details?"

I retrieve the invitation and hand it over.

Sherilyn scans the card. "It's an all-white party, meaning you must wear white."

The last time I wore white, a sniper laid down gunfire.
"I have a white dress but wore it to a party last month."
"Since Bryce's is closed, do you have anything else?"
"No idea."

Within a few minutes of entering my walk-in closet, Sherilyn picks out a pair of white pants and a flowing white blouse with elaborate sleeves and lays them on the island.

"Pair this with gold earrings and a necklace, and you'll be fine."

"I argued with Bryce about buying anything white because I'm sure to spill food or drink down the front."

"Don't be silly."

"A drunk at Adair's bash dumped a glass of red wine on my pants. I expect disaster."

Sherilyn does a quick rub with her hand on my upper arm. "It never ceases to amaze me what a stress case you are about parties and events. Go have fun and stop being so apprehensive. Attending this shindig will be tame compared to your top-secret job."

"Famous last words."

SIX

On Friday morning, I enter Salon Divine.

"Hi, Bambi," I greet the willowy blonde receptionist. "I have an appointment at ten with Ramon."

"He's not here yet because he's so stressed out from what happened to Bryce's store. He hasn't been booking early appointments and is often late, which is so unlike him."

"When will Bryce be able to reopen?"

"Not for several more weeks. He and Ramon are flying to New York tomorrow to review some inventory from designer friends' collections. Bryce is popular, so many in the fashion industry want to help him get back on his feet. What's new with you? I saw your photo on the front of the *Suprema Gazette* with Kincaid Foxx. Was Adair there?"

Was he ever.

"Yes." I think of listening to his steady heartbeat while he held me.

Bambi picks up a magazine on her desk and flashes the cover of Adair kissing me at the Ladies' League gala beneath the headline 'Who's Adair's Mystery Girl?.'

"I *screamed* when I saw this cover," she says. "Ramon came in, worried. But when he saw this, he also screamed. You two are such a stunning couple."

We aren't a couple; we aren't a couple.

Ramon rushes in. "I'm sorry I'm late. Give me a minute, and I'll bring you back."

Bambi lifts her long hair into a stylish twist in one move, securing it with a clip.

I can swim half the length of a football field underwater, but I can't manage to fix my hair.

Bambi observes my envy. "If you want, I can teach you how."

"I'm sure I'll be inept."

Ramon reappears. "Come on back."

I don a black smock and sit in his chair. "How are you and Bryce doing?"

Ramon lifts a shoulder, mouth downturned. "Bryce can restock, but he put his whole soul into the business."

I picture Bryce zipping around his store, selecting perfect outfits for exacting customers, or helping a clueless person like me. "The first time I went to his boutique, I didn't plan to buy much but left with almost more than I could carry."

"We joke his skill is to make customers *buy*-curious."

"I spend way more than I intend each time, so his strategy works."

Ramon scrutinizes my hair. "Your extensions are holding up rather well. Have any memories come back?"

"I get a hazy image of someone jumping over me, but I'm unsure how much is real. What did Jensen's lose? Do you know?"

"Everything, same as us. The thieves cleaned out all their inventory and removed their safe."

"They took a safe?"

"A full-sized one."

"They weren't there long, so they must've planned. Perhaps they cased the store before the theft."

"Bryce's store got some recent publicity from an online TikTok influencer's viral post, so there's been quite a number of new customers."

"Did anyone seem suspicious?"

"No, and most purchased expensive items."

"What was in the post?"

Ramon scrolls up a video on his phone and hands it to me.

An attractive young woman films the exterior of Bryce's Boutique while she narrates with excitement. The clip cuts to the interior, where she pans the store and fusses over some costly items. She makes Bryce smile into the phone before he rushes away to help a customer. The video has over 500,000 views, with many likes, comments, and shares.

I hand the phone back. "The video could've put his store on some criminal's radar."

"We were excited by the flood of new business, not realizing the downside. When we restock, we'll install an upgraded security system."

"You might also install bulletproof glass because it's tough to break."

"Good idea."

Several hours later, my hair is glamorous perfection. Annette, the manicurist, gave me a mani-pedi after Ramon finished. Now, layers of blow-dried blonde hair spills down to my shoulder blades, and my nails are French-manicured.

"We're going to hire an esthetician soon, so be sure and book an appointment," Ramon says. "In addition to micro-needling, chemical peels, and other treatments, we're bringing in a buccal facial massage expert to release jaw tension and increase lymphatic drainage."

Another service I didn't have a clue about.

As I pay the exorbitant fees, Bambi says, "You're radiating a major glow up. Is Adair taking you somewhere tonight? "

"He's in Europe."

"Too bad. I can't wait for more photos of you two."

I manage a tight smile. "I doubt there'll be many."

"Davia, please come back if you want to learn a few easy styles," Bambi says. "I'm not the best at much, but I have a talent for hair."

———

I'm waiting for the gates of my property to open when my phone rings.

"Hey, Kyle."

"What's happening?"

"Guess."

"In the old days, when you were my neighbor or worked with your team, I had clues, but since you moved to Rancho Suprema, the options in your community make predicting what you're doing impossible."

"I'm off to another party."

Kyle chuckles. "Last time I came out, I went to enough to last a lifetime."

"You went to *one*."

"One too many. Do you have a weapon?"

"I brought my 9mm, extra ammo, and a knife."

"You might need more."

"True."

"Anything else happening?"

I idle my Rover in the driveway, happy for an excuse to delay my arrival at the party. "I'm point for the Ladies' League Home and Garden Tour."

"Another mission fraught with peril."

"You have no idea how right you are." I describe Stacey Templeton and her turkey. "Bob Brooks will accompany me to one of the pricier estates."

"Give him my regards, and tell him I plan to test his golf game again soon."

"I will."

"Other than all this society nonsense, how's life treating you?"

When I don't respond, Kyle says, "What happened?"

I tell him about the burglaries and my injury, and his exhale is so clear it's like he's sitting next to me.

"Have you figured out how some thug got you?"

"No. And before you lecture me, I didn't court danger."

"Are you telling me the truth?"

"Warden asked me the same question, which led to a conversation about how we should be more open with each other."

"Bet that went well."

"About as you'd expect. Not complaining is our norm, but we're in a relationship now. I don't want secrets."

"Are you ready for that?"

"I think so."

"What about Warden?"

I pause. "He's less inclined."

"He's still in the mix. I wouldn't push him."

"We plan to vacation in Colorado when I'm free from this Ladies' League obligation. Discussing anything over the phone is limiting."

"That's true. How's your gunshot wound?"

"I've been taking it easier with workouts and spending time in my sauna. So far, so good."

"I should let you go so you don't miss the party."

"I think not attending would be best all around, but since the fashion show and my rumored relationship with Adair, the stack of invitations is at least a foot high. No one has my email, or the evites might exceed my storage limits."

"Why don't you ignore them?"

"I got advice if I don't attend at least one, people will continue to pester me."

Kyle doesn't say anything.

"Kyle? You're laughing, aren't you?"

"I clamped my hand over my mouth, but you might have heard my shoulders shaking."

"Thanks for the sympathy."

"Anytime. Text me when you're home."

"It'll be late in South Dakota."

"I don't sleep much and never sleep until you make it back alive."

Tears well in my eyes when he utters the phrase he used before my missions.

"I'll report when I'm clear; I love you."

"Love you, too, kiddo, be safe."

SEVEN

A long line of Mercedes, Porsches, Bentleys, and other expensive vehicles move up a drive to where valets wait. I suck in a deep breath for four seconds, hold for four, release for the same amount of time, then don't intake a breath for another four, a calming exercise from my operative days.

Grocery stores, hair styling, parties...my recent fears are absurd.

Once I surrender my Land Rover, I follow chattering attendees clad in white toward the front of a sprawling multi-level mansion.

"The Huntly-Harts may be nouveau-riche, but that doesn't stop me from enjoying their expensive wine."

"We bought a cheetah for a pet and bribed people to bring it into the country. Why is having one illegal? They're only big cats."

"I heard Adair Monroe's engaged to some woman no one's ever heard of. She must be a gold digger."

Were my grinding teeth audible? I hang back until the crowd enters the stately home, mulling whether I should leave, the valet ticket still in my hand.

The invitations will only continue.

An average-looking man and a statuesque blonde in a white sequined dress paired with dazzling diamonds smile as they welcome people. The entry features twenty-five-foot high ceilings and white oak floors. When the woman sees me, her face brightens, and she grasps both my hands.

"I'm honored you're our guest today, Ms. Glenn. I'm Samantha Huntly-Hart." Her diamond cluster ring is so massive I'm concerned the edges might scratch me.

I remove my hands and step further away.

"Christopher, this is Davia Glenn," Samantha says to her husband.

"Oh?" He cranes his neck toward the entry. "Is Adair with you?"

My eyes are slits. "He's in Europe on business."

Momentary disappointment crosses their faces.

Samantha says. "Before you go in, you're required to sign a media release." She motions to where their staff holds clipboards with documents.

"A media release?"

"We're influencers, so professionals are filming this for use on our live stream."

Before I can say anything, a hand touches my back, and Alex Gordon is beside me. "She's not signing anything, and if you use Ms. Glenn on your social media without permission, Mr. Morgenstern, her New York lawyer, will make a call to his West Coast branch of litigators."

"But, she's engaged to—" Samantha begins.

"How would you like to own this place?" Alex asks me. "*Or*," He rolls the word and extends it. "perhaps these kind people won't have you sign anything."

"But, but..." Samantha sputters.

Alex arches an eyebrow at the Huntly-Harts.

The line of people behind us watches with avid interest. "She won't need to sign," Christopher says.

"Please enjoy yourselves," Samantha says with complete insincerity.

We make it several feet when two men bar our progress and thrust clipboards at us. Alex glowers at the hosts, and Samantha excuses herself, grabs the staffers by the elbows, and marches them away.

"Ready for some wine?" Alex wears a white V-neck t-shirt, white pants, and neutral leather sneakers.

"I'm beginning to believe you're a wolf in sheep's clothing. You came to my rescue again."

"My pleasure, LT. I thought this party would be yawntastic, but scaring the hosts was amusing."

A server approaches, and we each take a glass of white wine from his tray. "Dinner's being served in a tent on the lawn in the back," he says.

We pass bouquets of white roses, hydrangeas, and other flowers, scenting the air with delicate perfume. More staff circulates with silver trays of hors d'oeuvres filled with white cheeses on crackers.

"How are you doing since I last saw you?" Alex says when we make it onto an extensive patio.

"The first few days, I needed to nap more often, but I'm okay now."

"I'm not surprised you bounced back fast."

"Or I have a hard head. Do you know the Huntly-Harts?"

"Not well. Encountered them at a local concert and thought it might be an opportunity to sign new clients for my business, but I think I'm out of favor now."

"I'm sorry."

"Don't be. Influencers can be a pain with their over-inflated sense of self-worth. I've worked with a few and got tired of the hand-holding real quick. Want something to eat?"

"Sure."

We cross a lawn to a tent where tall, clear vases of white flowers sit between silver chafing dishes on a serving table. White chairs surround circular tables with white floral centerpieces, and masses of white balloons with LED lights float on the tent's ceiling.

"Would you like some cod, lobster, and scallops?" a server inquires. "The side vegetables are cauliflower, white asparagus, mashed potatoes, or rice."

"Why do I want ketchup?" Alex says to me, and I stifle a laugh.

The final server in the line details a separate tent with desserts on the opposite end of the lawn.

"Want to place bets on what the desserts are?" Alex says as we find a table and sit.

"Okay. What's the prize?"

His eyes move along my body in a slow once-over. I stiffen, but his lips quirk. "Relax, LT. I'm messing with you. Two men almost came to blows at the Ladies' League fashion show because they each desire you, so I'll wait until your little love triangle works itself out."

Adair and Warden. "Then what's the bet?"

"Hm, how about you take me to the pistol range if you lose?"

"And if I win, what do I get?"

"I already offered you the best—myself— so how about a day at the Safari Park? Have you been?"

"No."

"It's part of the San Diego Zoo, east of here."

"That would be fun."

Alex hands me his phone. "Type your guesses, and I'll put mine in yours."

Between bites, we enter our list of possibilities and trade back.

"Either way, I win," Alex says.

"What do you mean?"

"More time with you."

Before I can respond, two women approach our table.

"Alex, Davia!" Brittany Guinn and Kennedy Connors speak almost in unison. They're rail-thin influencers who modeled with me at the fashion show and carry plates of food I know from experience they won't touch.

"Davia, we heard you and Adair got engaged," Brittany says as she sits. "Congratulations!"

"You must be *so* excited," Kennedy says. "Picture seeing him naked on a daily—"

"Ladies," Alex interrupts. "Do you think Adair Monroe's a cheapskate?"

"Of course not," Brittany exclaims. "His generosity's legendary."

Alex takes my left hand and points to my empty ring finger. "Then why isn't Davia wearing a rock the size of Gibraltar?"

A flush creeps over my face at the thought of an actual engagement to Adair. Alex is right. He would splurge on a spectacular ring.

Put Adair's aquamarine eyes, dark with desire, out of your mind.

"I guess our sources were wrong," Kennedy pouts. "Excuse me. I'm going to do a video of the food." She throws down her napkin and leaves.

Brittany leans forward. "I saw how Adair couldn't keep his eyes off you when you modeled and thought the news was true."

Alex slings an arm around the back of my chair. "Davia's saving herself for me."

"Pshh," Brittany says. "If I heard *you* were engaged, Fboy, I'd never believe it. Excuse me, but Kennedy and I are commenting on the party and interviewing the hosts for our YouTube channel."

Alex reaches for one of their two plates of untouched food when she's gone. "You still hungry?"

"Actually, yes."

We each take one and continue our meal while the tent grows more crowded.

When we finish, Alex says. "Wanna take a walk?"

"I'm never sure what to do, so that sounds good."

"All you have to do, gorgeous girl, is smile and nod. Talk about the weather. Ask about golf scores."

"I don't know anything about golf."

"You don't have to. People like to hear themselves talk, and most men want to stare at you."

"I'll keep that in mind."

Outside the tent, the number of attendees surprises me, packing the lawns and patio above us. Servers somehow manage to wend their way through the crowd carrying trays of food and glasses of wine.

Music plays on an outdoor audio system. "Isn't that 'White Wedding?'" I say.

"And right before that, 'Never Worn White.'"

"I wonder if this party will go on long enough they'll be forced to play 'White Christmas.'"

Alex grins. "Before we go too far, I must find the men's room."

"Shall we meet near the dessert tent to see who won?"

"Great idea."

He heads back up the stairs toward the house, and women surround him, halting his progress. He leans in to kiss a few cheeks, favoring them with his devilish smile.

Who is Alex Gordon? Having him beside me is more of a comfort than I want to admit.

Pivoting, I find the dessert tent's location, sidestep people, and do my best to avoid being bumped into the pool before finding a bench near my destination. Behind me is an area cordoned off by white ropes where children in white outfits enjoy assorted entertainments. There's a miniature train, an inflated rubber bounce house, a crafts table, and pony rides. An adult twists white balloons into animal shapes, and a person in a unicorn costume and another dressed as a fairy hand out twinkling white wands with stars to the kids. Their joyous laughter rings through the air, cutting through the event's artificiality.

Two little girls dive under the rope barrier and head toward me, frantic. One says, "Excuse us, but have you seen our dog?"

"I haven't. What happened?"

"We wanted to introduce her to our friends, but I dropped her," the other says.

The girls, approximately six-year-old identical twins, possess a profusion of blonde curls.

"First, what are your names? I'm Davia."

"I'm Evie Huntly-Hart," one says, spinning around to try and spot their pet.

"I'm Emily Huntly-Hart," the other says.

"And your dog?"

"Bluebell."

I get up. "What's Bluebell's size and color?"

Evie holds out her hands to about twelve inches. "She's a Maltese, white."

Did the hosts buy a dog to coordinate with the theme?

"Where did you last see her?"

"We were in the play area when a noise scared her," Evie says. "I think she came in your direction."

I ready myself to begin a full-scale search likely to destroy my white outfit when a dog trots up to the twins.

"Naughty Bluebell!" Emily cries, and the dog shrinks back at her harsh tone.

"She's not naughty," I correct. "She came to find you because you're her people and make her feel safe."

Emily hangs her head while Evie picks up the panting dog.

"Give her some love," I encourage Emily, and both girls fuss over their pet, praising her for being good and finding them. The dog wriggles with delight, licking them and making them laugh.

"You should give her a treat after you put her back," I suggest.

"We will! Thank you, Davia!" The twins carry Bluebell toward the house.

Retaking my seat, I eavesdrop on the conversations of people strolling toward the dessert tent or some formal gardens.

Are you attending Cannes, the Formula One races in Monaco, or both?

The top Argentine polo player's on my team now, so we'll win our next match.

Let's go to Thailand. I crave sex with five-year-olds.

I rocket to my feet, attempting to identify a man whose voice dripped with pleasure, but the cramped space is a sea of white with no way to identify the black spot inside whoever spoke. What should I do? What *could* I do? Was it a sick joke?

A hand touches my arm. "What's going on?" Alex says.

I continue my futile search for a few seconds, then give up. "Uh, nothing."

"I don't believe you."

"You don't?"

"I'm adept at reading people and situations due to growing up with a psycho sibling."

"That must've been rough."

"The daily possibility of death made me hypervigilant, which I often discuss with my therapist. But, back to the now. What's wrong?"

Deciding to relent, I say, "I overheard an unsettling conversation."

"What?"

"I'd rather not repeat it."

Alex's hazel eyes are intent, but he relents. "Okay."

"While you were gone, I helped the Huntly-Hart's twin girls find their lost dog."

"You fit the hero role, LT, so I'm not surprised. Let's go find out who won our bet."

———

A multi-tiered cake with white frosting flowers is the centerpiece of the other all-white dessert offerings. Plates of white chocolate truffles, white fudge, white chocolate eclairs, vanilla rum eggnog marshmallows, powdered sugar donuts, vanilla macaroons, coconut bars, and more fill the table. In a corner is a machine where a server dispenses soft serve vanilla ice cream into cones.

"I think I'm getting a contact sugar high in here," Alex says.

"I can't believe we both guessed the same number of items."

"We can agree to a tie-breaker."

"Whatever we do, I need some fresh air and fast." The cloying atmosphere makes me almost gag.

Once outside, Alex hands me one of the vanilla shakes he carries. "Our tie-breaker could be who can consume theirs faster."

"I don't need another headache. I'll go with each of us paying up."

"You've got a deal."

A few weeks ago, if someone told me I'd voluntarily agree to spend time with Alex Gordon, I would've laughed in their face.

An announcement comes over the property's sound system. "Please make your way to our recreation pavilion for some entertainment."

"Recreation pavilion?" I question, putting my half-full glass on a tray.

Alex sets his empty glass next to mine. "Live here a while, and you'll grow used to the unexpected."

"I saw a turkey wearing a custom couture hat, so I'm in the deep end already."

Inside a separate structure beyond the dining tent are chairs on a basketball court facing a multi-level stage. I position myself near the back and scan the building's interior. Alex props himself against the wall, his shoulder touching mine. "What are you doing?"

"Waiting."

"For?"

"The unexpected."

The hundred or more partygoers filter in, with children sitting on thick mats near the front of the stage. After analyzing all the exits and possible hiding places, I scan the crowd. I want to find the man I overheard, drag him into an anteroom, and interrogate him. Was he fantasizing about the innocent children waiting for the entertainment to begin?

Christopher and Samantha take the stage holding hands beneath a spotlight. Camera crews pan them and then the audience, and I melt into the darkness, pleased to be far from the action.

"Thank you again for coming!" Christopher says. "We've been blessed to find a global audience through our social media accounts. Tonight, we're broadcasting live to our paid subscriber fanbase, exclusive VIPs who deserve a first look at what we're doing."

"We announced to our fans that some of Rancho Suprema's classiest and most beautiful residents would attend, so thank you all for being here tonight," Samantha says to enthusiastic applause while Alex makes choking noises. "And now, what you've all been waiting for—a performance by the Huntly-Hart Bedazzled Beaus and Beauties!"

"Bet you can't say that five times fast." Alex is so near my ear that his stubble grazes my cheek.

When I turn in his direction, our faces are inches apart. "Is this another bet?"

"No." He slumps back against the wall.

Christopher and Samantha move into the wings. Music begins, the crowd applauds, and the curtain rises to reveal five children from ages six to fourteen years, two boys and three girls. They're in the color *du jour* from tallest to smallest, wearing headsets like professional singers. They launch into "Do-Re-Mi" from *The Sound of Music*, singing with choreographed dance moves while their parents sing along with them from the left side of the stage.

"I think our hosts copied Angelina Jolie," Alex says. One of the boys is Black, a boy and girl are Asian, and the youngest are the Caucasian twins I assisted with Bluebell's rescue.

When the song finishes, they wait for the applause to end and announce their names from oldest to youngest: Michael, Sophie,

Mason, Evie, and Emily. The music swells again, and a peppy number I don't recognize plays. It's a hit with the kids below the stage, who are dancing and singing along.

"I don't recognize this song," I say. "I'm old."

"We haven't hit thirty yet. We can leave if you'd like."

"That would be rude."

"You've already disappointed the hosts by not arriving on the arm of your billionaire. It's okay to bail."

"This isn't the worst I've endured."

An off-key note by one of the less-talented singers makes us wince. "Are you sure?" Alex says.

I hesitate, then say, "Let's go."

We sneak toward the door, moving as silently as burglars in the night, to where valets take our tickets and hurry to retrieve our cars.

While we wait, I say, "You're not a good influence."

"You might reform me, LT." Alex's car arrives as he says this. He brushes his lips against my cheek, hands the valet some cash, and drives away.

EIGHT

José has my black gelding Ace on the wash rack near the barn. He sprays water high on his head and neck, and the horse curls his lips to reveal blocky teeth.

"I wouldn't have washed him if I knew you were riding this morning," he says.

"I'm not. Haven't been down to give Ace a treat since last week, so I wanted to begin my morning with a positive. The rest of my day will be a trial."

"Why?" José runs a hand through his thick hair to whisk away water droplets.

"I'm having lunch with Bob Brooks, but we're also going to check a property for a Ladies' League tour I'm stuck handling."

"You'll love that." José shuts off the spray and picks up a sweat scraper to remove excess water from the horse's coat. "How're you doing?"

"No lingering issues." I retrieve a comb from a bucket with grooming tools and remove snarls from Ace's long tail. "I'm sorry my life's spilled over onto yours."

"Do you mean when I got choked unconscious by an assassin, helped you tie up the same assassin, or when I got myself tied up by a different assassin?" he says, but with a smile.

"Yes, all of that." My property manager isn't yet twenty-five but has backed me up without hesitation since I bought my residence.

"I'm tough. Don't worry about me, *jefa*."

"Sherilyn mentioned I need a housekeeper, but I'm reluctant to let anyone access the property and my home because of issues like you listed. What do you think?"

José unties Ace to lead him back to the barn. "It would have to be a special person. Let me ask around."

———

Bob Brooks steps out the front door to his sprawling ranch-style home before I'm out of my car. Alexandra appears beside him, her brown hair in a stylish pixie cut.

"Davia, why don't you come in before you two take off," Alexandra invites. "I haven't seen you in forever."

"I hear you're busy with your daughter's wedding."

"Jessica's guest list grows by the day, so it's been overwhelming but exciting." She gestures for me to enter.

The home's interior is sophisticated but comfortable. The living room décor is in rich, neutral tones with colorful orange, green, and cream pillows on the couch and chairs with potted plants and framed botanical prints dotting the cozy space. A floor-to-ceiling window reveals a serene Koi pond and a bronze sculpture of an Asian goddess.

"Can I get you a drink before you go?" Alexandra offers.

"We don't need anything, hon." Bob leans on his cane near the entrance. "We're heading to the club for lunch before our appointment and must leave."

"All right. I'm happy to have a moment before making more calls to vendors to confirm orders for the ceremony and reception."

"Where will the wedding be held?"

"In Los Angeles. Jessica and her fiancé, Darren, are finishing their residencies at Ronald Reagan UCLA Medical Center," Alexandra says.

"They're doctors?"

"Yes. Darren's going to specialize in plastic surgery, and Jessica's going to be an orthopedic surgeon. It was her goal since childhood because a doctor botched the surgery on her beloved daddy, and he's used his cane since."

"I'm sure you're both proud of their achievements," I say.

"We are," Bob says, "But if we don't go now, Alexandra will take you to the study and show you a framed certificate from when Jessica was the best student in kindergarten and every honor since. We won't have time to eat."

Alexandra hugs her husband. "You're as proud of our daughter."

"I am." He plants a kiss on her head.

"Davia, when this wedding's over, we'll invite you for dinner," Alexandra says.

"I look forward to it."

————

"Inside or out, Mr. Brooks?" a hostess at the Rancho Suprema Country Club says.

"Any preference?" Bob inquires of me.

"Out, if you don't mind."

"This is Davia Glenn, Julia," Bob introduces. "Julia's been a fixture at the club for how long?"

"Almost ten years." Julia takes us to a table on a covered patio over-looking the golf course. "There's a breeze, so you shouldn't be too warm."

She places the menus at a table for two, and another server brings glasses of water and takes our orders of iced tea.

I say, "I relayed your message to Kyle. He said you need to up your golf game because he plans to beat you the next time he's out."

"He does, does he? I guess he didn't tell you that we don't keep track of our scores and alternate who the winner is."

"He doesn't compete? Your friendship is good for him, then. Most of Kyle's friends are—" I stop. I almost said 'deadly operators.' "Uh, not like you."

Bob observes me over the rims of his glasses. "Kyle said parts of his life were off-limits. Rather like yours, I suspect."

The server takes our orders. Bob decides on a Mahi-Mahi plate, and I choose a Maine lobster salad. Golfers practice their swings nearby, and one launches a ball down the course.

"I have no idea whether they're good players," I say.

"If anyone says their score is lower than 90, it's likely a lie unless they're a pro."

"To be safe, I'll act impressed no matter their claim."

While we await our orders, the patio tables surrounding us fill. Most patrons wear golf attire, but some well-dressed women pile birthday-themed gift bags in front of a lady. Two men are engaged in a serious discussion, perhaps business, and the Huntly-Harts inhabit an area with their children, all clad in navy and red, while their parents take videos with their phones.

"You and Kyle are a lot alike," Bob says.

"What do you mean?"

"He noticed details about everyone wherever we went."

I pick my words with caution. "He taught me to be observant."

"Please give Jessica some pointers about personal safety when you meet her. She'll listen to you more than me because parental advice brings on the eye rolls."

"From what Alexandra says, she's a daddy's girl. She became a surgeon because of you. What happened to your leg, if you don't mind me asking."

"I got in a car accident and shattered my upper thigh bone. They said I needed surgery, but the injury became infected and didn't heal in alignment. Specialists evaluated me for correction and performed another surgery. Believe it or not, I'm way better than before, but the cane will always be necessary."

Could I deal with a body limitation and stay as cheerful as Bob? Kyle almost ended his life when he lost part of a leg, unable to accept the end of his Delta Force career, and the thought that nerve damage from my gunshot wound might end my operative days scares me.

An older man in a police uniform I recognize as David Sterling of Rancho Suprema's Private Security emerges from the building. A younger man in a suit with black wavy hair is behind him.

"Hey, Bob," Officer Sterling says, coming to where we sit. "Haven't seen you in town lately."

"Been busy with listings," Bob says. "Have you met Davia Glenn?"

Officer Sterling pauses. "You found Willie Weston's body."

"Yes," I confirm. My hair was short then, and Willie Weston's corpse was the main event, so I'm impressed by his recall.

Sterling introduces the man beside him. "This is Detective Robbie Rodríguez from the San Diego Sheriff's Major Crimes Unit. He's investigating the commercial burglaries downtown."

His name's familiar, and I make the connection. "Bryce gave me your business card, and I meant to call, but it slipped my mind."

He tilts his head. "Oh?"

"I reported the Jenson's Jewelry thieves but got knocked unconscious outside Bryce's. My full memory hasn't returned, so I have little to add."

Bob places a hand on my forearm. "Are you okay now?'

"Yes."

"We haven't gotten leads on who did this yet. I had a meeting with business owners to discuss bolstering their security," Detective Rodríguez says."There've been some commercial burglaries in La Jolla and one home invasion, so we're concerned about community safety. "

Bob frowns. "Home invasions? Has anyone been injured?"

"The thieves struck when the owners weren't home, so no," the detective says. "Some security cameras caught their images, but the men wore ski masks."

"How many criminals were involved?" I ask.

"Five or six, hard to say." Detective Rodríguez removes a small pad from a coat pocket. "I'm working with the FBI, who assembled an interagency group in LA to help catch the bandits. Give me your contact number, please."

I recite my info, and Officer Sterling moves aside when our server brings our lunch plates. "We'll let you enjoy your meal," he says.

"Call me if you remember anything," Detective Rodríguez says.

The men join three people at a nearby table. I recognize Henry Adams, who serves with me on the Ladies' League board.

"That's the president of the Rancho Suprema Association, Henry

Adams, the Association manager, Brett Holme, and the local Small Business Association president, Libby Porter," Bob says. "Dave Sterling is the senior officer of our local police force. They call it private security, but the officers are all former law enforcement."

"Henry Adams is the building and grounds person at the Ladies' League." I put the names and faces of the other Rancho Suprema leaders into my mind, confident I'll see them again and have to pretend I care about their positions. I dip a piece of my lobster in a side dish of butter. "Bryce is a friend, and the theft hurt him deeper than losing his inventory."

"I'm sure." Bob cuts his fish. "Small business owners work hard, and the crimes are a real blow. And home invasions? I'll remind Alexandra to turn on our security system."

"Also, go through your home and find a place you both might hide. Think of somewhere that's not a typical target for thieves, like your pantry."

"Alexandra will be impatient with me, saying she's got more important things to worry about, like the wedding planning, but I'll make her listen."

While we enjoy lunch, more golfers tee off, and the twin Huntly-Hart girls, Evie and Emily, chase an inflated red ball and bump into the back of Henry Adams' chair. He retrieves the ball from beneath the table, hands it to Evie, and pats her bouncy blonde curls. Emily spots me and comes over, her sister right behind.

"Hi, Davia!" she says.

I indicate the ball Evie has in her hands. "Does everything escape from you two?"

"No," Emily says. "We kicked it too hard."

"Emily, Evie, this is Mr. Brooks."

"Hello, young ladies."

They give him shy smiles and bolt away again.

"Ah, to have their energy. Where'd you meet them?"

"Their parents hosted a party I attended, their dog escaped, and they enlisted me to help catch her."

"You and Kyle radiate a solid, trustworthy vibe. You'll both be stuck helping children and animals throughout your lives." Bob checks the

time. "We should finish up. We have twenty minutes until our appointment, and I'm sure tardiness isn't acceptable to the Kensingtons or their
representatives."

"Unless they're the ones making us wait," I comment.

"Truer words haven't been spoken."

NINE

"Who's our contact?" Bob asks on our way to the property.

"Linda Riley. She has some title, but I forget."

"Grand Poobah Riley, Mistress of Management?" Bob jokes.

Two men staff a small structure beside formidable gates, and I roll down my window.

"Who are you?" The guard's flat affect conveys he's not a typical minimum-wage worker.

"Davia Glenn and Bob Brooks. We have a one p.m. appointment with Ms. Riley."

"Show me your IDs."

Bob takes his driver's license out of his wallet while I locate mine in my purse. The man makes a careful comparison and hands them back. "I'm required to search your car. Both of you need to step out."

"Uh, okay." I'm relieved to drive the Maserati today. Maintenance technicians from National Security removed all exterior traces of a recent gun battle from the Range Rover, but I didn't thoroughly inspect the interior. The guard's aura of suspicion makes him the type to spot a dropped breadcrumb.

While the other sentry verifies our appointment, his cohort spends an uncomfortable amount of time probing the seats' nooks and crannies before searching the glove box, sun visors, and trunk.

"You should have him change your oil while he's at it," Bob says.

When he finishes and returns our IDs, the gates roll open.

"I wonder why the Kensingtons volunteered to be on the Ladies' League tour. You said they rarely host parties, and I understand why." I navigate a long, tree-lined drive. "I doubt anyone would be thrilled to go through such an extensive search upon arrival."

"At least they didn't make us submit to a body cavity probe."

The road meanders past acres of manicured lawns, shaped bushes, and gardens, but my training makes me scrutinize the incredible amount of security. There's high-tech fencing, cameras, and security officers with dogs. I'm sure many features aren't visible to the naked eye.

"How rich did you say they are?"

"A million or more to them is like a penny to us," Bob says.

"How did they make their money?"

"Probably the usual mix of inherited funds, laying waste to natural resources, insider trading, or arms deals," Bob quips. "But in all seriousness, they own houses worldwide, and there's a rumor they haven't been in some of them."

When we near the residence, astonishment crosses our faces. The U-shaped building resembles the Palace of Versailles near Paris, with its multi-storied façade and windows facing a courtyard of fine gravel. A tiered circular fountain sprays water onto a Grecian-style golden sculpture of a woman with an arm outstretched.

Bob's head swivels to take in the magnificent building. "On paper, I knew this place was around sixty acres with a 52,000 square foot primary residence, but this is spectacular."

A man in a dark suit hurtles out the front door, past four limestone pillars holding up an entry roof, and down some stairs. He waves his arms, indicating I shouldn't have the nerve to park in front. At least, that's how I interpret his frantic gestures and disapproving face.

"You have to be worth billions to park where we were," Bob says as the man directs us to a space much further away. Once we're out of the car, the man says, "This way," spins on his heel, and makes for the house.

"Can you keep up?" I say to Bob.

"I'm faster than you think."

We aren't far behind when the man touches a biometric entry device, and the front door clicks open. "After you," he says, and we enter.

An attractive, dark-haired woman in her forties waits in the entry below a skylight high in the vast ceiling. She clasps an iPad to her chest. "I'm Linda Riley. Welcome to Hazelton Manor."

We do introductions, then I say, "Before we begin, how do you plan to address security? We'll have several buses and around one hundred attendees."

"When Beatrice Gibbs approached us about the property for the Ladies' League tour, I went over our security concerns, and she assured me we could perform backgrounds on all the attendees, drivers, or other personnel. We're last on the tour for a reason. People can skip us if they don't want to go through our protocols."

"Will the Kensingtons be here?" Bob says.

"I'm not privy to their schedules, so we keep Hazelton in a constant state of readiness. Shall we?"

Linda moves down a corridor with an open domed ceiling casting sunlight on marble pillars and sculptures in display nooks. She stops at a sitting room and motions to a gold doorknob. "These were custom-made and cost $200,000 each."

Bob and I exchange glances while Linda polishes an invisible smudge from the knob with the edge of her sleeve.

"How many are there in total?" Bob asks.

"I've never counted them. Hazelton has twenty bedrooms, eighteen bathrooms, and countless other rooms. Not all have them, but most do. The home's furniture is custom-made for each room or curated from collections."

"First thing I noticed, didn't you, Bob?" I say.

He nods at me, eyes twinkling.

We continue past more golden doorknobs, marble-topped tables displaying ornate clocks and figurines, and dozens of rooms beneath Linda's notice. My injured leg twinges, my first flare-up since a few weeks prior, and I curse the heels I wear. Linda pauses beside another door and touches her tablet. Crystal chandeliers flash on to illuminate round tables surrounded by plush, red chairs. Oil paintings suitable for museums hang near dark brown-and-white marbled columns built into the walls.

"We use this room when we host fundraisers," she begins but stops when a blond man in his early thirties ambles down some nearby stairs, not putting his hand on the gold-filigreed banister.

"Mr. Kensington," Linda says when he nears. "I would never have scheduled—"

He raises a hand, and she stops.

"I'm Brant Kensington," he says to Bob and me, smiling to reveal white, straight teeth. He's in casual jeans and a polo shirt, but his fine features match the classy décor. We introduce ourselves, and he shakes our hands in turn.

"They're here to finalize the Ladies' League tour details," Linda provides, tucking a strand of hair behind an ear.

Bob says. "I'm sure your property will be the highlight."

"Will you be here for a meal? This room can seat over one hundred since it's around sixteen-hundred square feet," Brant says. "We also have a ballroom capable of accommodating three hundred."

"Another estate is hosting the lunch," I say.

"Linda, provide casual refreshments here or on the patio for the event, okay?"

"Yes, Mr. Kensington." Linda types into her tablet, head down.

"Your generosity's appreciated," I say, and Brant cocks his head to regard me. Thick lashes, darker than his hair color, highlight his amber eyes.

"You're Adair Monroe's fiancée, aren't you?"

I fight the urge to thrust my ringless left hand at him. "We aren't engaged."

"No?"

"It's a persistent but inaccurate rumor. Are you friends with him?"

"We've crossed paths a time or two, here or on other continents."

Another man descends the stairs, an older version of Brant. He's in a navy cardigan paired with loose-fitting pants, wears dark-framed glasses, and whistles an unfamiliar tune.

"Mr. Kensington, I'm so sorry to have booked—" Linda begins.

"You're too worried about inconveniencing us," the man says.

Linda gulps.

"Bradford Kensington." The newcomer thrusts a hand at Bob, who shakes it.

After I introduce myself and explain to the elder Kensington the purpose of the visit, Bradford says, "I'm sorry my wife, Hazel, isn't here. She'd want to ensure the tour's perfect, but Linda's an expert on the estate."

The manager colors at the compliment. "Thank you, sir."

"When's your event?" Bradford says to me.

"May 23rd, a Saturday."

"Will we still be here, Brant?" he says.

His son says, "Not sure. Weren't we attending Cannes this year? Dad, we shouldn't delay them."

They say farewell, and Bradford sinks his hands deep into the sagging pockets of his well-worn sweater. The men go toward another corridor, chatting, but Brant looks back at me with his brow furrowed.

Linda says, "I didn't realize they were in residence. The upstairs comprises the family's private bedrooms and bathrooms. It's too bad you can't tour the master. It cost over five million to finish and is breathtaking."

"That much? I'm sure it's magnificent," Bob says.

Linda opens a side door onto a spacious patio near a pool and sweeps an arm toward another part of the residence. "That wing contains a gift storage room, a gift-wrapping room, a beauty salon, a wellness center, a humidity-controlled storage room for the silver, a gym, a Pilates studio, a climbing wall, and more. Unless you have a particular interest, I'll keep them off the list."

"I'll ask Beatrice." I tap a reminder into my phone. "What's in the gift room?"

"Designer handbags, crystalware, fine linens, silk scarves, jewelry, etc. The Kensingtons pride themselves in having the best hostess gifts, or gifts for other occasions."

"Alexandra and I should invite them over," Bob says.

The estate manager ignores his remark. "Our miles of trails contain sculptures, and our two-acre formal garden has benches and fountains.

We also have an orangery and a rose garden. I can arrange for golf cart tours if there's time."

Bob indicates the massive pool we stand beside. "How big is this?"

"It contains 250,000 gallons of salt water, and a retractable cinema screen rises from a slot near the water. We have three pools, two outdoor and one indoor. The outdoor pools each have buildings with changing rooms, mini-kitchens, and lounges where guests can relax. Not too interesting. Let's go this way."

Bob catches my eye, and we clamp our lips together to keep from laughing.

"Another unique feature is our separate building with over $400 million in art," Linda says. "There's also a 150-seat theater with concessions, a 2,500-bottle wine cellar, and a "sweets suite" with over $50,000 worth of candy stored in glass containers."

"Is the candy for kids or adults?" I say.

"Both, of course."

"Of course," I echo.

"Hazelton Manor should be the only property on the tour," Bob says.

Linda beams. "It's one of America's finest residences. One floor comprises only closets with wardrobe storage because of the family's societal demands. There's also a vault for champagne, a 10,000-gallon aquarium, tennis courts, and more."

"You must have an extensive staff to care for this property," Bob says.

"We have housekeepers, gardeners, a master rosarian to care for the rose garden, security, private chefs, and others. Keeping Hazelton in top shape is a constant battle and my responsibility." Linda glances at her tablet. "I have to cut this short, I'm afraid. I need to brief the staff now the Kensingtons are in residence."

"We shouldn't keep you," I say. "Why don't you choose what's best and email the list to me? I'm sure the board will be thrilled with whatever you decide."

Whereas I want out of here before my head explodes.

"I'll email them to you by tomorrow afternoon." She begins to leave but turns back. "Oh, I almost forgot the gun collection."

I perk up. "Guns?"

"Bradford Kensington has put together both a historical and practical collection. He has period guns displayed by category, like flintlock, caplock, matchlock, etc. He also has a whole section of Holland & Holland, Purdey, and Fabbri shotguns and a storage room with military-grade ammunition."

Was I drooling? Some of the guns she mentioned cost hundreds of thousands.

"How large a space?" I ask.

"It's a separate building, like the art museum, about the size of a six-car garage. For security, the walls contain varied thicknesses of steel plates able to withstand a rocket-propelled grenade, and it has a custom safe vault entry."

We retrace our steps to the front of the house. Once we say goodbye to Linda, a man follows us to the car.

We buckle our seat belts. "What did you think, Bob?"

"Quite the eye-opening gander at a world I've only caught glimpses of, even after residing in Rancho Suprema all these years. When the Kensington's built this estate, the community was in an uproar because of the size but quieted down when they donated enough money for us to remodel the local library."

"What's the saying? If you want people to do anything, bribery's your best bet."

———

After dropping Bob at his residence, I drive home, mind still on Hazelton Manor. While Bob raved about the silk wall coverings from Dubai, the Michelangelo-like painted ceilings, and other features, I wondered about the multiple rings of security. Did they have heat sensors buried in their lawns? Automatic weapons built into the walls? A tiger in the back garden?

A middle-aged woman in a housekeeper's uniform carrying a heavy bag and an unfurled umbrella negotiates the steep road my home is on. The temperature's in the high 80s, and sweat stains the armpits of her white uniform. I roll down my window.

"*¿Necesitas que te lleve al autobús?*" I ask in Spanish, guessing she's on her way toward a bus stop about two miles away.

Relief crosses her face. "*Sí, gracias.*"

She folds her umbrella and situates herself. "My name's Camilla."

"I'm Davia. Do you work near here?"

"Yes, for the past five years."

"Does your employer ever give you a ride? "

"The missus is tanning by the pool and doesn't want to be disturbed. She don't know nothing about work. She calls me Ma Camilla, like I'm her *madre.*" She shakes her head, laughing to herself. "She must be thirty-six but doesn't cook or do much of anything except spend her rich husband's *dinéro.* Now she worries her *tetas* are saggy, her face is cracking, and her husband might leave her for a younger, prettier *chica.*"

Uncomfortable with the steady flow of unwanted information, I say, "I want to employ a housekeeper, but only once a week."

"What do you need besides cleaning? Laundry? Cooking?"

"I'm not sure."

Camilla hesitates, then says, "Papers? You know, U.S. citizen or work permit?"

"They would have to be documented because of my, um, job. And I'll need to conduct a background."

"Ah." She grows quiet.

We near a bus stop with stucco walls and a Spanish tile roof. Women in housekeeper uniforms talk to each other or stare at the road as if willing their buses to appear. I put my car in a nearby space, retrieve a notepad from my console, and scribble my info.

"If you think of anyone, have them call me."

"*Sí, gracias.*" She tucks the paper into her bag.

Some women put their hands to their mouths when Camilla emerges from my black Maserati MC20 and burst into laughter when she does an exaggerated swagger toward them.

Backing out, I wave as I head home.

———

My phone buzzes with a video call as I emerge from my infrared sauna, where I spent time hoping to stave off issues after a day in heels.

"Now *you're* in a towel," Warden says.

"I was in the sauna."

"You're sweaty, and I'm not the cause?" He says this in a teasing tone, but unhappiness underscores his words.

"I wish you could take the credit."

His hungry eyes drink in my features. "Me, too."

"What's going on? You seem down."

"We have a mission, and I'm unsure how long we're out."

Emptiness seeps into me. "You think you'll be gone for a long engagement?"

"We'll have a better idea when we're in country, but it appears complex right now."

Complex is code for too many variables until the team is on-site. I recall an insertion into an African country to support armed forces. The resolution took months.

"I need to see you." Warden's voice is hollow.

"I want to gear up and go with you."

"You want me to be honest, right?"

"Of course."

"Nine more months of separation from you might break me." His gaze is unfocused, his face bleak.

"Break you?" I repeat, struggling to believe his words.

"I said if you wanted that life, I wouldn't blame you, but it was a front, Davia. Being without you is killing me."

A heaviness strikes, and tears sting my eyes. "God, Warden, I don't know what to do."

"I lie awake, wanting you beside me, and try to find a solution to our situation," he says. "My responsibilities distract me, but not when I'm home alone."

"I lie awake, too, repeating a mantra that I'll recover, return to the team, and you'll be waiting."

"Does it help?"

"Honestly, no. Other than traveling to Virginia, I have no concrete solutions. Do *you*?"

"I've worked the problem from every angle, but each fix isn't fair unless it's what you mentioned, occasional visits. If you move in with me, you'll have to wait while I'm gone all day and disappear for sporadic periods. You'll want to be with our team during our daily training and on missions with me, and I'm afraid you'll be more unhappy."

"Which is worse? Missing each other long distance or when we're in the same place?"

"At least we could be together part of the time if you were here, but you promised your parents to spend a year trying your aunt's way of life."

"If it weren't for my injury still acting up, I would've ditched already."

"Do you know how few times in my life I've said I don't know what to do?" Warden says.

"Never?"

"If you leave me for—"

"Stop. Promise me when you're gone, you'll stay mission-focused. I don't want to lose you."

He attempts a smile. "I'm hard to kill, remember?"

TEN

On my way to tour Adair's estate, wariness inhabits me, and I roll my neck and shoulders as I drive toward his multi-story English-style home. Today's a stark contrast from my last time here when anticipation, confusion, and other tumultuous emotions filled me. Adair had bounded out the front door and rushed to the car to press his lips against mine. Now, his right-hand man, Jason McCall, is on the top step, leaning on crutches as he waits, gray eyes tracking me.

When I approach, I say, "I'm here for a property tour, not a fight, Jason."

He says, "You're armed."

"As I'm sure you are as well. Should I beat you to death with your crutches, or would you rather give me details about Adair's solid gold bathtub or his underground nightclub?"

A corner of Jason's right eye twitches. Is it amusement or a flicker of irritation?

"You're well aware he has neither." Jason's voice is stiff-upper-lip British as he extends an arm to indicate I should enter.

When he hobbles in after me, I say, "How's your leg?"

"How're your ribs?"

"What's with the hostility? Adair's alive, and he let you employ some adequate bodyguards."

"What do you mean 'adequate?' Those men are—"

"Scared to take on my team leader, so I suppose they possess some sense."

"When was this?"

"At the Ladies' League fashion show."

"Adair didn't mention it."

"Because Adair stood up for himself and didn't notice, but I did. If you want him to be safe, hire people with superior skills. Now, can we switch gears, and you become a tour guide and me a Ladies' League board member? After your time with MI6, you can be a chameleon, like you demonstrated when we took on those terrorists."

"And my cover got blown within minutes, leading to this injury," Jason grumbles, swinging forward. "Let's go this way."

I stop before a painting Sherilyn went into raptures over when we attended a party here. "Should this be something brought to the attendees' attention?"

"The Salvador Dali sculpture in the library might be of more interest, but we can include the painting if you want." He keeps going, and I rush to catch him, saying, "I don't recall the artist's name or—"

"It's a Thomas Gainsborough."

I imagine him thinking, "You idiot."

Marble-floored halls extend from the entry, and we go past a bedroom.

"Isn't this Adair's master?" Where, for a brief instant, I relaxed against him and pretended we were a couple.

"He likes to use it because it's closer than hiking up to the second floor, but no."

"On the plus side," I say, "if he wants a snack, he burns calories whenever he needs to find the kitchen."

"He has a kitchenette in his master." We take an elevator to the second floor, where Jason enters a wood-paneled room filled with bookcases. A circular stair accesses a second level, and light streams through bay windows. I inhale the scent of books and take in the comfortable chairs and reading lamps.

"He has over ten-thousand books in this 1,400 square foot room, and it's Adair's favorite location in the home. The Dali sculpture is there." Jason nods to a bronze on a side table. An Elmore Leonard novel is on a chair beside it, its place held with a leather bookmark. Was Adair a bookworm at heart?

Jason scowls at me. "You look like you want to move in."

"I love books."

"Perhaps we shouldn't include this. People might not leave." He stresses the last word.

He means me.

Continuing our tour, Jason reveals a gym, a movie screening room with twenty-five seats, and a spa treatment center. I picture Linda Riley saying, "Not too interesting," and I fight off a laugh.

Jason's cell phone gives an alert. After a brief conversation, he tells the caller he'll ring back. "Excuse me." He heads toward the library, and I remain before more oil paintings by artists I don't recognize. After a moment, classical music draws me to an open door further along the corridor.

At the center of a spacious dance studio, Adair is shirtless in white tights before a wall of mirrors. He performs a spinning turn, arms floating above his head and back, lost in the haunting music. He jumps through the air, lands, and takes another graceful leap.

I've never seen Adair bare-chested and bite my lip. A black abstract tattoo on his left side accentuates his six-foot, lean body's lines, while the fit of his tights leaves nothing to the imagination.

Damn. My dreams didn't do him justice.

Unaware of my presence, he approaches a floor-to-ceiling black pole, grips it with one arm, and ascends to turn with his legs in a scissor position. The move emphasizes his glutes and the defined muscles of his upper body and abs, now slick with sweat. He's a study in graceful masculinity, his body under iron control, and I press my hand against my mouth. Then Adair falters, winces, and bends over. He grips his side where his broken ribs still heal, and I stop myself from rushing to him.

After a few moments, his face eases, and he straightens, shoving away the discomfort in a way familiar to me.

Jason joins me at the door. "Let's go." He moves away with speed despite his crutches.

"I didn't know Adair was back," I express as I catch Jason, who pounds another elevator button.

"Neither did I."

Were these long-time friends not communicating? Were they estranged because of me or an unrelated matter?

"You're surprised Adair's back." My tone is neutral.

"You didn't know he'd be here either." He seems pleased.

The elevator arrives, and we board.

"Is he okay? The injuries from his abduction—"

"He left for England soon after, and all we've discussed is business."

I change the subject. "How long has Adair danced ballet?"

"He took classes at his mum's studio and has immense talent, but she left off pushing him when he focused on making money."

Adair grew up practicing his steps while I perfected my aim.

"He never mentioned it."

"He doesn't mention a lot of things," Jason says.

The elevator stops, we disembark, and Jason takes us through a door leading to a golf cart. "Let's decide where we can have the luncheon. Because of the heat, we can assemble tents in a shaded portion of the gardens."

He stashes his crutches in the cart, and we take seats. We travel along paved paths past an acre or more of raised beds and other vegetable gardens, then Jason stops. Ahead is a grove of trees. Many bloom with crimson and pale pink flowers surrounding a flat, grass-covered area. On one portion is a custom treehouse with a circular staircase for access and a wooden play structure with a slide and swings.

"This is almost straight out of a fairytale," I say, enchanted despite myself.

"Adair pictured his kids playing here one day and wanted it to be magical."

A future, idyllic scene presents in my thoughts, me in the role of Adair's life partner as we chase after our...I clear my throat. "Transporting one hundred people here and back might be a lot. We're touring Hazelton Manor right after and—"

"Hazelton?" Jason's face has a quick flare of some emotion.

"Yes, I went yesterday. Brant Kensington and his father introduced themselves and claimed acquaintance with Adair. Is that true?"

Jason delays his response. "Yes."

Are we back in our original roles, two operatives disclosing the bare minimum?

"Their level of security is what I'm sure you wish Adair would authorize. Do they have a reason for it beyond their wealth?"

"Let's find another location for lunch." Jason reverses the cart while I ponder the quick subject change. "Perhaps we can use the same area as when you came to Adair's last big affair, and we can open the garage with Adair's supercar collection."

Unwilling to let the Kensington topic drop, I say, "The attendees might tour Hazelton Manor's climate-controlled, one-hundred-car garage. I don't want to be repetitive."

Jason grunts in response, his granite features not giving anything away.

Did past billionaire bickering make him reluctant to discuss the Kensingtons? "I think the tour is more about gardens, art, and luxury, not cars, but I've never done this before."

"All you'll need to succeed here is for His Gorgeousness to appear. No one will care about much else." A tone of resentment colors his words.

"Jason, you're Adair's closest friend, and you've been in his life since you were a teen, and he was, what, five or six? What's happened?"

"None of your business." He slams on the brakes as we near the residence, lifts out his crutches, and dismounts beside a flat expanse of lawn. "Will this do?"

"Of course. Lunch will take an hour; if we leave an hour for a tour, that's plenty."

A man in mud boots carrying gardening shears emerges from the formal gardens, raising a hand to indicate he needs Jason.

"I know the way out," I say.

Jason doesn't respond, hobbling toward the gardener. After

traversing the patio, I enter the house and make for the front door. I put a hand on the knob but pause to contemplate the design in the marble foyer, wondering if Adair's family can trace their lineage to someone with a coat of arms or if the pattern is merely for aesthetic purposes.

"Davia? What are you doing here?"

Adair.

ELEVEN

His sandy-brown hair is disordered, and he wears a gray t-shirt, white jeans, and no shoes. My brain stutter-steps through thoughts. *You look so tired, no, exhausted, and your cheekbones are sharper than usual, but you still stop my heart.*

"I'm here because of my responsibilities coordinating the Ladies' League Home and Garden Tour," I explain. "Jason took me through the house and...."

Adair closes the distance between us and crushes his mouth to mine, demanding and desperate, as if he'll never be with me again. He drops an arm around my waist to bring me against him, and his signature spice cologne brings up memories like a slideshow. The day we met when Adair pushed me out of the way of a speeding car and landed right on top of me, when he stopped a gunman from killing me, danced with me at a gala, or raced me up the stairs of his yacht.

"I want you." His voice is husky. "I can't keep doing this, Davia."

"Doing what, Adair? What do you mean?" I put my hands on his forearms and step back. The close-up of the pain in his eyes and the dark circles beneath them is a shock.

He answers by placing his lips against mine again, and I respond without thought. When he lifts his face, he traces a path down the column of my throat with his lips, one long-fingered hand underneath my blouse caressing my skin.

"I won't go on without you." He takes my hand and strides with determination toward the inner space.

"Adair, you need to talk to me."

He doesn't stop or reply, propelling us forward. He understands I can incapacitate him but doesn't seem to care. We go through double doors to a bedroom, and Adair shuts and locks them. He spins around to pin my arms above my head and kisses me like a conqueror storming a castle.

And I'm lost.

Adair stretches back, tugging his shirt over his head, affording me a fleeting moment for my brain to scream, *What are you doing?* He draws me against his bare torso, and his piercing eyes are fevered as his mouth returns to mine, his tongue darting in leisurely, hot strokes. He backs toward the luxurious four-poster bed, maintaining our lip lock as he unbuttons my blouse.

I place my hands over his, signaling him to stop.

"We should—" I begin, but he brings me into his arms and onto the bed, his weight pressing me into the soft comforter. He brushes my hair from my face, the blue of his eyes darker.

"We should do what we've always wanted." He administers more mind-numbing kisses, and I reciprocate with equal fervency until a tiny part of me grabs for the remnants of my self-control. I shift from under him until we lie facing each other, and I brace my hand against his shoulder to distance us.

"Adair, you know the situation. Warden—"

"I don't care about him." He attempts to remove the barrier, but I immobilize his wrist.

"I do."

"Do you? You fight your attraction to me whenever we're together, so mentioning that guy is irrelevant." He yanks his hand away and props himself on an elbow, breathing hard. "You've always wanted me."

"On some level, I have," I admit.

His heated look would set a forest ablaze. "Then why are we still talking?"

"Because your behavior is different and not true to who you are. I need you to explain."

An irritated rumble comes from deep in Adair's throat, and he moves to the side of the bed and sits up. "All right, fine. Let's have the talk we should have had after you left me at the hospital and didn't return my calls."

"I agree we're long overdue to discuss what happened." I sit beside him, fighting my desire to caress his chiseled stomach as I struggle to regain control over my stampeding emotions. "Are your injuries healing?"

He shrugs. "As expected."

Unable to stop myself, I trace a finger along the black swirl on his side. "Isn't getting inked in this area painful?"

"Yes, but if you keep touching me, we won't talk much more." His voice is rough, and I drop my hand, standing to straighten my blouse so I don't give in and touch every inch of him.

The man who owns my heart is in Virginia, so why do I feel this way?

Adair rises and nestles against my back, wrapping his arms around my chest as he runs his lips along my right ear. "And no, I won't make this easy for you." He nuzzles a spot on my neck, but I unwrap from his embrace and face him.

"Explanations first," I say.

He gestures to a nearby couch. "Let's sit."

I perch on its edge. "You need to tell me what's happened to you."

Adair flings himself down beside me. "I survived days tied to a chair, got the crap beat out of me, and thought I might die. You took on like a zillion gunmen to save me, and what did you do? You cut communication."

"I told you I regretted my decision when we spoke at the fashion show."

"Well, now's the time to explain why you bailed on me."

"You wound up in the hospital twice because of my past, and I don't want you to go through anything like that again."

"You do realize I'm an adult, right?" His tone cuts. "Believe me when I say I've given the pluses and minuses plenty of thought."

"You can't begin to—"

"Let me finish." He straightens. "The whole time I was gone, all I could think about was you, and when I found you here..." His words trail off as he takes my hand, lacing his fingers through mine. "I refuse to pretend I don't want you for myself."

"I—"

Adair makes an exasperated sound, stopping my words. "Don't you understand yet, Davia? I'm in love with you."

In love?

He cradles my face in his hands and brings his lips to mine again, but his touch is tender; the previous frenetic intensity vanished. His embrace is unhurried, intimate, and proprietary. My heart pounds as I reflect on his words.

He looks into my eyes. "I mean it. You're better with me than—"

"Someone you know nothing about," I interrupt. "You don't know my history with Warden, what we've been through together, or anything about him."

"True, but if you loved him, you wouldn't kiss me like you do."

Before I respond, Adair says, "Tell me you don't think about me, dream about me, want me."

Avoiding his statement, I say, "Adair, our acquaintance is recent. Can you explain why you like me beyond this attraction, infatuation, or whatever it is?"

"Like you? I *love* you." He retakes my hand. "You're beautiful, intelligent, and real, unlike anyone I've ever met."

His sincere words cause my chest to grow tight, and I drop my eyes. Adair lifts my face. "And what about me? Is it only infatuation?"

Coming up with an explanation for my mixed emotions is a challenge. "You helped introduce me to a way of life I never envisioned, but...it's not that simple, Adair."

"Is anything? I'd still be abroad if I doubted your feelings for me."

If I'm unsure of my feelings, how is he so confident?

"But—"

"Before you launch into the 'other guy' argument again, at least sleep with me."

"Sleep with you? Adair—"

"Just sleep. Come on, I'm exhausted and need to hold you." He rises and extends his hand. "I'll behave. I promise."

I hesitate, but his tired eyes cause me to slip my hand into his. While I kick off my shoes and unstrap my ankle holster, Adair draws back the bedcovers and lets me in first before climbing in after me. He raises an arm so I can lay my head against his chest. He's slim and doesn't encompass me like Warden, but lying against his bare, smooth skin somehow banishes all my discordant thoughts.

Adair kisses me on the forehead, and sooner than I expect, we fall asleep.

Twelve

Neither of us has moved when I wake. I relax into Adair's warmth, my hand on his chest, where his breathing is deep and steady. When I raise my head, Adair's dark lashes flutter, he opens his eyes, and a contented smile raises the corners of his full lips. I begin to sit up, but he locks his arms. "Not yet, please. I haven't slept like that since before, well, you know."

The anguish in his words causes me to lie back against him.

He strokes my hair. "My days of wasting time are over, Davia."

"After-effects of an event like you went through can be different for everyone, but I get it."

"Having seen what you're capable of, I'm sure residual trauma haunts you."

Trauma is part of my job, not yours.

When I don't respond, he says, "You don't want to talk about it, do you?"

I shake my head and disengage from him. He doesn't stop me, raising his arms to stretch.

"Adair, I'm unsure what to say."

He sits up and runs his hand down my cheek. "Promise you won't tell anyone going to bed with me is a complete snooze fest."

I can't help but smile. "I promise."

The nap has restored some of Adair's bountiful, light energy, and my conscience eases, but chagrin at my disloyalty to Warden gnaws at the edges of my mind.

I never should've let things go this far.

"I need to go."

"Do you?" Adair bends forward to brush his lips against my cheek. "I warned you; I'm not playing fair from here out."

"I'm going to need time to—"

"To what?" He traces his lips along my jawline before grasping both sides of my face and sliding his tongue between my parted lips. My thoughts fade, and I don't want him to stop, so I ball my hands into fists, struggling against this inexplicable attraction.

A loud pounding on the door makes Adair lift his head. "Adair, are you in there?"

Jason.

Adair releases a harsh groan, and his voice is a knife's edge. "Unless this is a business emergency requiring my most urgent attention, you should back away and leave me alone."

"It is, or I wouldn't disturb you, Mr. Monroe," Jason emphasizes the last two words. 'Mr. Monroe' is Jason's code for 'bloody tosser.' What's happened between these two?

Adair launches himself off the bed, picks up his discarded t-shirt, and puts it back on while I feel like a naughty child caught by an adult. After running his hands through his messy hair, Adair unlocks one door, goes out, and shuts it behind him. The men's heated conversation is audible enough for me to discover the subject is a business problem, not me. Going to the en suite bathroom, I smooth my hair, straighten my clothing, and replace the holster on my ankle. Adair's ardent kisses have swollen my lips, and I put my fingertips against them.

The door reopens, I step back into the bedroom, and Adair rushes to take my hands. "Must dash. As angry as I want to be with Jason, this is an emergency."

"I—"

His lips are on mine before I finish, and my hands find his tousled hair. He makes a frustrated moan but releases me.

"To be continued." He flashes a grin as he heads for the door. "I'll call when I'm free."

I don't move until I can calm my racing pulse and steady myself enough to go to my car.

I can take on multiple assailants, defuse a bomb, and charge into hell without thought, yet this confounding man has slipped past my defenses once again.

———

Sherilyn's white Mercedes fills a spot near my garage. She emerges from the gate leading to the guest house, waves at me, and I roll down my window. "Are you in a rush?" I say.

"No, and this is perfect timing because I finally finished those window treatments in the guest house! How many months has it been with the measuring, fabric orders, delays, and more delays? Hurry, so I can show you the result."

When I rejoin her, she hugs me in greeting.

"Mm. You smell delectable. Wait a minute, there aren't any perfume bottles in your home, or I would've found a tray to display them." She steps close to me again and takes a long whiff. "Davia, this is men's cologne, not women's. Did you decide to go for an androgynous scent because, if you did, I need the name of this tantalizing aroma. I mean, this is—"

"I was with Adair."

"With Adair? *With* with Adair?"

"Uh, it's—"

"Complicated, right?" she finishes. "Okay-dokey. Let's skip the window treatment reveal. You only pretend to be interested in décor for my sake. We should go inside and, do you have any wine? We might need some, or at least I will."

In the kitchen, Sherilyn removes a bottle of Merlot from a decorative rack, finds an opener, and removes the cork while I lean against the kitchen island, lost in thought. She shoves a filled glass into my hand, and we sit in patio chairs beside a table.

"Okay, I'm ready to hear the whole story."

I take a sip of wine, delaying, and Sherilyn remains silent for once, waiting. Unsure what to say, I begin with facts. "I went to Adair's today to meet Jason McCall, his right-hand man, in readiness for the Ladies' League Home and Garden Tour. I needed to review the details for the luncheon and what Jason thought should be highlighted. I assumed Adair was still gone, but he was back."

"He was? And?"

My cheeks grow warm. "He was practicing ballet in his dance studio."

"Is he good?"

"He could've been a professional."

"What was he wearing?"

Not much.

"Only some tights."

"Go on."

"When I finished up with Jason, Adair stopped me. He showered and changed, and I began to explain my reasons for being there when he rushed forward and kissed me."

Sherilyn lowers her wine glass. "Like a 'Hi there' peck on the cheek or—"

"The other kind."

"The other kind? Davia, seriously, the suspense is already unbearable without you making me extract every detail."

"He wasn't his typical restrained self, put it that way. He seized my hand, dragged me into a downstairs bedroom, shut the door, and...." My words trail off, hands covering my face.

"And?" she prompts, squealing with excitement.

"We took a nap."

"A *nap*? Is this code for 'had epic sex'?"

"No. We literally slept together."

Sherilyn stares at me. "I'm super confused. The major make-out session and progression to a bedroom did not lead my thoughts to a nap. What happened? Never mind, I know. You went all guilt-ridden, didn't you? We've talked about this before. Warden lives across the country, you haven't dated that long, and he hasn't said he loves you. He also said he's fine with you dating other men to meet the will requirements."

"You're right, but he called last night and said he's at a breaking point without me."

"Warden? That hardcore hunk admitted that?"

"I wanted him to be more upfront about his inner emotions, and he was. I'm sure it was tough for him."

"Since you don't acknowledge emotions, let alone tender feelings, if he's the male version of you, this is difficult to process. He must care about you a lot."

"He does, and I feel the same, but whenever I'm around Adair, he's all I desire. I don't know what's wrong with me."

Sherilyn pats my back. "You might be invulnerable, but your heart isn't."

"My heart's with Warden."

"Not all of it."

"What makes this harder is Adair said he's in love with me."

"What?" The word almost shatters the sound barrier. "Did he say this before or after the nap?"

"Before."

"Girl, you're not normal, but this is beyond my comprehension."

"Warden—"

"Warden? I adore Warden. I do. And he adores you, but he's in Virginia. He had a little over a week here and then came out for the fashion show, but that was an in-and-out quickie, not a stay. Now Adair's declared his love...."

"You don't know about Warden and me."

"Tell me."

I grip the wine glass. "I can't."

Sherilyn bobs her head as an idea comes to her, and she says, "My parents are lawyers, remember? When they discuss their cases but can't come out and say anything, they say 'hypothetically' before describing the facts."

I say, "All right. Hypothetically, I've worked with Warden for three years, and he's my team leader."

"And your team comprises the four gorgeous men who accompanied him to the fashion show?"

"Yes. Hodge is the blond guy larger than Warden, and he's from Texas; K is the Black man who resembles a young Idris Elba, the medium-build one with his hair in a bun is Ned, and the brains of the team, the skinny one, is Savant."

"They give off a deadly vibe even wearing suits, which now makes sense. So, hypothetically, you're the only woman."

I nod. "We handle missions I can't discuss, no matter what terms I use. Hypothetically, we've saved each other countless times, and the man I trust most in this world is Warden. He's calm and in control when anything goes wrong, no matter how disastrous, and I owe him my life."

Memories of my last mission flash past. Warden shouting orders as enemy combatants overwhelm us, staying controlled despite the desolate circumstances, and staunching the blood from the bullet wound to my thigh.

"I appreciate you admiring him, as I can't begin to understand what you achieved together, but having him as your man is another story. Were you always attracted to him?"

"His cocky attitude overshadowed his movie star looks. I put him in the hotshot, alpha-male category and made it my mission to beat him at anything possible."

"Like what?"

A memory of me ready to engage him in close-quarters combat on my first day with the team, awed by his sheer size and strength, surfaces. His face held scorn when he stared down at me. It surprised him when I kicked his ass.

"Fighting, knives, firearms, you name it. We began to keep track in an unofficial 'who's better' contest."

"Did you win?"

"The only thing Warden beat me at consistently was running because he's six-three and fast." I recall him shooting me a smirk as he blew by me each morning. "I leveled up in other areas, though."

"This is like an enemies-to-lovers romance novel."

"A what?"

"Right. I doubt you read romances. As I said before, Warden could be Jacob Elordi's twin brother, and I get why you desire him. Who wouldn't? How did you get together?"

"Warden kissed me out of the blue, taking me by surprise at the time, but when I thought about it more, we touched each other on a ruse of supportive friendship, held eye contact too long, or found reasons to hang out and talk, but it was against our orders to fraternize."

"And you went against orders?"

"Yes, and it's another testament to how much we wanted each other. The dangers we endured created an unbreakable hellbond between us."

"Until Adair."

I take a long drink. "Adair's not part of my world."

"You mean your secret government, or whatever it is, world. But now you're in the one most of us inhabit. Perhaps it's time for a new life chapter."

Hummingbirds flit nearby, enjoying fragrant hydrangeas; the sky is a rich blue and cloudless, and mansions dot the valley across from where we sit.

"Most people would trade lives with me for this, but I want to recover from hypothetical life-changing injuries and return to my job and Warden."

Sherilyn makes a disbelieving sound and picks up her wine again. "I found you injured with bloody clothing and a bulletproof vest in your bathroom a few weeks ago. Since Adair called me from a hospital, desperate for me to check on you, I deduced your injuries involved him somehow. Am I hypothetically correct?"

"I think you and Detective Montoya are perfect for each other with your super sleuth brains."

Sherilyn rolls her eyes. "And you dodged the question."

"Okay, hypothetically, you're correct."

"So you saved Adair, took two bullets to the vest, but aren't sure how you feel about him? You're making me crazy."

"I'm going to Colorado for a vacation with Warden. He wants to introduce me to his parents, and we'll have time to discuss our future."

"My advice would be to hurry. You can't keep living a split existence now Adair has said he loves you."

"Warden isn't in the country."

"Boo-hoo. Poor Davia, having to spend time contemplating which incredible man would be better. How many girls in the real world get choices like this?"

"I deserve that," I say.

"Are you ready for more wine?"

"Sure, I'll get the bottle."

Sherilyn hugs me. "I realize you're tough and all, but remember, I'm your friend no matter what you decide."

THIRTEEN

"This meeting is called to order," Beatrice Gibbs declares to the Ladies' League board members. She wears Chanel, her go-to designer, radiating the warmth of an iceberg. I sit between Francis Downs and Henry Adams, doodling on the agenda.

Francis reports on attendance at the recent fashion show and announces my operative teammates, who she refers to as 'five fine gentlemen,' attained a new record in sales of raffle tickets. Next, Fred Smith, a dreary man, goes over the profit and loss statement slower than motorists calculating who goes first at a four-way-stop intersection.

I zone out, thinking about Adair.

Last night, my heart skipped when my phone buzzed around nine p.m. with Adair's name on the screen.

"You still up?" he asked. "Want to come over? Want me to come over?"

"I'm already in bed," I lied. "I have an early meeting tomorrow at the Ladies' League."

"I don't believe you."

"Which part?"

"I'm getting the lay of the land with you, Davia. It's that other guy again, isn't it?"

"Warden and I have a history, yet you expect me to drop him."

"How long have you dated him?"

"Not long, but we worked together for three years."

"Has he said he loves you?"

When I don't respond, he presses, "He hasn't, has he?"

"I'm going to Colorado to see him."

"Why?"

"He's an important part of my life."

"Okay, but I have a proposal. Let's date, no pressure."

"Date? That's—"

"All right, I'll change the semantics. He's been in your life for three years, so give me time."

"Let me think about it."

And here I sit, thinking about it, not paying attention to anything around me in a meeting I don't want to attend, in a community I don't want to live in.

"On to new business," Beatrice says. "Davia, have you arranged the Spring Home and Garden Tour?"

I want to say I haven't, but I go through the details, and Beatrice blinks rapidly, her mouth partly open when she can't find anything to criticize. When I finish, she moves on to the board member coordinating the transportation.

In the time it takes a seed to grow into an oak tree, the meeting concludes. Henry Adams turns to me. "Say, Davia. I'm having a gathering tonight with some of the leaders of Rancho. We learned you called in the Jenson's Jewelry burglary, and we appreciate your actions. We'd love for you to join us for dinner. Oh, and please bring Adair."

"I don't know his schedule."

"But you'll come, won't you? I'll text you our address."

With reluctance, I accept, thinking I might gain more information about the thieves and find the person who got the jump on me.

"Davia," Beatrice says as I make for the door. "Your thorough report was unexpected."

"Thanks?"

"I spoke with Kincaid Foxx, and he committed to introducing his next collection with us. He plans to have a unique creation for you."

Will he design another haute couture horror like he forced on me at the last fashion show? "Can't wait."

Since the Ladies' League building is on the edge of downtown, I decide to stop by and see if Bryce has reopened. A crew is busy installing exterior security cameras, and a heavy door has replaced the old one.

"Is Bryce here?" I ask one of the men.

"Yes, he's inside, but the store's not open for business."

"I'm a friend," I say, and he resumes working.

Bryce hangs blouses on a rack with speed. "*Bonjour*, Davia! I reopen in two days."

"Anything I can do?"

"*Non*, other than buy some new outfits. Ramon and I employed your suggestions for security, and I'm much more confident now."

"Henry Adams invited me to his home tonight with Rancho's leaders, and I'm unsure what to wear."

"Who else will be there?"

"He didn't share his guest list."

"Henry Adams is CEO of a high-level hedge fund company," Bryce says." And he's got a clique of people he's friends with. They deemed themselves the power core of the community, the rulers of this fiefdom. All old money, all confident they're in a club you don't belong to."

The usual Rancho condescension on steroids.

"What should I wear?"

"The pale blue sheath dress I sold you when you first moved here with pearls and flats. Drape a cream sweater over your shoulders tied in front if it's chilly. The classic never fails," Bryce advises, stepping back to scrutinize the now-full rack.

"Do you have one?"

"Of course." Bryce zooms to the back and returns with an ivory garment.

"Anything else you found in New York that should be in my closet?"

He puts the sweater on the counter, disappears again, and returns with an armful of items. "These would be perfect for you."

Each piece I try on provides a classic profile I never thought possible, so when I come out of the dressing room, I tell Bryce I'll take them all.

"*Naturellement.* You're embracing the lifestyle at last." He totals my purchases, and after I pay the insane bill, he hugs me. *"Au revoir, belle fille."*

On the way to my car, a text vibrates.

Adair: *Want to see me?*

My mind screams yes, but my self-restraint forces me to hesitate. After berating myself, I type: *I got invited to a dinner tonight. Want to go with me?*

Adair: *What do you think?* (Wink emoji.) *Text me your address and the time. I'll pick you up.*

I picture a smile spreading across his face, him believing he's winning me over.

Is he?

———

José climbs out of his truck and waves for me to stop. When he nears my car, I roll down the window.

"I talked to my mom and aunt, and they're trying to find a housekeeper for you," he says. "I stressed they have to be legal and submit to a background check, and since I'll also work with whoever they choose, I told them they need to be picky."

"Spoiled boy. Have you spoken to a housekeeper named Camilla who works up the street? I gave her a ride to the bus the other day."

"Yes. She talks too much."

"I got that."

"Whenever I see her, I give her a ride, but that doesn't happen often."

"She has to walk to and from the bus each day?"

"Think so."

Would I ever become so self-involved I'd let someone who worked in my home all day make that long trek?

"Where are you off to?" I say.

"Meeting a cousin for lunch. He works in the kitchen at Las Palmas."

Las Palmas is a Mexican restaurant on the edge of Rancho Suprema.

"Grr. Now I want tacos," I say. "Don't let me keep you."

"Want me to bring some back?"

"A chicken taco combo plate with rice and beans would be perfect." I dig into my purse and hand him money. "Do you have a service fee?"

"No, but I'll keep your change as a tip." José grins. "Be back in a little over an hour."

————

By the time José returns, I've laid out my dress, shoes, and sweater, plus retrieved Aunt Lilah's pearl necklace and earrings from the safe. The stress from attending a party with problematic people worsens at the thought of Adair accompanying me.

You're only getting to know him.

A delicious odor emanates from a white bag José hands me, but his pensive expression telegraphs he's worried. "Do you have time to talk?" he says.

"Sure, come in. What's going on?"

"*Mi primo* told me about a situation I want to run past you."

"Okay." We sit at the kitchen table, and José tells me to go ahead and eat. As I remove the foil-wrapped plate from the bag, he says, "My cousin, Emilio, has worked in restaurants for a long time, and many kitchens in San Diego staff Mexican-American employees. He began working young and is now head chef at Las Palmas. When we were kids, he'd make *chilaquiles* for breakfast before we woke or surprise his family with experimental recipes. He was happier at a farmer's market than on a playground. Today, he acted troubled, and it took a lot of quizzing before he opened up. Said he heard rumblings a restaurant stopped paying staff wages because they lacked immigration status."

"What do you mean?"

"Some foreign citizens get lured here by employers who give them work visas and promises of good salaries, but they take away their passports and make them work for excessive lengths of time and pay them nothing."

"Does he know where they are?"

"He's not sure."

"Is it happening in Rancho Suprema?"

"He thinks it might be, but he doesn't have time to investigate because of his duties. He said it could be rumors and exaggerations, but what concerns him most is hearing some of the women might be used for sex."

My appetite leaves as I think of the missions my team went on against a terrorist code-named Badger, who engaged in the trafficking of children.

"How can I help?"

"You have by listening, and if I learn more, I'll let you know. I'm a U.S. citizen, but I grew up as a minority. My family's successful, but we've known many who've suffered, so this situation bothers me."

Fourteen

Adair's hands are behind him when I open the front door. "Hi, beautiful. I brought you these." He flourishes a small bunch of California poppies, not a bouquet from a florist, but what he might have stopped and picked. As I take them, I focus on the flowers, not the hyper-awareness and head-to-toe tingles his presence causes.

"Did you make your gardener gather them?"

"They're for my girl, so I picked them myself."

"I'm not your girl."

Adair disputes my words with a knowing smile.

"Come in; I'll put them in some water."

While I hunt through cabinets in the kitchen, hoping Sherilyn thought to stock a vase, Adair says, "You've got a spectacular view. Mind if I go out back?"

"No, be out in a sec."

He opens a French door to the patio while the reality of having him in my home increases my turmoil. Warden brought me against his large, solid body, saying, "Let me demonstrate what you'll miss if you dump me for one of these moneybags," and claimed my lips right where I now hold Adair's flowers. Jolted like someone dumped cold water over me, I give up my search and put the blooms in a drinking glass.

"It's peaceful here," Adair says when I join him. He's in dark slacks with a subtle plaid pattern and a fine long-sleeved cream t-shirt.

"It's not as grand as your place."

"I wondered where you lived, what it would be like. Why did you choose this property?"

"It fit my needs at the time."

"Let me guess, defensible high ground?"

I ignore this. "What made you choose yours?"

"The size was a key feature. I can host charity events yet also have some peace. It's freeing to be away after handling business demands."

"Did you ever get lost when you first bought it?"

"Of course. I loved to torment Jason by hiding myself somewhere he couldn't find me."

"Speaking of Jason, did you two argue?"

He folds his arms. "I don't want to talk about it."

"Okay, none of my business. Are you ready to go?"

Adair runs the back of his hand down my bare arm. "Would you like to be more than fashionably late?"

My mouth goes dry. "Did you want to sit out here and talk?"

He ignores my question. "Remember when I texted you from Europe and asked which you liked better, conversation or sex? You never responded."

"It's not a fair question."

"I'm not playing fair from here out, remember?" He puts his arms around me.

"I've been honest with you, Adair, Warden and I have to discuss our future."

"Where's your phone? Give him a call. I'll wait."

"Adair—"

He grins mischievously, releasing me. "I'm winding you up; let's go."

In the driveway is a sleek black sports car. "This is a McLaren Artura, a hybrid," he says. "It lacks the roar of some of my other cars, but I'll forgive it."

"How gracious of you." As I buckle in, I say, "Are your bodyguards waiting outside my gates?"

"You're my bodyguard tonight, and I want you to take your job seriously."

———

Adair parks in a paved courtyard fronting a sprawling, single-story structure with stone-covered walls and a tiled roof. He opens my door, takes my hand to assist me, and doesn't let go as we approach the house.

"Do you know our host, Henry Adams?" I say.

"Not sure, but I'm not here year-round. I've managed to stay as below the radar as possible, turning down invites to serve on committees or attend most community or private events. It was simply good fortune we crossed paths." Adair rings the doorbell, and Henry answers.

"Davia, so pleased you could make it," Henry says, then to Adair, "I'm Henry Adams. We met at a golf tournament last year, but I don't expect you to remember."

Adair shakes his outstretched hand. "I must have been more concerned with trying not to make a fool of myself on the course."

We pass beneath a wrought iron chandelier and proceed along a tiled corridor. The walls are a warm shade, and the rooms have arches made of brick for openings.

"Here we are," Henry pauses before a room where people visit with each other. "Everyone, this is Davia Glenn and Adair Monroe. Please make them welcome."

The women stare at Adair. Three men split their regard between us, and I drop my eyes.

"I'll let you all introduce yourselves, but first, they need some booze," Henry says. "The bar's outside, so come this way."

On the patio, a middle-aged, distinguished man waits before an array of liquor bottles at a built-in bar. Four women in white uniforms check the food held in chafing dishes and trays with glass coverings.

Henry says, "Let Luís know what you'd like, then come back and get acquainted."

"We'll take some red wine, please," Adair tells Luís.

While he pours, Adair softly says, "I never thought I'd see you unnerved by anything."

"You found my weak spot. I'm a failure at parties."

"Let's reverse our roles tonight, then. I'll be your knight in shining armor, and if you need rescuing, either put your arm around my waist or scream, 'I can't take this anymore!'

"Deal," I say.

Adair hands me one of the filled wine glasses. "Ready to face the enemy?"

We re-enter the house, and Henry approaches with a fine-boned woman in her fifties. "This is my wife, Minerva."

"So lovely to have you join us," she says. "Dinner will be a serve-your-self affair, as the people here tonight are old friends, and we don't stand on ceremony. Davia, I'm sure Adair would love to talk man stuff, so will you let Henry borrow him?"

"Of course."

Adair squeezes my hand. "Remember what I said."

"I will."

Minerva says. "We're waiting for more people to arrive, but let me introduce you to who's already here." She takes me toward two sofas. "This is Jennifer McMillan and her daughter, Hannah."

A blonde woman in her sixties raises a martini toward me, saying, "So you're Adair's latest."

His latest? What did that mean?

"Mom, don't be so rude," a blonde near my age says. She wears a black cashmere lounge outfit and doesn't look up from her phone.

"And this is Nicole Wolfe," Minerva says.

Nicole's sweep of brunette hair frames a fair face with dark eyes. "You must be quite the catch to be here with Adair. Your last name's Glenn?"

"Yes."

"Who are your people? Are you related to Senator John Glenn, the astronaut?"

"No. My parents are from South Dakota."

"Nicole will search for you in the blue book," Jennifer says. "She lives by the social register."

Footsteps sound, and four more people enter. Bradford and Brant Kensington accompany Amelia Meadows and Kenneth Clayton. Adair lifts his head with his chin jutting forward, a display of superiority in the face of...what? Did he remember my disastrous date with obnoxious Kenneth when I moved here?

"You made it!" Minerva hurries to welcome the newcomers.

"We didn't bother to knock," Amelia says in her low Southern voice.

"You don't have to, my friend." Minerva hugs her while Henry shakes the men's hands.

"Amelia's family is from Savannah, Georgia. They've been in the register longer than your husband's, haven't they, Nicole?" Jennifer says.

Nicole flicks her eyes toward the ceiling before giving Jennifer a venomous glare. "Around the same time as yours, darling."

"You can sit here, Davia," Hannah says, patting the cushion beside her but continuing to scroll on her phone. I move a coaster on the coffee table and put down my still-full glass.

"I heard you and Adair are engaged," Jennifer says.

"We aren't."

Nicole sits forward. "Before you get married, be sure to find a storage unit and have it lined with cedar." At my uncomprehending look, she says. "You know, for the wardrobe, accessories, and jewelry you buy and want to hide from Adair."

Amelia and Minerva join us, and Minerva says, "What are you talking about?"

Jennifer keeps her voice down. "We're advising Davia to rent a place to store the items she doesn't want Adair to discover. We all have our off-site closets. For the men, it's out of sight, out of mind, and no lectures on spending too much money."

Amelia says, "I don't have to do that."

"You don't have a man, Amelia," Minerva says, and Amelia goes rigid.

"She's lucky," I interject. "She has her own money and can do whatever she pleases. I think it suits her."

A Latina woman appears in the doorway. "Dinner is ready, *Señora* Adams."

"Thank you, Maria." Minerva announces everyone can fill their plates and eat in the dining room.

Adair beckons me, and I excuse myself. He takes my hand. "How's it going?"

"Doing my best to stay out of the infighting."

"There's a battle you might not win. Are you hungry?"

"Not much, but I can pretend."

Bradford Kensington cues up behind us, saying, "You were at Hazelton the other day, weren't you?"

"Yes." I reintroduce myself.

"'Sorry, I'm not as good with names as I used to be. Did Linda provide you with all the information you needed?" He pushes his glasses up and jams his hands into the pockets of another well-worn cardigan, giving the appearance of a forgetful professor.

"Yes, thank you."

"Good, good." He pats my shoulder. "What's new with you, Adair? Haven't crossed paths with you since last year's Dubai World Cup."

"Is that a soccer game?" I ask, and Adair says, "You mean football, don't you? No, it's a horse race. We'll have to go."

Brant joins his father. "I thought you two weren't engaged."

"We aren't yet, Brant." Adair's tone is cold, and the men lock eyes.

"Don't pressure these young people, son," Bradford says. "Countless women will wail when Adair's off the market."

"Of course." Brant's tone mocks.

Kenneth Clayton is at the bar chatting with Luís, waiting for his drink. The women come out together, laughing, and Kenneth glances at them. He sees me, lays a hand flat against his face, and turns away, much to my satisfaction.

Perhaps stepping in a rope trap on my property and hanging upside down made you rethink life? Or was it my gun?

We fill our plates with grilled shrimp, carne asada, fresh corn tortillas, and mixed vegetables. "Are these people old money?" I say to Adair.

"All I know is they're way out of my league. Makes me wonder why we got invited. Most of the people in this room have as much money as the economies of small countries."

"I thought from what Henry said this would be a community safety meeting, but I'm never sure of anything around here."

Henry waits inside the dining room door. "Davia, why don't you sit with the men? Adair can charm the women with his presence."

At the thought of Adair leaving my side, my appetite disappears. "Okay."

"I'll introduce you to the boys." Henry deposits his plate at the head of the table and pulls out a chair for me. "Davia, on your right is Josh Whittaker, Naomi's husband, and on the other side is Mike McMillan, Jennifer's husband and Hannah's dad."

Josh Whittaker has a receding hairline and heavy jowls, while a blond Mike McMillan appears as tall as Warden but not as fit. After I put down my plate, I tuck my arms in as I sit.

Mike glances at my chest. "Henry told us you called in the Jensen Jewelry burglary."

"I did." I stay true to my habit of scanning the room and noting any object I can use as an improvised weapon instead of elbowing him in the ribs.

The pair tuck into their meals, and Josh says, "I wouldn't have bothered to call the cops. Stores have insurance. I'm more concerned about the home invasions. From what we've been told, wealthy global enclaves are targets, the crimes perpetrated by organized teams out of Chile with Colombians used to fence the stolen items."

"The good news is they wait until people aren't home," Mike says. "Do you live alone?"

"Uh, yes." I force myself to take a bite of food.

"Adair should review your security system," Mike advises. "I'm sure he wouldn't want anything to happen to you. Hell, he's got enough money; he could hire you protection."

I almost choke as I swallow. Coughing to clear my throat, I say, "That's unnecessary."

The room becomes a hum of laughter and conversation, and Kenneth sits far from me. The women are intent on Adair as he tells a story.

"Will there be any entertainment tonight, Henry?" Josh says.

A relaxed smile crosses Henry's face. "Not until later."

I think of my team's favorite way to unwind. "Do you play poker and smoke cigars?"

Mike and Josh exchange smiles. "We like to mix things up."

Who knew what multi-billionaires got up to for fun? Not me.

"Did Detective Rodríguez discover any leads on the burglaries?" I say to Henry.

"He got some surveillance footage from a business adjacent to Bryce's Boutique. Said it's pretty grainy and unclear because of the heavy rain."

I make a mental note to call the detective and find out if the video caught the assault on me, desiring to discover who did this and why I failed.

After the meal, Henry invites the men into a side room while the women troop off in a different direction. Hannah, still staring at her phone, is beside me.

"Are you as bored as me?" She plays a video and wears wireless earphones.

I dodge her question. "Why did you come?"

She makes a face. "Mom controls the purse strings to my trust, so if she insists, I go. She talks about me learning to manage my future by becoming better acquainted with her super-rich friends, but they talk about the same subjects whenever I'm around."

"Do you know why we're separating from the men?"

"It's some moth-eaten tradition from centuries ago. I don't know who renewed it, but the men want to discuss their side pieces. My dad's the worst of the bunch, and poor mom pretends not to know, but she does."

"That must be tough."

"I think I've seen you before," she says. "Did you go with Alex Gordon to the Huntley-Hart's white party?"

"We didn't attend together but wound up in each other's company."

"Thought you might be having a fling with him. He's super sexy. He'd inspire me to get up to all kinds of things."

"He's my wealth management advisor. He inspires me to learn more about investments, but that's all."

Our destination is an outdoor patio decorated with plush furniture and lit by decorative candles in free-standing sconces. A table has coffee and hot water canisters beside a tray of tea packets and desserts.

"Are you redecorating?" I say to Minerva when she picks up a slice of chocolate cake.

"No. Why?"

"Several rooms didn't have furniture, so I thought...."

"Oh, this house is so large; we leave them empty because we don't have any use for them."

"I see," I say, not seeing at all.

While I make some tea, I listen to the women's conversations.

Did you hear Eleanor paid a gardening service $1,500 an hour to move some plants around her garden until they suited her?

That's nothing. Marla called her housekeeper to drive an hour from her home, stressing she needed an urgent matter resolved, but she only wanted the trash taken from the kitchen to the outside bin.

Would Adair hear me if I screamed?

As if on cue, he appears in the doorway. "Sorry to disturb you, but Davia and I must leave. I have an early flight tomorrow."

The women make disappointed noises.

"Travel is exhausting," Minerva says, "Let me escort you out."

"My sincerest apologies, Minerva," Adair says as the others call farewells.

"I don't think I'd travel if we didn't have our jet," she says. "Please join us again next month."

When we're back in the car and away, Adair says, "Do I get props for rescuing you?"

I smile at him. "Yes, I neared my limits. How'd it go with the men?"

Lines crease his forehead. "I'm not sure. They appeared to be judging me, deciding whether to welcome me into their club."

"Those are some powerful people with significant connections."

"Who knows if they'll let me in or, more importantly, if I want to be part of their posse."

"I sensed you don't like Brant Kensington."

"I'm not uber-wealthy like his family," Adair says. "so he looks down his nose at me."

I believe this isn't the whole story, but don't press. When he stops outside my home, Alexandra Brooks calls my phone.

"Davia, I need your help." Distress fills her voice. "I'm with my daughter in LA and can't get ahold of Bob. Could you go by our home? It's almost ten, and he's not answering his phone, which isn't like him."

"Could he have fallen asleep?"

"He hosted a showing this evening, an open house. I'll text you the address. Perhaps he got talking with a potential buyer, and they went out afterward. It's likely nothing, but this upcoming wedding's made me a bundle of nerves."

"It's no problem; I'll go now."

Adair says, "What's wrong?"

"I need to check on a friend, the man who sold me this house. His wife's in LA and is worried she can't reach him."

"I can drive," he offers.

"I think it's best to part ways. You said we're getting to know each other, and I prefer to say farewell here."

"Text me later, okay?"

"Will do."

———

A quick outfit change delays my departure, and I don't speed to the Brooks' since many simple explanations exist for Bob's non-communication. The residence doesn't have a security gate, so I drive in. A motion sensor light comes on when I approach the front door and ring the bell. After several attempts with no response, I peek in the windows and gain entry to the backyard by pulling myself up and over the locked gate. More motion lights blaze to life, shining on the peaceful reflecting pool.

The home's interior is dark, and I bang on the sliding glass door, but there's no sign of anyone inside. The stillness of the property makes me believe no one is home. A panel of decorative windows tops the garage door, and I jump to look but only glimpse an empty space.

Exhaling, I scroll up Alexandra's text with the address of the open house. My Range Rover's GPS places the property about three miles east, on the edges of Rancho Suprema. While I drive, I ring Bob's mobile, but it goes to voicemail.

The property's wrought iron security gates stand open at the location, and a twinge of apprehension nudges me.

He might be inside, chatting with a potential buyer. He loves people and learning about them.

The colored concrete driveway is steep and ends at a Spanish-style home where Bob parked his car off to the side to not interfere with people coming to view the property. The house's lights are off, and I touch the 9mm handgun secured in my waistband before stepping out of the car. Short palm trees line a paved walkway to the front, and I stay close to its edge as I progress.

The front double doors are shut, but the right side isn't locked. When I first toured my property, Bob locked the house when we went to view the barn. Knowing he's meticulous about security intensifies my disquiet.

I step inside, not making a sound. Like Bob's home, the stillness makes me conclude no one's here. Perhaps Bob did go out for a drink with a buyer, got preoccupied talking, and they took the other person's car.

Snapping on my compact tactical flashlight, I shine it around a spacious, furnished room featuring a sizable abstract painting on a wall. The next room is a less formal family room with a television, fireplace, and pool table. Inside the door, a figure lies on the floor in a dark pool of blood.

FIFTEEN

My flashlight's beam glints off the red liquid surrounding Bob's upper body. He lies on his stomach, head facing left and eyes closed, glasses askew. His cane is beside him on the tiled floor, and his hand is near the top.

Did he fall and hit his head?

"Bob?" I crouch to check his neck for a pulse, pressing and searching, and put my finger under his nose. His skin is pale and waxy, and I call his name again but louder. I try a second time to find a pulse, willing one to be there, but find none.

I fall back on my heels.

He can't be dead. He can't.

Despite knowing the time for CPR is past, it takes all my willpower not to flip him over and begin emergency measures. At last, I force myself to dial 911. When the call concludes, I press a hand to my mouth, working not to cry.

"Oh god," I breathe, helpless, frozen beside Bob's still form.

My phone vibrates, and I jump. Alexandra's name is on the screen, and I gulp a deep lungful of air.

"Davia, did you find him?"

"He, uh, is Jessica with you?"

"She's right here and has been badgering me to call. She had a premonition about her daddy, and we're worried out of our minds."

"Alexandra, he's had an accident."

"An-an accident? Is he okay?"

"I've called 911, and help is coming."

"What happened?"

"I'm not sure. He might have fallen."

"How serious is it?"

I squeeze my eyes shut, my heart breaking. "I can't find a pulse, and he's not breathing."

Sirens wail and grow near while Alexandra sobs. In the background, her daughter demands to know what's happening.

"I'm going out to meet the paramedics," I say. "I'll call you back."

A fire truck, ambulance, and a Rancho Private Security SUV come to a halt in front of the residence. Four men gather gear while Officer David Sterling exits his vehicle. I tell the paramedics where Bob is but don't go back inside.

"Ms. Glenn?" Officer Sterling questions as he approaches. "What's going on?"

"It's Bob Brooks, and he's dead."

Sterling stares at me, then stumbles past and enters.

I wait on the front step. Wispy clouds cover a crescent moon and stars, and a coyote howls in the distance while I wipe my eyes and lock down my distress.

Sterling rejoins me, grim-faced. "I've called Sheriff's Homicide. Someone ransacked the bedrooms, so I'm closing this as a crime scene."

The firefighters and paramedics file back out, and Sterling says, "Let's put our vehicles on the road. Everyone needs to stay for elimination prints."

We back out, and I wait beside my car. Sterling comes to me, and I explain why I checked on Bob.

"Did you tell Bob's wife he's dead?"

"No, only he wasn't breathing, that I couldn't find a pulse, and help was on the way."

Sterling lowers his head. "I can't believe this. Bob and I have been friends since I began working for Rancho Security over twenty years ago. He shook my hand and said, 'Let's grab some coffee; I want to learn about your life.' Afterward, we got together every week or so to catch up and share our troubles or triumphs."

About half an hour later, a sheriff's patrol car and two plain wrap vehicles come up the road. Detective Ricardo Montoya drives the first car, and Detective Worth, a female homicide detective I recognize from several other crime scenes, is in the passenger side. When Montoya sees me, his brows knit, and he rolls down his window to listen to Sterling.

"Montoya said for you to wait," Sterling says while the new arrivals park along the road. A fair-haired man with a towering presence gathers the detectives around him, gives directions, and the patrol deputies cross the driveway entry with crime scene tape.

"That's Detective Sergeant Hurst." Sterling indicates the man who directs the detectives. "This is his team."

"Detective Worth was at the Weston scene, and Detective Montoya interviewed me later." I don't bring up the other crime scenes where we crossed paths.

Alexandra rings me again, and I turn my phone toward Sterling. "What should I do?"

"Let me," he says, and I hand him the phone.

"Mrs. Brooks? It's David Sterling with Rancho Private Security. Where are you? LA? The paramedics came and—no, he's not at a hospital. I didn't want to tell you over the phone, but he didn't make it."

Her scream pierces the night.

———

A crime scene tech team and the medical examiner arrive, and a technician takes everyone's fingerprints and photographs our shoes. Sgt. Hurst shakes the responders' hands, and they leave.

"When the evidence team finishes, my team will go in. I'll need you at the station for an interview," he tells me.

"Why?" I question. "The victim's wife requested I try to find him, and I called 911 when I saw his condition. I'm happy to give you a statement now."

"You think I don't know who you are?" Hurst seasons his words with a sprinkle of condescension. "I ran the Myles' murder case, and you were first on the scene. I don't believe in coincidences."

"I also called 911 there, saved one of the victims, and caught the Myles family murderer. Or did you forget?"

He steps into my personal space to intimidate me with his size. Since he's got nothing on Warden and Hodge, I don't react.

"I bet you're a pampered princess playing detective in your posh community. Listen up, little girl, you won't skate around our questions this time. Detective Montoya should've taken you in at the Myles scene."

"Did you just call me 'little girl'?"

Sgt. Hurst is so near the scent of his body spray mixes with his toxic masculinity, sparking a clash between my disbelief and despair. "I'm sick of spoiled brats with attitudes attempting to mimic Nancy Drew," he continues. "You wouldn't dare exhibit such sass if you ever did a day's work."

"Oh?" My tone's indifferent, a sure way to provoke a charging bully.

The clatter of wheels causes the sergeant to raise his eyes toward the house. "The ME's going to be coming down with the body," he tells the patrol deputies, who hurry to detach one side of the crime scene tape to allow the vehicle to leave.

"You stay right there," Sgt. Hurst orders me, returning to the house.

Officer Sterling joins me, and the taillights of the ME's van carrying Bob's body disappear.

"Do you think he meant right on this spot when he told me to stay here?"

"Hurst's a prima donna, all bark and no brains. I need to get an idea of how long this will take. Will you be okay?"

"I'll wait in the car."

———

Because of the time difference, it's three a.m. in South Dakota when I call Kyle Kavanagh.

"What's happening?"

"I'm unsure how to say this."

His voice sharpens. "Did Warden get hurt? Is your team okay?"

"Bob Brooks is dead."

"What? How?"

I tell him, and we sit in silence for a time.

"Do you think it was an accident?" he says.

"Dunno. He could've fallen on the tile floor and cracked his head open, but someone ransacked the house. Hard to say."

"How are you handling this?"

"Not well. You?"

"I don't know how to feel right now," Kyle says. "Friends have died, but most were special forces like me. Bob was such a terrific guy..." his words trail off. "Are you home?"

"No. Still waiting for a sergeant to decide if I can make a statement here or at the station."

"Terrific way to treat a helpful citizen," Kyle says.

"Montoya's on the team, so at least one intelligent person is working the case."

Kyle met Detective Montoya last month and says, "He's sharp. He'll catch the killer."

The strain of Bob's death envelops us as we share a few memories of Bob.

"Montoya's coming to talk to me," I say when the detective approaches my car.

"Let me know about the funeral," Kyle says. "I'll come out."

I climb from the Rover into the chill air.

Montoya's brown eyes lock on me. "What did you say to my sergeant?"

"Nothing confrontational."

"Whatever you said ticked him off, and it took some persuading, but I talked him into letting you give me a statement here and coming in for another one if he requires. Which, I want to warn you, he will."

"Sorry you have to work for a guy like him, but I'm not too concerned since you run mental rings around him."

"He's been a thorn in my side since I first became a detective in another unit. Once, I got a report some guy was cruising around with a loaded shotgun in his trunk. His girlfriend reported she was concerned he would kill her, and she'd been an informant for me when I worked narcotics. I informed Hurst, and he said, "He's not doing anything illegal."

"*Not* illegal? Even I know that's incorrect. What did you do?"

"Copied the relevant section of the Penal Code, highlighted it, and put it on his desk. I stopped the guy and took the gun."

"Mediocrity appears to be on the list of desirable qualities for leadership in some places."

"True. Now, let's go over what happened." Montoya takes out a recorder and notepad for my statement, brushing a lock of dark hair off his forehead with a weary hand.

When we finish, he says, "I'm sorry for the loss of your friend."

"Bob was a wonderful man. Do you think he was murdered?"

"We won't be sure until the autopsy."

"Officer Sterling said the house was ransacked. Do you think one of those Chilean gangs targeted the place?"

"Also, can't say. We don't have contact information for the owners yet, so we don't know."

"Bob wouldn't have shown an unkempt house."

My phone vibrates.

Adair: *You didn't text me. Are you okay?*

Montoya says, "It's late. You should bail before the sarge changes his mind and makes you stick around."

On the trip home, I call Adair.

"Davia, did you find your friend?"

"He's dead. I've been waiting for law enforcement to clear me to leave."

"Oh no, who was he?"

"Bob Brooks."

"Bob Brooks? I met him and his wife once at the Ladies' League. What happened?"

"Can't say. He might have fallen, struck his head on the tile floor."

"What can I do?"

Let me cry into your shoulder? Hold me all night?

"I'll be okay. I'm going to take a shower and go to bed. " When he doesn't reply, I say, "Adair?"

He sighs. "I'm waiting for you to stop armoring up around me."

"I'm not."

"Sure you're not. You shouldn't be alone."

"I'm going to crash."

There's another long pause. "All right, but call me if you need anything."

When I'm home, I text Sherilyn about Bob, and she calls within minutes.

"Ric and I were on the phone earlier, but he got a call and had to leave. Was he there?"

"Yes." I relate what happened, and Sherilyn says, "How are you doing?"

"I don't know. If I got there sooner—"

"Stop. You can't change what's already happened."

"Their daughter's upcoming wedding must intensify Alexandra's grief since he now won't get to attend."

"He was such a good man and interested in other people. I'm not processing this yet."

"Me either."

"Need me to come over?"

"No, I'm going to stare into nothing for a while and try to fall asleep."

"I'm glad you broke your 'I can handle anything alone' rules and reached out."

"I wanted you to hear the news from me."

"It's a start."

Sixteen

"I was thinking about you. How's everything?" Mom says when I call after a restless night with little sleep.

"Uh, not good. You remember my real estate agent, Bob Brooks?"

"Yes, you said he was wonderful to work with, and when Kyle returned from his trip, he shared lots of stories, mostly wild golf tales. Why?"

"He died."

Mom draws in a breath. "What happened?"

After relaying events, I say, "Bob's daughter's getting married next month, and the family has gone from celebration to mourning. I don't know what to do for them."

"Send a card and flowers, take over some food so they don't have to cook, listen if they want to talk. Grief differs, so you need to gauge the situation as you go. But are you okay?"

Was I? "I will be. Kyle said he'll come out for the funeral."

"Do you need me to come? I realize your dad and I haven't, but his farming and my job at the school keep us busy. On weekends, I volunteer at the health clinic and have my Presbyterian Women's group."

"I would love to have you out, but I'm meeting James Warden in Colorado soon, so I might leave without much notice."

"The international affairs consultant who lives in Virginia?"

"Yes." I'm unhappy I can't share his true profession. "He wants me to meet his parents, who live near Boulder, but we don't have firm dates yet."

"Are you that serious about him?"

"He's not proposing, so don't get too excited. He's taking me to Rocky Mountain National Park, where he enjoys hiking and fishing."

"Your dad and I would also love to meet him. I don't think you've introduced us to anyone you've dated except Bobby Riley, and that was high school stuff. You didn't date him for more than a month after the prom."

"You don't need to remind me I'm old."

"For heaven's sake, you're only twenty-seven. If you call yourself old again, I'll come out and swat your behind."

"I'll remember that's a way to make you come to California."

Mom laughs. "I know Lilah forced this new life on you, but do you like it any better?"

"I've made some friends, but I'm still a fish out of water. I have to coordinate the Ladies' League Spring Home and Garden Tour, and a woman who keeps a pet turkey owns one of the properties. She has a 3,500 square foot closet, part of which is storage for numerous matching couture hats for her and her pet turkey."

"The turkey wears hats?"

"Yes, and it has its own elevator and playroom."

"People waste so much money on frivolities, like Lilah. She went through a period when she became obsessed with bonsai trees. They were in every room of her home, and she paid a staff to care for them."

"I need to contact Mr. Morgenstern and ask why I only receive twenty percent of the inheritance annually. Think of all the turkeys, hats, and bonsai trees I could buy. Wait, I keep forgetting to ask, but you visited Aunt Lilah's Upper West Side penthouse in New York a few weeks ago. Do you want to keep it?"

"I have no attachment and got all the personal items I wanted."

"I'm meeting with her wealth manager later today, so perhaps he'll have insight."

"He'll have a better idea than me. I have no regrets about being a small-town nurse and farmer's wife."

"Why did you want me to try this lifestyle? I'm much better suited to how you and Dad live."

"I think so too, but if you have financial security, I wouldn't stress so much about your future."

"But I have a good job and—"

"You have a good job, but Lilah's money gives you a lifetime of security. Oh, I meant to ask, what happened to the British billionaire?"

"How did you segue from jobs to Adair, Mom?"

"I'm curious."

"He's been in Europe handling a business emergency." I'm unwilling to continue this topic and change the subject. "Thanks for listening and advising me on how to handle Bob's death."

"Call me anytime. Remember, I love you."

"Love you, and please tell Dad the same."

———

I stand next to Alex Gordon at United Shooting's outdoor pistol range. Temperatures in the high eighties make us the lone shooters, as most opted for the indoor air-conditioned practice areas.

"This is a better place to discuss your finances than my office." He loads a .380 automatic, his ear protection headset looped around his neck. "I'm not in a suit and can hang out with you."

I load my Sig Sauer nine millimeter. "And I can pay off my end of our bet and gain some financial guidance; it's two birds and all that."

"True. You're swimming in a different stream now."

"A stream where the water comes from an exclusive, insiders-only source, I'm sure," I say.

"You're catching onto this already, but I want you to stop acting like a wild animal with a paw caught in a trap. You should reframe how you view the inheritance."

"How am I supposed to do that?"

"Your attitude needs to change. Think about your dreams and aspirations and what those look like."

"Dreams and aspirations? Since finding out about Aunt Lilah's inheritance conditions, my primary concern has been to comply with them. I moved to Rancho Suprema because of the clause I needed to live in an expensive zip code, got a position at the Ladies' League to fulfill the 'serve on a non-profit board' requirement, and made it into the society pages as she specified."

"Your magazine cover with Adair Monroe was the chef's kiss."

"I don't see it that way."

He sends me a questioning look. "Lilah required you date a millionaire or better every quarter, so why not him? Oh wait, there's the other guy. I do have a solution for you."

"Oh?"

"Learn the rules and break them, baby. I meet the money requirements if you ever need a date without the drama."

"Isn't that a conflict of interest?"

"As your wealth manager, think of it as another, more personal, service I provide." He shoots me a flirtatious glance.

Was he safer than Adair or treacherous in a different way?

"My aunt also left me the use of her penthouse in New York, but I won't use the place. Any ideas on how to handle it?"

"You can sell or rent the property out, but if you turn it into a rental and sell later, you might be taxed differently. As to the trust, there's no hurry on what to do with the money. You can store and accumulate your wealth over time."

"I'll think about it more. Are you ready to shoot?"

We expend four loaded magazines each, and I'm surprised by how accurate Alex's aim is, the center of his target shredded, like mine. He tugs off his ear protection and says, "Gotcha, didn't I?"

"You did. When you carried a concealed gun at our initial meeting, I put you down as a poser."

"Never let them see you coming," he says. "It's one of the reasons I find you so intriguing, unlike the boujee babes I usually put up with. You sized up the situation, distracted me with your sultry faux-seduction, and disarmed me. Quite the turn-on."

"My actions had the opposite effect of what I intended."

Reading my disapproval, he says, "Back to your finances. You bought two expensive vehicles; how did that feel?"

"Good, coupled with guilt."

"Guilt?"

"People buy houses for the cost of either."

"Have you put those vehicles to good use?"

I raced the Maserati at high speeds to find Adair when a terrorist kidnapped him, and the Rover survived a rocket-propelled grenade and numerous rounds yet kept running so I could save him.

"Yes, they've helped me a lot."

"So, they served a purpose. My advice? Go out and experience all this life offers. Let go of your past and guilt. Decide what this money might bring that's a positive, rather than focusing on the negatives."

I realize I haven't viewed the money and conditions as anything but a weight around my neck. "I'll consider what you said."

Alex removes his eye protection to wipe sweat from his brow with the back of his forearm. "Lilah Latham talked to me about you and her plans to give you a different option for your future. She lived by a 'her way or the highway' motto and scared most of the upper-crust crowd, but her heart was in the right place."

"Did you ever find proof she possessed a heart?"

Alex snorts. "I sense lingering animosity toward your aunt. Do you want my therapist's number?"

My head pounds, and I rub my temples.

Alex frowns. "Are you okay?"

"I think the explosive noise triggered a headache. I should've worn in-ear and outer-ear protection, but I forgot about my concussion."

"How bad is it?"

"Three aspirin bad."

"Perhaps we should quit for the day."

"Davia!" Arlene Knecht calls, and her trailing family waves as they approach. The hillbilly clan isn't any cleaner or better dressed than when I first encountered them here, but they all have broad smiles. Alex rubs the side of his face, looking at me for clarification.

"Your 'never let them see you coming' rule applies to these people."

I hug Arlene, the seventy-something matriarch, a tiny woman dressed like America is still in the 1800s.

"How'd you do on your CCW trial with your pea shooter?" Arlene refers to the .22 Magnum revolver she helped me master before my concealed weapons shooting test.

"I did much better than anyone expected."

"We still have the ear protection you gave us. It's way more comfortable than musket balls and wadding," Chester, Arlene's son, says, and his three teenage kids nod with enthusiasm.

"Hi, Davia!" Bobby Jr. greets while his brother, C.J., and sister, A.J., give me shy smiles. A.J. gestures to Alex. "Is he the boyfriend who tried to shoot you last time? If he is, I get why you forgave him."

"I would never shoot at Davia." Alex's charming smile makes A.J. blush, and he introduces himself.

We pack our gear while the Knechts put out their targets. Alex says, "A man tried to shoot you here? A boyfriend, you say?" His eyes glint with humor. "No wonder you went right after the gunman at my sister's. Not a new experience."

"Let's go back to you advising me about Aunt Lilah's money, okay?"

"Boyfriend subject dropped. As for your future, you're still becoming accustomed to the inheritance. Over time, you should go from aware to involved and engaged in your fiduciary approach. I want you to embrace the idea that wealth and happiness can go together."

"And if I don't?"

"Do I need to remind you that if you don't comply, the money goes to lobbying efforts so the rich pay no taxes?"

"More evidence my aunt's heart, if she possessed one, was black."

My phone rings on our trip back to Rancho Suprema.

"Miss Glenn? Detective Montoya. As expected, the boss wants you in for a formal interview."

"Does this mean someone murdered Bob?"

"Yes."

Alex gives me a startled glance.

"Does his family know?" I ask.

"Yes. Forensics said Mr. Brooks died from several hard blows to his head, caving in his skull."

Alex briefly rests his hand on my shoulder to give me support.

"Does Sergeant Hurst have a timeframe for this interview? Do I need a lawyer?" I say.

"Can you come in tomorrow? The lawyer's up to you."

"What time?"

We make an appointment for the afternoon and conclude the call.

"Did you know Bob Brooks?" I ask.

"I handle his investments, although they're more modest than yours. Some people stopped working with me after my sibling got arrested, but he called to say he liked my work. He was a stand-up guy. Why is the sheriff requesting an interview with you?"

"I found his body." I relay the rest of what happened. "The sergeant thinks I'm a rich girl playing detective, and I'm also pretty sure he thinks women are a subspecies."

"He'll be in for quite a surprise. Do you want a recommendation for an attorney?"

"No. I didn't do anything wrong and..." I stop, almost saying my training makes me a pro at handling interrogations. "I'll be fine."

"Want to have a late lunch? We can stop at a location that doesn't mind sweaty, dirty customers."

"I don't have much appetite right now," I admit.

"And I wouldn't mind a shower."

Alex lives in a ubiquitous Rancho Suprema home, Spanish-style, with perfect grounds. He didn't ask me to come in when I picked him up, and he doesn't now, for which I'm grateful.

"Let's plan a day at the Safari Park when temperatures drop," he says as he offloads his gear from my Rover into his garage.

"Okay."

"Be good to yourself so you won't land back in the hospital. I'm not always available as a nursemaid."

"I'll be fine."

Alex says, "I'll see you at the funeral, if not sooner. Don't forget to think about what I said regarding your inheritance, and try not to let any ex-boyfriends shoot you."

SEVENTEEN

The Sheriff's Homicide Division is in a multi-story tan building with the logo emblazoned on the glass entry. After going through security, I receive a visitor's badge. Will it be Detective Montoya or Detective Sergeant Hurst who retrieves me?

An elevator dings and its door opens.

"Happy to see you, Detective," I say to Montoya.

"I bet you are, but Hurst's aware of your interview time, so expect him to appear."

"Can't wait. Have you been able to take Sherilyn on a date since the fashion show? She mentioned Cinco de Mayo."

He perks up at her name. "We managed to enjoy Old Town without interruptions."

Sherilyn never mentioned their date. Was my voluble friend tight-lipped regarding time with her detective? Or had I been so caught up in my dilemmas that she hadn't wanted to share her happiness?

In the elevator, Montoya takes a moment to fix his loosened tie and check his image in the shine of the doors, squaring away like he's still a Marine.

"Buffing up for the sarge?"

"He's a stickler when interacting with civilians, reads all the department's PR, and believes it. 'We provide the highest quality public safety service to the people of San Diego,'" Montoya mimics. "Memorizing the mission statement might've been key to his promotion. After you."

On the second floor, Montoya takes me to an interview room. "We've done this drill before. Water, right?"

"Good memory." I sit at a table with a voice recording device and a legal pad on its surface.

"I recall you don't drink coffee though you own a fancy espresso machine. Wonder how you live." Montoya brings me a small paper cup of cold water, turns on the recorder, and recites the date, time, and our names. I tell him about the call from Alexandra, the futile trip to their home, and driving to the address where I found Bob's body.

"Let's take it slow from when you neared the property," he says. "When you got to the address, were the gates open or closed?"

"Open."

"Did you find this unusual?"

"It made me more cautious." I describe seeing Bob's car and going to the front door.

"Why did you try the door?"

"Thought he was out with a client since his car was still there. The house seemed empty like the showing was over, so if he locked the house, I would've concluded he was with a client, either celebrating or working to make a sale."

"Were both of the double doors unlocked?"

"I only tried the one on the right."

"Did you turn on any lights when you went inside?"

"No. I keep a, um, flashlight with me," I say.

"What kind of flashlight?"

"Small, LED rechargeable." The word 'tactical' is innocuous, but not with what Montoya has deduced about my past.

"Did you think there was trouble?"

"No. I keep flashlights in my vehicles, and the house was dark."

"What did you do next?"

"I went inside."

"Why?"

"Concern. Bob's a stickler for security, and I thought he either got distracted talking and forgot or something worse happened."

"After you went in, what did you do?"

"Stopped and listened."

"Did you call out for Bob?"

"No."

"Why not?"

"I wasn't sure of the situation and didn't want to alert anyone to my presence."

"Were you armed?"

"Yes. I like to be careful."

"When you saw Mr. Brooks' body, what did you think?"

The scene rolls into my thoughts, and I swallow. "I thought maybe he fell, and I went to render aid."

"The amount of blood was extensive. Did you have any suspicions it was foul play?"

"I didn't think about it because I focused on whether he was alive. I checked his pulse and his breathing and called 911."

"You didn't attempt resuscitation?"

"I knew he was dead and had been for some time."

Montoya's eyes snap to my face. "Do you have experience determining how long people have been dead?"

"I'm not a medical examiner."

"You're not, but—"

The interview room door bangs open, and Sgt. Hurst fills the opening with his bulk.

"So, you came for the interview," he says.

"Obviously."

Montoya pauses the interview and turns off the recorder. "Did you have questions for Ms. Glenn?"

The big man hesitates, and he's good-looking enough he might believe women find him irresistible. Coupled with his position of authority, I don't want to think about the possibilities.

I take a drink of water.

"Are you giving my detective any problems?"

"Wouldn't that be a better question for your detective?"

Hurst lumbers forward, his heavy cologne preceding him. I take another sip of water and keep my eyes on Montoya, whose slight head movement warns me.

"Ms. Glenn's consistent with the details of her previous statement and cooperative," Montoya tells Hurst, who is inches from my side. I rub my left eye with my middle finger, and Montoya fights to school his features.

"Is that right?" Hurst says. "I find that hard to believe."

Smiling like an indulgent parent, I say, "What do you need, Sergeant?"

He takes a step back. "What do you mean, what do I need?"

"All I can give you today is the truth and cooperation. Did you need anything else?"

His hand goes to his chin, puzzled. "I suppose what you're doing now, giving a statement."

I rise and extend my hand, which he shakes. "I appreciate the high quality of public service you give the citizens of San Diego."

"You're...welcome?"

I resume my seat while Montoya coughs and fiddles with the recorder. Hurst backs away, saying, "I'll let you continue the interview." He closes the door on his way out.

Montoya stretches. "Shrewd moves."

"Is there anything else?"

"I could wait for an explanation about how you recognized Mr. Brooks was dead and get some vague nonsense so far from the truth it's not even a cousin or call it a day."

"Up to you. Do you know Robbie Rodríguez, a detective in Major Crimes?"

"Why?"

"He's investigating the business burglaries in downtown Rancho and mentioned some home invasions. I reported men carrying crowbars who burglarized Jenson's Jewelry, and someone breaking into Bryce's Boutique cracked me in the head, knocking me out."

Montoya is incredulous. "Someone managed to knock you unconscious?"

"Don't rub it in. My recall's wonky, and I only have glimpses of what happened. Rodríguez has some grainy footage that might help me remember."

Montoya makes a call on his cell. "Robbie's not picking up. I'll talk to him, though. We joined the department at the same time and are good friends."

"Am I done?"

"Yes. Reading between the lines of conversations with you gives me eye strain."

———

As I turn onto my street, Camilla, the housekeeper, appears for her daily journey toward the bus stop.

"Need a ride?" I say.

"*Sí, gracias.*" Inside, she drops her bags at her feet and buckles her seatbelt.

We've traveled the length of the street to turn onto the road into downtown when I realize she hasn't said anything.

"How's your day been?" I say in Spanish.

Camilla's hands come together, and she fidgets. "I, I worry a lot."

"About?"

She stares at her lap. "*Tres chicas han desaparecido.*"

Three girls have gone missing.

"Who? When?"

She relates the maids worked in Rancho Suprema, and one used the same bus stop as her.

"Olivia's fifteen, *muy bonita.* She work hard, support *su familia en Mexico.* Gone since last week."

"Is she documented?"

Camilla shakes her head.

"Did ICE pick her up?" ICE is the acronym for U.S. Immigration and Customs Enforcement.

"We don't think so."

"Any news of the other girls?"

"No, but they all suddenly had *mucho dinéro*, won't say how."

I don't want to mention the apparent explanation, the desperate choices women make. "Did Olivia say anything that might give you an idea of what happened to her?"

"No. She happy with money, but also troubled."

This time when Camilla gets out, her head is down as she goes to where the other women huddle together. Were the girls' disappearances related to labor trafficking?

José's on a utility tractor discing the arena, and I stop to relay the information.

"I'll talk to my cousin again and find out if he's discovered anything. My mom might have a housekeeper for you, but she's finding out more about her before giving me the name. Mama's like that when it comes to me."

"Are you telling me you're her favorite?"

"She'll never admit it, but it's the truth."

EIGHTEEN

What should I take to Alexandra? She texted to say she was back in Rancho with Jessica and sent her gratitude. For what? Failing to stop Bob's murder haunts me, as I obsess and second-guess what might have happened if I had arrived sooner.

My thoughts are interrupted by a text from Adair. *How are you?*

I'm seeing Bob Brooks' widow & daughter in a few hours.

Adair: *I'm free if you need me to go with you.*

Wanting to hear his voice, I call him.

"Davia, how are you dealing with Bob's death?"

"I've never been in this situation, have you?"

"No, but I've lost a few business associates before their time, and it can be quite a shock."

"Mom advised me to take some food, flowers...it all comes across as inadequate."

"You're beating yourself up, aren't you, that you couldn't save him?"

"A little."

"You mean to say a lot. No one expects you to save all of humanity, although I'm sure you believe otherwise. Look, why don't you let me arrange what to bring, and I'll pick you up."

"You don't have to."

"It'll be my pleasure, and I'm a distance removed since I only met the Brooks at the Ladies' League."

When Adair arrives, he's in a black BMW SUV and wears a gray suit and tie. He brings me into his arms for a comforting hug saying, "It'll be okay." I wrap my arms around his waist as I choke back unexpected tears.

"Let me show you what I brought." He opens the rear to reveal a gift basket filled with self-care items, a freezer bag containing an assortment of reheatable meals, and a basket bouquet arrangement of white roses and other flowers.

"This is perfect, Adair."

"Here," he hands me a sympathy card and removes a pen from his pocket.

"Thank you." I write a message and sign my name.

"You can thank my staff. They got excited to do something other than respond to emails or take phone calls." He shuts the back. "Are you ready to go?"

"Do you think this is suitable?" I'm in a navy jersey knit skirt and matching top.

"Yes, it's exactly right."

After pushing the ignition, he takes my hand, and my sadness eases a fraction. "Do you know what to say?" Adair questions as we wait for the security gates to open.

"No," I admit.

"My mum told me to say, 'I can't imagine how you feel,' because we can't know what another's loss is like."

"Moms are an endless resource, aren't they?"

"They're ahead in the life experience curve, so deferring to their wisdom is a safe bet."

As Adair pulls up before the Brooks' residence, I halt the memories of the last time I futilely searched the property or when Bob opened the door with a welcoming smile before we left to have lunch and toured the Kensington Property.

Adair hands me the flowers and card and carries the gift basket and food container. I ring the doorbell, and a woman opens it. She's hollow-eyed and a blend of Bob and Alexandra, taller than her mom but with matching features and thick brown hair.

"I'm Davia Glenn, and you must be Jessica," I say, and Adair introduces himself.

"Mom said you might stop by. I'm sorry, I'm not...Do come in."

I place my items on a side table, and Adair puts the self-care basket beside them.

"Where's your kitchen?" Adair holds up the meal bag. "I can put these away."

Alexandra appears from a doorway, so diminished it's all I can do not to react. She comes toward me without a word, taking my hands.

"Davia, it means the world you're here."

Adair and Jessica go toward what I presume is the kitchen while I say, "I can't imagine how you feel, Alexandra."

"Let's sit down."

We take seats on the couch, and she keeps one of my hands in hers. "Will you tell me what the police didn't?"

"What do you mean?"

"Did he suffer?"

"He lost consciousness right away, I'm sure. When I arrived, he-he...."

"When I called you, he was gone, wasn't he?"

I wipe a hand across my eyes. "Yes."

"It's not your fault, Davia. You did all you could."

Adair and Jessica return with an attractive dark-haired man. Adair sits beside me, and Alexandra says, "Davia, this is Darren Freemont, Jessica's fiancé."

As the couple sits, Darren says, "Thank you for coming and for the gifts."

The light catches the water spilling into the reflecting pool beneath the endless benevolence of the Asian goddess statute. We sit in silence, the sorrow of Bob's death stifling us. Alexandra is the first to emerge from the fog of grief and says, "Your presence means a lot, Adair."

"Of course."

Jessica says, "Davia, Dad said you're well-versed in personal safety, and he wanted to introduce us so you could give me some pointers. Me living in Los Angeles made him concerned."

"The last time we had lunch, he told me about you and Darren and how proud he was of you both."

Jessica fights back tears, and Darren presses a tissue into her hand. The doorbell rings again, and Alexandra returns with Officer Sterling and some patrol officers I recognize. We get up to give them room.

"Ms. Glenn, Mr. Monroe," Sterling says, and we nod at him.

"I'll come by again soon," I say to Alexandra, hugging her, and we make our farewells.

We file past the new arrivals and leave.

———

In the car, Adair says, "Want to get some food?"

"I'm not the best company right now."

"Why don't we go to my place? I'll text my chef and have him fix a meal for us, nothing fancy."

"Your chef?"

"If I cook, it'll be fish and chips microwaved from a box."

"It's a comfort you're hapless at something."

"I can compensate for my cooking skills if I serve you in the formal dining room to make it a grander experience. We can shout at each other from opposite ends of the 1300 cm table."

"A forty-plus foot table?"

"Yes. Jason can act as a footman, and we can talk by trading missives on a silver tray if you like."

"I think he's a millisecond away from strangling both of us, so no."

Adair types out a text. "All set."

"It meant a lot you went with me."

"Spending time together isn't limited to having fun. Doing life is how we get better acquainted."

Manicured trails, flowers, and mansions whiz by while I assure myself we won't cross lines today, the familiar guilt playing like a radio on low. Why did I want Adair with me, not Sherilyn, who knew Bob well?

We enter through the back of the house, Adair removing his tie. "I should've asked if you wanted to go home first and change; sorry." He throws the tie around the neck of a Grecian statue in a nook.

"Didn't your mom teach you to put away your clothes?"

"I'll grab it on the way to my room later," he points at the ceiling. "Let's have some wine while Alain cooks. By now, he'll have an assortment of appetizers, soup, salad, entrees, and ten desserts prepared."

"That fast?"

"I'm joshing; come on." We take a corridor until we reach a glass room. Inside, at least five hundred or more wine bottles decorate the walls, resting on aluminum brackets.

"Red or white?" He touches his thumb to a security device, and the door unlocks.

"Are you afraid someone will steal your alcohol?"

"Feature came with the house, but it's a prudent measure when I have parties. This one," he indicates a bottle of red, "cost around $7500, so I wouldn't want just anyone pulling the cork."

"I had no idea."

"Always a smart investment, and this price is nothing compared to some rare vintages going for the hundreds of thousands."

"Is there a trick to becoming used to this life?"

"I was initially bewildered, but then Mum told me I'm in a new world, one I earned, and to have fun since life is short and could end anytime."

"More wise advice."

"What about you? Are you used to Rancho Suprema yet?"

"I don't think I ever will be. My aunt left me some money with conditions, so moving here wasn't what I wanted."

"Conditions?"

"I prefer not to talk about them."

"I won't push. Alain readied a table on the back veranda, but we can eat in if you'd like."

"Outside's fine."

Adair carries two wine bottles to our destination and picks up an opener from a table with white linen, flowers, dishes, and trays with net covers. He uncorks the wine and pours some into heavy crystal glasses. "Here you go."

The patio overlooks the formal gardens and a variety of roses in full bloom. We sit, and Adair uncovers one of the trays to reveal a plate containing what he tells me is duck breast, rhubarb, and *foie gras.* Another tray has roasted cherry tomatoes paired with prosciutto and cream cheese on thin slices of toasted bread, and the final plate contains grilled shrimp on wooden skewers in what Adair says is a glass filled with chilled mango puree.

"He made this in the time it took us to get here and choose the wine?"

"Alain's the Michelin-starred chef I coaxed out of working in Paris, the one who cooked for us on my yacht. We grow most of the herbs and vegetables he uses and keep chickens for fresh eggs."

I take a bite of the duck appetizer, savoring the rich meat contrasted by the tart rhubarb.

"He's worth every penny, isn't he?" Adair says.

"I'm pretty sure you don't pay him in pennies."

After the appetizers, a thin blond man in a black chef's uniform approaches, carrying two plates.

"Ready for salad, sir?" he says. Adair stands and takes the dishes, and the chef rubs his neck, avoiding eye contact.

"Alain, this is Davia Glenn."

I begin to get up, but the chef's horrified look stops me. "The food is wonderful, thank you."

"*Merci.*" After another disapproving glance at Adair, he departs. Adair hands me a plate, then places his on the table.

"He thinks I shouldn't lift a finger. More wine?"

"I should pour instead of you so he doesn't scold me," I say, but relent and allow Adair to give me more of the excellent vintage.

When we finish the salads, Alain reappears, and I quickly survey the roofline and pillars for hidden cameras but spot none. The main course is sea bass paired with grilled artichoke hearts and caviar, plated so beautifully it's an art piece.

"Wait on dessert, please," Adair tells him, and Alain says, "*Oui, Monsieur,*" before departing.

The sun drops below the horizon, and Adair says, "Are you cold? We can go in."

"No, this is pleasant." Lanterns wink on in the gardens, and I think of hiding in them when I first attended one of Adair's parties, trying to recover from the effects of a drug an assassin injected into me.

"Let me turn on some music." He goes inside, and soon a soft, relaxing tune plays. Adair comes to my side and holds out his hand. "Why don't we dance?"

He sweeps me into the slow-tempo music, his touch igniting a trail of electricity where his strong hand entwines with mine. Adair's other hand rests on my waist, a tender anchor in this intimate embrace. The sultry voice of a female singer fills the air, her melancholic plea of "Stay with me" putting voice to my unexpressed desire for him. Every moment triggers a collision of emotions within me, but I find solace by laying my cheek against his shoulder and surrendering to the security of his arms. The melody shifts, carrying me further away from anything but this moment as the sky transforms into a tapestry of stars, as if nature paints a backdrop for our private universe.

Nineteen

Amelia Meadows says, "Henry Adams gave me your number. I'm hosting a small gathering tonight and would love it if you and Adair would stop in."

Me and Adair. He drove me home the night before, and I said, "A car's following us."

"Those are the new bodyguards Jason hired. They're unhappy because I wouldn't let them ride with us."

"I'll make sure and test them out later."

"Please be gentle. If you beat them up, word will get around, and I won't have anyone willing to take the job."

He walked me to my gate and hugged me, saying, "Reach out whenever you need me."

Now, I tell Amelia, "I'm not sure what he's doing today."

Part of me wishes I knew, already spending much of the night pondering his restraint. Was this a new tactic? Kyle once said, "The only tactics men should use with you are when you're on an operation. They have no value anywhere else."

Amelia says, "No matter. Before I forget, I want to say I appreciate you standing up for me. In these circles, defending someone is a rarity."

"I've experienced some animosity myself." From you when we met, but that was right after your former boyfriend was murdered.

"So, will you come?"

"What do you mean by small gathering? The term can mean five to five hundred."

Amelia lets out a throaty laugh. "I mean ten or less."

"I might not be the life of the party due to Bob Brooks' death."

"Such a tragedy. He was one of our community's kindest, most genuine people."

So far, Francis Downs, Alexandra Brooks, and Adair were the only consistently decent people from the Rancho crowd. Stop. Don't think about him again.

Should I call Alex and get his therapist's number?

"See you tonight," I say, and we conclude the call. Why did I accept an invitation when I'll spend the whole time counting the seconds until I can leave?

My doorbell rings, and José waits outside. "Mama's found the right person to be a housekeeper for you. You're hesitant, but she's reliable and discreet."

"I did some research, and I can't request a background until I offer employment, so a preliminary interview's a requirement."

"She can be here this afternoon."

"You know, working here can be dangerous. Is she as skilled as you with a machete or shovel?"

"Doubtful, but I can call her and inquire."

"Let's not scare her away yet. Say, did you talk to your cousin?"

"Left him a message. He's busy, but I stressed he should contact me if he finds out more about the rumor."

A workout, sauna session, and a shower kill time while I wait for the potential housekeeper to arrive. I leave my phone in a drawer in the office so I don't give in and text Adair, begging him to be my society shield again. After eating some yogurt, I do pantry memorization drills, rearrange the items, and rerun the mental exercise to keep from calling

Adair. Why does my ability to compartmentalize and lock away my problems never work with him?

What now? Clean my closet? Read a book? Go to the office, retrieve my phone, and call Adair?

I pick up a mystery novel I haven't finished and, before settling into a chair near the pool, I take a few minutes to unlock the guest house and survey the window treatments Sherilyn installed. It's good she isn't with me, as I doubt I could've faked excitement. The quiet, the sun reflecting on the pool's blue water, and the twists and turns of Detective Fox Argall's adventures in *Ruin of the Watcher* keep me engaged. When it's almost time for the interview, I go inside to ensure I'm presentable and end my phone time-out, but no one's contacted me.

Am I back in high school, waiting for a guy to call?

At the appointed time, José appears at the front door with a fiftyish Latina woman he introduces as Ana Sanchez before he leaves to go back to work.

"Please call me Davia, and come in. Would you like some tea?"

"Yes, please. You have a beautiful home, Ms. Glenn." Her black hair's in a tidy bun, and she's clad in a white housekeeper's outfit paired with sturdy shoes.

"Call me Davia."

"All right, Davia."

"Why don't you tell me your background?"

"I was born in Mexico City, and a relative petitioned for my family to come to the United States and was our sponsor. I arrived when I was fourteen, so long ago." She smiles. "I graduated high school, married, and have cleaned houses since."

"Tell me about your last job."

"I worked for an elderly couple daily because they needed me to cook, shop, and do household chores. They recently sold their home and moved into a retirement community."

"Did José tell you this is only once a week?"

"I needed to cut back my hours. My husband has a well-paying job, and I want to spend more time with our grandchildren."

We go through the house. "What do you think?" I say when we finish.

"You're a tidy lady, and your home won't require much except dusting and vacuuming, maybe some window washing. I can do your laundry and some cooking if you like."

I want to tell her I won't need her to, but Alex Gordon's words replay: *Let go of your past and guilt. Decide what this money might bring that's a positive rather than focusing on the negatives.*

"Do you like to grocery shop?"

Ana nods. "I did all the shopping for my last employers at the Suprema Market."

"Really?"

"If you tell me what you like to eat, I can prepare some meals for the remainder of the week you can reheat. That will give you more time to devote to other things."

We review the salary, and Ana says she'll get a background check done that week.

"Before you go," I say, "A woman who works near here told me some Rancho Suprema housekeepers have disappeared. José said Olivia, your niece, is one of them."

Ana crumples, shoulders sagging forward. "I blame myself. I got her the job, hoping to find a way for her to become a citizen. She hasn't been in the U.S. long, lured across the border by some boyfriend who, like a fool, she trusted. He ditched her."

"Do you have any idea what happened to her?"

"She used to tell me all about her job, what she did, and funny stories. About two weeks before she disappeared, she got home later and later from work. When I attempted to learn more, she said she was with friends but didn't give me specifics.

"Do you think it was a man?"

"Could be. Olivia came home with a new phone, an expensive one, and new outfits. She wouldn't tell me how she got them. I don't think she bought them because I took her to send money to her family in Mexico weekly, and she never had much left over."

"Anything else?"

Ana stares at the ceiling, lost in thought. "Her personality went from enthusiastic and bubbly to anxious, even afraid."

"Did she have any bruises?"

"Not that I saw, but I was busy helping my employers pack for their move and working extra hours, so I came home exhausted."

"Do you know the other girls?"

"I don't, but they're all young, in the country without documentation."

"Do you have a picture of Olivia?"

Ana scrolls up a photo on her phone. Olivia is a striking young lady with thick black hair and playful doe eyes.

"She's pretty." I hand back the phone. "Do you mind texting the photo to me? I'll keep an eye out."

Ana sends me the photo and slips the phone into her purse.

"Sorry for all the questions."

"I've been worried sick but haven't found a trace of her. Her phone is turned off, and her belongings are still in her room. She lived with us."

"Perhaps she'll come home."

"All I can do is pray."

As I go with Ana to her car, I contemplate whether the similar age and vulnerability of the undocumented girls could have made them targets, but by whom? Human traffickers? Men? I don't give voice to these thoughts.

———

A sloping driveway takes me past an open security gate, and I back my car into a space where I can't be blocked. I'm an hour past when Amelia mentioned I should arrive, planning a late in-early out strategy.

"Davia, do come in," Amelia welcomes, and the scent of her wine glass and floral perfume covers me when she leans in for a hug. Her signature red lipstick marks her glass's rim like a vampire's kiss. "Sorry Adair couldn't make it."

"So am I." I was proud of myself for not calling him but regret my restraint.

Light wood floors, white walls, ivory couches, and an immaculate kitchen make up an open floor plan. I thought Amelia's home would resemble a Southern plantation, given she's from Georgia, but the décor is ultra-modern. Another preconceived notion shattered.

A blue-sky view through a floor-to-ceiling retracted wall allows air inside. Invitees are on the patio, talking.

"You know everyone already, so get some wine and mingle." Amelia indicates the kitchen where a man and woman prepare a meal. Various bottles of wine are open next to glasses on a white marble counter. When the woman pauses chopping vegetables, I wave her off.

How slowly can I pour and delay talking to anyone?

Since the chefs send me concerned glances, I pick up the filled glass and move to the opposite side of the room, where a TV broadcasts a golf tournament with the sound muted.

Brant Kensington pauses beside me, holding an empty wine glass. "Do you like golf?"

"I know nothing about golf."

"You date Adair, and he hasn't talked golf?" His rich voice contains disbelief.

"Not at length, but—" *We aren't dating; we're getting to know each other.* "I'm sure he'll expound on the topic eventually."

"Still in the not-much-talking phase? He has that effect on women."

Sudden irritation hits me. "Have you known him long?"

Brant's deep-set amber eyes gleam like golden honey. "We've crossed paths for five years or so. You're new to all this, aren't you?"

"All what?"

He jerks a thumb at the others. "The never-ending games of the rich. After a time, you're bound to rub someone the wrong way. For Adair and me, we knocked heads over a burgeoning beauty on the continent, nothing major. He won, of course."

My head grows light, and I admonish myself to keep it together. Why would Adair vying for other women bother me? Brant doesn't perceive my discomfort and says, "How long have you known him?"

"A few months."

"Having seen him operate, let me give you a word of advice. Get away from him before he shatters your heart into that cliché of a million little pieces."

Steadying myself, I say, "What makes you think I have a heart?"

Brant's bark of laughter turns heads. "Adair might lose this time."

Before I can formulate a response, Jennifer McMillan calls, "Davia!

Don't let Brant monopolize your time, come join us." At her side is Hannah, head down, phone-obsessed.

Brant says, "I'll let the others have you but be careful. You'll be their plaything until the newness dissipates. They'll invite you to fundraisers, nominate you to serve on boards, and make you tell stories about your life for their amusement."

"One of my favorite words is no."

Brant laughs again, then goes toward the kitchen.

"Tired of Adair and moved onto Brant?" is Jennifer's opening when I approach. She drops her voice. "I mean, I don't blame you. Brant Kensington is worth a hundred Adairs."

"Is he? In what way?"

"Besides the Kensington money, rumor has it he's an absolute stud in the bedroom."

"Are you saying Adair isn't?'

Why am I defending him?

Jennifer snakes a hand adorned with glittering rings onto my arm. "We've tried to find out, but no one's ever given us details."

He's a real snooze fest. "I can't say."

Jennifer narrows her eyes. "Can't or won't?"

"Don't bother her, Mom," Hannah's thumbs fly over her phone. "I'm tired of listening to people speculate what it would be like to bang Adair and complain when none of the women he's been with will talk."

Jennifer steps back. "I'm going for more wine. Amelia should hire servers; she's got plenty of money. Instead, she bought this place last month and filled it with beige furniture to match the bland walls, kitchen, and floors. Not a trace of personality anywhere."

With that pithy remark, Jennifer stalks away, and I take a drink of wine, gazing at the view of the ocean as the sun casts fading colors on a long swimming pool in another part of the yard.

"You can tell me," Hannah says, not taking her eyes off a video.

"Tell you what?"

"About Adair."

"He's thirty-one, from England, and donates much of his money to charity. His mom danced ballet as a professional, and...."

"I can read Wikipedia." Hannah turns her back.

I wander to the patio's edge, enjoying the sky's vibrant hues instead of fixating on Brant's words.

Get away from him before he shatters your heart into that cliché of a million little pieces.

Were Adair's actions a long game to make me his, and then...?

Before I can examine the minutia of my encounters with Adair, Minerva Adams joins me, saying, "Did that pair irritate you already?"

"No, I'm admiring the view."

"A better choice than dealing with the McMillans. Jennifer's kept Hannah in the playpen her whole life, but they can both be problematic. Were they needling you about Adair? Jennifer's wanted him for Hannah *forever*. Hannah doesn't care; she only wants to continue receiving trust fund money from Mommy and Daddy to fritter her life away."

"I'm surprised they haven't tried for Brant Kensington. Isn't he the bigger catch?"

"You get Brant; you get the Kensington family, which is another deal. Hazel would make Hannah's life miserable for daring to touch her darling, only son."

"Bradford's pleasant," I nod to where the elder Kensington's in another disheveled cardigan and his thick black glasses talking to Henry Adams and Mike McMillan.

"Don't let his appearance fool you. He's a ruthless businessman, uncaring whether it's a friend or foe when he wants an asset. His ascent began when he desired his best friend's company, some software tech business. Bradford worked as a CFO, the chief financial officer of some other corporation, and was a whiz with numbers. He somehow used insider information from his friend to purchase a controlling interest in shares, fired his friend, and stole his wife, Hazel. He chooses companies for a hostile takeover like a serial killer stalks prey, fires employees, and exerts aggressive oversight." Minerva shivers, rubbing her arms.

"Are you cold?"

"I'm going to borrow a wrap from Amelia."

She goes toward the house but glances at Bradford, her face displaying...fear? I'm not sure. Did Minerva suspect the elder Kensington might try to take over her husband's hedge fund company?

Amelia announces dinner is ready, and everyone files into the kitchen, where the chefs offer thin slices of steak and roasted potatoes, scallops on baby spinach covered with pomegranate sauce, and roasted vegetables steeped in browned butter.

"Hello, Davia," a man says from behind me, and I find Bradford Kensington beside me. "Where's Adair tonight?"

"Busy."

"That'll allow time for us to get better acquainted. Why don't you sit with me?"

We take our plates to where two plush chairs are before an outdoor table. Bradford pushes his glasses up his nose and regards me with the same amber-colored eyes as his son's. "How long have you lived in Rancho Suprema?"

"Only a few months."

"And before?"

"I worked as a personal assistant for a CEO and traveled a lot."

"What's his name?"

Of course, you think the CEO's a man.

I mention the name from my cover story, and any inquiries will back up my false position.

"Never heard of him." Bradford takes a bite of steak.

"Your property manager said you don't live here full-time."

Bradford chews and swallows. "Oh, we have homes scattered on most continents, and I go where business takes me. How about you?"

Inside, I loathe the ping-pong of the conversation but say, "I only have a home here."

"Your aunt was Lilah Latham, right?" He spears another bite of steak.

How had he come up with the connection? "Yes. Did you know her?"

"No, but Hazel might have, New York, right?"

I nod.

"I did business with Edwin Latham a time or two. Shrewd fellow, but he sputtered more than he talked."

As a kid, I thought my uncle resembled a walrus. He accompanied my aunt to South Dakota only once to support her disapproval of my childhood home and life path.

"Mind if I sit with you?" Nicole Wolfe drags a chair over, assuming she's welcome, but the annoyance on Bradford's face says otherwise. "Davia, Henry said you were friends with Bob Brooks. I'm so sorry. I intend to send flowers but don't know his wife's name."

"Alexandra Brooks and their daughter is Jessica."

"I'll try to remember to tell my personal assistant."

"Officer Sterling told me you found him, Davia," Bradford says, and Nicole's hand flies to her chest.

"How are you here? I'd still be in bed or at the Golden Door Spa for a month,"

"Davia's made of sturdier stuff than most of us, right?" Bradford's mouth is full, so the words aren't distinct.

"I haven't lived here long enough to make that judgment."

"But you've worked a real job," Bradford persists, "unlike so many in this community. Wait, Nicole, weren't you a spin class instructor once? Isn't that where you began your campaign to marry Josh?"

Nicole flushes but doesn't address the apparent dig. "Weren't we discussing Bob Brooks? Did you ever meet him, Bradford?"

"Yes, at Hazelton Manor with Davia, and ran into him somewhere later. Pleasant man."

Amelia joins us, only a wine glass in hand, her wrist flicking to swirl the contents. "I have a psychic in the study who'll read tarot and predict your future. Come find me when you finish eating, and I'll take you to her room, first come, first served."

Bradford says, "You ladies are likely more interested than me."

Josh Whittaker beckons to his wife, "Nicole, I need you to settle a bet for me with Henry."

"Excuse me." Nicole leaves her plate of food and goes to where her husband sits at another table with Henry and Minerva Adams and the McMillan family. Brant eats alone inside, watching the golf game.

Amelia goes to the other table, where the conversation is loud, interspersed with hoots and laughter. I poke at the spinach beneath a scallop with my fork.

"You're not much of a talker, are you?" Bradford observes.

Mustering a smile, I say, "I prefer listening."

"You and my son are perfect for each other." He nods toward Brant.

"Is he also an introvert?"

"Brant marches to his own beat. Say, what did you do to Kenneth Clayton? He avoided you at Henry's, acting like a scared rabbit. Bet that's why he's not here tonight."

"We went on a date once and didn't have much in common."

"You give meaningless answers, don't you?"

"Do I?"

Bradford's soft eyes harden for a flash. "I'm going to discover what's revved the others up. You should ask the psychic what your future holds."

As he leaves, I wonder why his words came across as threatening.

———

Amelia takes me to a secluded room. "Kim Meredith came from Los Angeles and is a psychic medium so revered I spent a fortune to hire her."

A plump woman with curly blonde hair in a flowing dress sits behind a table containing ornate cards. She's lit candles, and a heady fragrance from incense wafts through the room.

"Kim, this is Davia. She's here for a reading," Amelia says.

"Welcome, come sit down."

After a moment's consternation, I do. Is seeing a psychic better or worse than small talk?

"I'll hang the 'Do not disturb' sign on the outer handle," Amelia says and departs.

"I sense you haven't done this before?" Kim shuffles the deck.

"No."

"Don't be nervous; your aura is a deep cobalt blue, so you're already interested in the unexplained. I'll do a general reading first; then we'll commune with Spirit, okay?"

Unsure what she means, I shift in my chair.

"Here, I want you to shuffle this deck and cut it into three piles, three times, with your left hand. When you cut, let your fingers tell you when to stop to divide them."

As I carry out the task, Kim says, "Are you allowing your energy to flow into them?"

My confused expression is her answer. Kim takes the deck and arranges ten cards in rows. As she turns them over one by one, her eyes flick to me with surprise. "You have a lot of major arcana among these."

"What does that mean?"

"Major arcana are destiny cards, while minor arcana pertain to day-to-day issues. Here," she taps a card in the center covered by another, "this one is The Tower in reverse, positioned to represent who you are. The image symbolizes a human ego-created tower struck by lightning. It suggests your life has undergone significant changes, possibly accompanied by some discomfort. The card covering The Tower indicates your challenges and what's hindering you from achieving your desires. It's another of the major arcana, The Hanged Man. It signifies that you're in an uncomfortable position where fighting and resistance won't work. See how he's hanging? It won't help if he struggles. You need to let go of circumstances that no longer serve you."

Is my essence an exploding tower, putting me in a position my warrior self can't fight?

"Now, here's the immediate past, a three of swords. You've experienced pain."

Bob died, and I couldn't save him. Did she somehow figure this out from the media coverage of his murder?

"This," Kim thrusts an illustrated square my way with a woman surrounded by a wreath, "represents The World, symbolizing potential outcomes of your future. The world's at your feet once you choose a path, which is invigorating. However, the other cards in your reading are dominated by swords, representing action, change, power, courage, and conflict."

One of the sword illustrations showcases an individual seated on a bed, palms shrouding their face, with swords mounted above them on a wall. The association between swords and conflict is the first item I can relate to since the reading commenced.

She considers her layout, emitting contemplative sounds. "I'm hesitant to share this, but some vexing scenarios are on the horizon. You'll battle some potent, malevolent forces."

"You're making my life sound like an action movie," I say, but Kim continues to frown at the spread, a hand on her chin, ignoring my words. "You must be an old soul to have signed up for this many tests and trials. Come around here and take my hands."

She scoots over on the loveseat. I sit and reluctantly place my hands on hers, wondering what I'm doing. Will she snatch them back when she glimpses my past?

"A man is here; he wants to thank you for finding him and says to tell his wife and daughter he's fine and at peace. He's doing a little dance, wanting me to let you know he doesn't need—a cane, I think."

My eyes fill with tears.

"Do you know someone who fits this description?" Kim asks.

"Yes. Did he say who killed him?"

Kim appears to listen. "He's not sure. He says it happened fast. No, you wait your turn. Some woman's here trying to push the sweet man aside. Her name is an L word."

Aunt Lilah.

"This lady claims to be your aunt. She talks about revelations, understandings, and awareness she didn't have before she died. She wanted to contact you and tell you you're loved. She's proud of the person you've become, how you've handled life, and what's been thrown at you. You had a strained relationship with your aunt, right?"

"Yes, I did."

"She was desperate to tell you what I said, which is why she was so assertive. She apologized to the gentleman, and they left together."

I remove my hands from Kim's, mind racing.

"You can sit back in that chair." While I resituate myself, she says, "Shuffle and cut these one more time."

When I finish and return them, Kim says, "Spirit keeps shouting at me, 'Men, men, men.' Do you have men problems?"

I want to laugh but give a non-committal shrug. She lays out more cards, draws her shoulders back, and taps a finger on the deck before casting more.

"You have three men in your life who are important. One is a dark-haired, action-oriented, quick-thinking powerhouse, another is charming, romantic, a visionary, and the last is a financial power with a hidden, troubled undercurrent he covers with a relaxed attitude."

Warden, Adair, and Alex.

She selects a card from the deck, spins it in her hand, and places it on the table.

"One of these men is your soulmate. Do you want to know which?"

Did I?

She tells me.

TWENTY

"How set in stone is all of this?"

Kim says, "You have free will, but your primary spirit guide is smiling."

"My what?"

"We all have spirit guides for different needs; for instance, an Asian man with a beard from ancient times is here. He's in a military uniform and says he guided you during your warrior training." Kim's eyes go to the side as if listening to someone invisible, then return to me. "Good gracious, and you appear so demure."

I examine the space where this warrior allegedly is but see nothing.

This is so far beyond my comfort zone; it's in another dimension.

There's a knock at the door. "Are you finished yet?" Amelia inquires.

"Almost!" Kim calls, then says, "Remember, although you can change your path, the one with the least resistance, without obstacles, means you're going in the right direction."

———

I'm home, slumped in a chair in my bedroom, staring at nothing as my thoughts spiral. How much of Kim's reading was real, and how much was complete fantasy? Excess energy forces me up, and I pace the room. When my phone rings with a video call, I hustle to answer.

"Warden, are you back?"

"We're not going to be for some time. I'm where I can make a secure call, but we'll have to put off the Colorado trip."

Ned appears on the screen. "And he's been a big pussy about it too, Bombshell."

"So much for the new, improved you, Ned," I comment. The scruffy beard he shaved off before the Ladies' League fashion show has grown back.

"I can always shave, but our team leader can't do anything about his ugly mug." Ned nudges Warden.

"You keeping your guns greased, Dav?" Hodge drawls, replacing Ned and towering over Warden's right shoulder.

"Went shooting a few days ago, so yes."

"I'm going to test your skills in Colorado," Warden says. "Loser— and that will be you—will owe me a special tribute, and I'm sure you know what I mean by special."

Hodge acts mock-scandalized. "Don't say things like that in front of Savant. You'll scar his virgin ears. Hey, K! Want to say nothing to Davia?"

K appears on the screen and winks at me. Warden turns the phone to where Savant types at high speed on a laptop, and he raises a hand.

"Now you boys have greeted our teammate—" Warden begins.

"Wait, I need to say hello." Craig Kilburn appears, a big hand on his bald, scarred head. "So you saved your boy toy, Bombshell? Thought for sure he died...and I think someone here wishes that were true."

Kilburn wanders away, chuckling, looking pleased at sowing discord.

"Hang on a sec," Warden says. "I'm stepping out and away from these buffoons." He goes to another room. "No shock, but Kilburn's still an asshole. When I have a better time frame for our return, I'll try to call. You know how these campaigns go, bored to death, then facing death. Anything new?"

"I found the body of the man who sold me my house. He was murdered."

"Murdered? What happened?"

I tell him about Alexandra's call and my actions.

"God, babe. We deal with death in our jobs, but finding him must have been rough."

"I called Kyle Kavanagh, a South Dakota neighbor who became friends with Bob on a recent visit, and he's coming out for the funeral."

"This isn't meant to be funny, but murders in Rancho happen so often that you'll soon be the only resident."

"I'm shocked, too. I expected little to no crime."

"How's your concussion?"

"Been doing memory drills, but I think lack of daily practice is more of a problem than my injury. I got a headache at the range but didn't bring my best ear protection."

"And the nerve damage from your wound?"

"Plan to begin running again."

"Be careful. I don't want you gone longer than necessary."

"Kyle will be here soon to counsel me on potential issues. He's like a protective parent but with better weapons skills."

Warden drops his eyes. "And what about your 'boy toy?'"

"He's got PTSD issues from the kidnapping and torture."

Now Warden's gaze is unwavering. "He's back in Rancho?"

"His estate is on the Ladies' League Home and Garden Tour."

"Why are you giving me a 'facts only' response? Have you seen that Brit?" His voice is a threatening rumble.

"He helped me take some flowers and gifts to Bob's widow and daughter and accompanied me to a gathering hosted by community leaders. They said they planned to discuss the burglaries, and I hoped to get a lead on who attacked me."

"And did you?"

"No, the people were more concerned with inner circle bickering than the crimes."

"You're talking to him, going places with him...he has home-field advantage." Melancholy permeates his words.

"Warden, no. Time with you is my priority."

"Is it?"

"Yes. I don't want to upset you, but I'm responsible for what those terrorists did to Adair. It made matters worse when I stopped talking to him after the rescue."

"Worse for who? You went in to save him alone, risked your life, and now you're worried because *he's* traumatized? He's lucky he's still breathing."

"Warden, we've fought enough about his rescue. I gave you my reasons and—"

"Whatever, Davia. While I'm gone, you need to figure out why you're with a man who isn't me."

He disconnects.

———

Sleep eludes me most of the night. Why would I destroy Warden for—whatever Adair brings into my life?

Warden will leave you.

I get a call notification early the next day and pray Warden is ready to talk. My body deflates when the ID reads Beatrice Gibbs.

"Davia, we have an emergency," she declares. "Stacey Templeton was the victim of a home invasion, and heaven knows what that will do to our tour. Go to her house now and determine if it's still suitable."

"Won't Stacey tell you what happened?"

"I can't reach her. I can't believe how inconsiderate she's acting with the tour almost upon us."

"I doubt she'll welcome—"

"Please do your job." Beatrice ends the call.

———

"This is ridiculous," I mutter, driving toward Stacey's address. Her security gates stand open, and I hesitate before turning in, sure the Ladies' League tour will be the last thing on her mind.

Tiberius Torston Templeton IV doesn't greet me as I go to ring the doorbell. While I wait, Detective Robbie Rodríguez arrives.

"Detective," I acknowledge when he nears.

"Ms....Glenn, right?"

"Call me Davia."

He removes his sunglasses, deep brown eyes regarding me with curiosity. "Montoya related what you did to Detective Sgt. Hurst."

"You mean when I thanked him for his service?"

"Montoya got a kick out of it, but I'm sure he remained inscrutable. He mentioned you'd like to see the burglary video at Bryce's?"

"Yes. Perhaps it will help me remember what happened."

Stacey Templeton opens the door outfitted in a black pantsuit, a black velvet hat, and an elaborate black lace veil covering her face.

"Ms. Templeton, I'm sorry to disturb you," Detective Rodríguez says, "but you were so distraught last night. I thought now would be a better time to take your statement,"

"Oh, Davia, it's so kind you're here as support." She clutches my arm, mistaking my presence. "I'm hardly coherent since losing T4."

"The turkey—I mean, T4 is dead?" I say.

"Isn't that why you're here?"

"Uh, yes," I improvise as Stacey collapses against me, sobbing into my shoulder. When she can regain control, she straightens, removes a handkerchief from a pocket, and wipes at her red eyes. I pat her back, saying, "Let's sit down." We shuffle to a couch in a nearby room, and she crumples onto it.

"Do you want some water?" I say, but she latches onto my hands, hauls me down beside her, and weeps anew.

"I'll find some," Rodríguez volunteers and goes toward the kitchen.

"I-I can't believe T4's gone. He was so brave."

"I can't imagine how you feel," I say, grateful for the phrase, as I wonder what happened.

Detective Rodríguez returns with a water bottle, twists off the cap, and hands it to Stacey before sitting in a chair opposite us.

"Do you think you can answer questions now, Ms. Templeton?" He keeps his voice soft as Stacey drinks some water, oblivious to the snot pouring from her nose.

"Here." I take the handkerchief from her, reach under the veil, and clean her face like a child's. "Now, blow." She does, and I fold away the mess, place the soiled cloth beside her, and notice an embroidered turkey on one of the corners.

Stacey props her bottle on the couch and retakes my hands like a drowning woman clinging to a life preserver. "I'm ready, Detective."

Rodríguez turns on a recorder and recites the date, time, location, and people present. "Why don't you tell me what happened last night?" he says, and Stacey shudders.

"I attended an opera downtown because I've patronized their programs in the past and received an invitation for a pre-performance meal. When I left, T4—"

"T4 is?" Rodríguez asks.

"Tiberius Torston Templeton the fourth, my-my..." Stacey stammers, "My faithful turkey companion, rest his soul."

"Where was T4?" I say to keep the conversation on track and away from another cascade of tears.

"I tucked him into bed in his playroom before I left. I should've hired a sitter, but he's been less destructive when I've been out. I told him how long I'd be gone, he indicated he understood, and then I read him a story, and he went right to sleep."

Rodríguez is impassive, but I wish I knew what he was thinking. "About what time did you leave?" he says.

"My driver picked me up around six p.m."

Rodríguez taps his pen on his pad. "Is this driver someone you're familiar with?"

"Branson's been my driver for over ten years. He's with the limousine service I employ whenever I need to go somewhere distant."

Distant? Downtown San Diego is about twenty miles.

"You don't use Uber or Lyft?" I ask.

"What are those?"

"I need details about your driver and service." Rodríguez takes notes as she recites the names. "When you left, were the security gates to your property open or closed?"

"Open, I think. My gates need repair and don't automatically shut when cars leave. I took a vintage Judith Leiber couture beaded bag and wouldn't dream of cramming a gate remote in it."

Rodríguez says, "About what time did you get home?"

"I promised T4 to be back before midnight and knew he'd be pacing if I were late, so I made sure to arrive home on time."

"What happened after you got back?"

"The lights in the house were off, which I found odd. Tiberius doesn't like the dark, so I leave them on at night."

"Did you enter through the front door?"

"Yes."

"Was it locked?"

"Yes, and when I flicked the switch..." Stacey pauses, face paling. "Tiberius lay on the floor. At first, I thought he fell down the stairs because his neck was at an odd angle, and I wondered, 'Why didn't he use his elevator?'"

Rodríguez's eyes open a fraction at this, but Stacey continues her story, oblivious. "Then I saw the blood."

The detective clears his throat. "Let's go back. The turkey, I mean T4, has an elevator?"

"Of course."

Rodríguez flips some pages before managing to say, "You saw some blood?"

"Yes, there was quite a lot trailed throughout the foyer. Amelia, my housekeeper, mopped it up this morning after your evidence team finished. And god, they left fingerprint powder *everywhere*. She's still cleaning upstairs."

"We think the tur—T4 attacked the burglars," Rodríguez says.

"Is that why you took his body?"

"The evidence team wants to ensure they have adequate samples from his beak and claws."

"When will I get him back? I need to make funeral arrangements."

"Within the next day or so, I'm sure."

"Have you ever seen a turkey in a state, detective? I'm sure he went ballistic when Tiberius saw it wasn't me. T1 used to body slam my father when angered and peck at our hands. He also attacked with his spurs. My other companions have been less volatile."

"DNA will help us arrest whoever did this," Rodríguez says.

I withdraw my hands from Stacey's. "You must be proud of T4 for trying to protect your property."

"Oh, I am. I've already contacted my artist to alert him that he needs to add T4 to the sculpture in the yard."

"Have you compiled a list of what was stolen?" Rodríguez says, but he's struggling to keep his voice level.

"They cleaned out my closet. With all the premium bags, shoes, and clothing taken, I put the loss at over two million from that area alone. They also somehow took my jewelry from a wall safe, so that's another five to seven million."

"The Ladies' League did a recent video as part of their Home and Garden Tour promotion if that helps establish what's been taken," I say. Did the break-in occur because of online publicity?

"I'll make sure to take a look," Rodríguez says. "Why don't we go through the home?"

"You'll stay, won't you, Davia," Stacey implores.

"Of course."

The detective picks up the recorder, and we go through the residence room by room. Although the thieves cleaned out many items, the empty closet is a shock.

"They took the champagne, too," Stacey says. "I had at least six cases of 2000 Dom Perignon Brut Rosé by the bar in preparation for the Ladies' League tour. They cost nearly $1800 per bottle, with six bottles per case. If they drink it, I hope they choke."

"Stacey," I say, "I don't mean to be insensitive, but will you withdraw your home from the tour?"

"What would T4's death mean if I did? He gave his life for his beloved property, so I must move forward to honor his bravery. I keep extra clothing and accessories in a separate storage building, and the thieves missed it."

"I'll let Beatrice know," I say.

Several hours later, we complete the inventory.

"The thieves were quite discerning," Rodríguez concludes. "They only took items of high value. Do you have any security cameras?"

"No, I never bothered. My insurer will be unhappy, as I do a policy review yearly to ensure adequate coverage, but no amount of money will bring T4 back to life."

"I'm sorry for your loss," Rodríguez says as we leave.

I hug Stacey and trail the detective toward our cars.

"Make an appointment to come in and see the footage of the Bryce's Boutique burglary, okay?" he says. "But if you mention the turkey right now, I'm warning you I might start laughing and be unable to stop."

Twenty-One

"Are you ready?" Kyle wears a charcoal black suit and a somber expression. His red-gray hair is short, and his muscular frame conveys power.

"Think so," I smooth the hem of my black dress.

Bob's funeral service is at a local church where he was a long-time member. We arrive early to a nearly-filled parking lot. People stand together in a courtyard, speaking quietly and waiting for the doors to open.

"Hi, Davia," Alex Gordon says. "Good to see you again, Kyle, but not under these circumstances."

"Alex was Aunt Lilah's wealth manager and now mine," I explain to Kyle, who encountered Alex when I first did and didn't hold him in high regard.

"Oh?" Kyle reassesses Alex. "Did you get along with her?"

"Did anyone?" Alex says, which makes Kyle grin and say, "I'd like to meet the person who could."

The crowd stirs, and Adair comes straight toward me, oblivious of his effect. He's in a black suit that fits him like it was custom-made to flatter his trim body, which it likely was. When he's beside me, he takes my hand and says, "Sorry I'm late."

I remove my hand from his and say, "Adair, this is Kyle Kavanagh, my neighbor in South Dakota and a friend of Bob's."

The men shake, Kyle scrutinizing Adair with the same intensity he has when setting a tripwire or squeezing off a .50 caliber round.

"A pleasure." Adair smiles, and it takes a long moment before Kyle says, "Likewise."

"Do you know Alex Gordon?" I ask Adair, and Alex says, "Yes, good to see you, Adair." José joins us, and I introduce him to Adair.

The crowd parts so Alexandra, Jessica, and Darren can enter the sanctuary. They go inside, and a staff member announces the church will reopen once the family is situated.

"How did you know Bob?" Adair says to Kyle and José.

"When the previous owners listed Davia's house for sale, Bob was the agent," José says. "He was sure the new owner would keep me on as property manager, and he was right."

Kyle tells of me pairing him with Bob as a golf partner, and Adair says, "We should play if you're here for a while."

Alex listens, and his lips twitch at Kyle's continued appraisal of Adair. He says, "You might be stuck with the big guy if your wingman doesn't approve of your glamour boy, LT."

"At least you don't think Kyle's my boyfriend this time." I refer to when Alex accused me of having daddy issues because Kyle's in his late forties.

"I'm having trouble keeping up with two."

The church opens, and people move in that direction. Adair retakes my hand, and his presence reassures me. Why has he become my go-to support system? Unable to explain why he's a comfort, I tell myself now's not the time to solve this mystery.

As we enter, a church staffer invites us to sign one of the guest books for the family. Adair stands beside me, hand on my lower back as I write my name and a brief message. I hand him the pen so he can do the same, and he smooths a bit of hair back from my face, saying, "Are you going to be okay?" I nod, and he signs the book and hands the pen to Kyle, who's unreadable.

After everyone signs, we move toward the sanctuary, receiving programs with a photo of Bob on the front. Alexandra, Jessica, and

Darren sit in a pew, hunched over, eyes down. Darren drapes his arm around Jessica's shoulders, and she holds her mom's hand. We find seats on one of the numerous curved benches facing a dais with a lectern and table. A circular stained glass window casts light on the steel and wood arches overhead and a waiting choir.

The pews fill, and I recognize many faces from the Ladies' League membership and others in the community. Adair moves his program to where we can read it together, his shoulder solid against mine.

The church's pews hold at least six hundred people, and it's standing room only at the rear. A pastor in black with a white collar climbs the steps of the dais and puts his arms out, saying, "Let us stand."

We all rise, and he performs a call to worship and prayer. "Eternal God, our help in time of trouble, send your Holy Spirit to comfort and strengthen us, that we may have hope of life eternal and trust in your kindness and mercy, through Jesus Christ our Lord. Amen."

A chorus of amens from attendees resound, and we sit. After some scripture readings, a slide show of Bob's life plays on a large drop-down screen. Photos of Bob as a child, graduating college, on his wedding day, and holding baby Jessica go past with Louis Armstrong singing, "What a Wonderful World." I wipe at tears, and Adair hands me a handkerchief. Kyle touches my arm; his eyes also rimmed by tears.

A series of residents, some of whom grew up with Bob in Rancho Suprema, share stories, all with a similar thread. He was an easy-going, caring man who loved his family. Some share humorous stories, one a fun tale of Bob trying to rescue the family cat from a tree but winding up stuck and the fire department bringing a ladder to help him down.

The pastor gives a brief sermon, the choir sings several songs, and the Lord's Prayer is recited. The service ends with an invitation to go to the Fellowship Hall to enjoy a post-memorial luncheon. Attendees wait as the Brooks family proceed up the aisle. Alex excuses himself to talk with some people, and we continue into the courtyard, where José receives a call and steps away.

"I wish I'd spent more time with him," Adair says.

Kyle shakes his head. "Only the good die young and all that. Be right back. Going to the men's room."

Sherilyn and Detective Montoya join us, and the handsome detective's typical stoicism lessens in Sherilyn's company. "That was sad," Sherilyn says, and I hug her.

When Adair retakes my hand, Sherilyn's eyes shine, but Montoya rubs his chin, and I picture gears grinding in his brain. Warden informed him I was his girlfriend at the Ladies' League fashion show, and Adair's beside me now.

Before I spiral into another endless guilt loop, the Kensingtons approach.

"Hello, Davia, Adair." Bradford says, Brant beside him. Adair's deep inhale is audible.

I tell them, "I didn't think you knew Bob well."

"As I said, ran into him a few times and at Hazelton. Felt we should pay our respects," Bradford says.

Brant focuses on Sherilyn, a wolfish smile coming and going like a dark cloud. Bradford pushes his glasses up, perhaps at a loss for what to do with his hands since he's in a suit instead of his usual cardigan sweater. His ruthless undercurrent is more evident now his casual camouflage is gone, his impatience palpable.

Henry and Minerva Adams wave the Kensingtons to their group, including the usual suspects. Nicole Wolfe and Josh Whittaker visit with Jennifer and Mike McMillan while Hannah is near them without her phone for once. She taps a foot, arms crossed.

José returns and says, "That was my cousin. He found out more about, you know, so I'm going to talk to him."

"Okay," I say, and he departs.

When Kyle returns, we enter the Fellowship Hall, where Bob's family greets people. When Alexandra sways, Darren places a steadying hand beneath her elbow, and Jessica puts an arm around her mom's waist. I think about Bob's message from the spirit world, picturing him beside his family, and I blink back more tears.

"Kyle, we appreciate you came all the way here for this," Alexandra says.

"It was my honor."

Church members serve a buffet of casseroles, salad, rolls, vegetables, and desserts. From the little we take, it's apparent none of us are hungry.

"Glad to see you're working this case," Kyle tells Montoya when we're seated.

Montoya's lips twist. "Getting nowhere, though."

"If anyone can solve it, you will," Kyle says.

"He will," Sherilyn agrees with pride.

"Is Kyle your Jason?" Adair says to me in a low voice.

"They are rather similar, except Kyle likes me."

Across the room, Hannah swivels her head as if finally noticing other people exist. Bussers clear plates, but none are Olivia.

Amelia Meadows is at a table with Beatrice Gibbs, Francis Downs, and others from the upper hierarchy of the Ladies' League. Alex is at a distant table and smiles when our eyes meet. Appropriate to the circumstances, people keep their conversations muted, a solemn atmosphere settling over even the most entitled attendees.

After the meal, we regroup in the courtyard, preparing to leave, when a girl's squeal makes heads turn.

"Davia!" Evie Huntly-Hart races toward me, trailed by Emily.

"Evie, Emily! Come back here." Samantha uses a strangled stage whisper and hurries after her daughters, with Christopher right behind. The other children don't join the twins but laugh when they throw their arms around me, faces beaming.

"Fans of yours?" Adair says.

I introduce the girls, and they say to Adair, "Are you a prince?"

"I'm afraid not. Crowns are heavy, and castles are cold and drafty."

The twins break into tinkling laughter.

"He's my knight in shining armor," I tell them.

"Where's your armor?" Evie asks Adair.

"This is a serious event, and armor makes a lot of noise. Besides, I don't expect any dragons."

More laughter erupts from the twins.

"I'm so sorry," their mom apologizes. "Girls, this is a solemn occasion."

"But this is our friend, Davia. She helped us find Bluebell at the party," Emily says.

Samantha frowns. "Bluebell? Why would she need to help you find Bluebell?"

Emily recognizes her error. "Um...."

"Bluebell is their dog," I explain. "Samantha, the dog escaped the room somehow, and I helped retrieve her. She was only loose for a few minutes."

"Oh? Well, thank you," Samantha says.

Christopher takes his girls by the shoulders, saying, "You need to promise to behave."

"We will," his daughters say, then run back to where the other children wait, nearly bowling over Brant and Bradford Kensington as they do. Hannah is nearby, back on her phone.

Christopher and Samantha shake Adair's hand, expressing disappointment that he couldn't accompany me to their event, as Alex rejoins us.

"Davia had Alex for company," Samantha says, and Adair looks between me and Alex.

"Don't stress, Adair," Alex says. "I kept your fake fiancé from having her face plastered all over the Huntly-Hart's channels."

Samantha and Christopher redden at his words, then head back to their children.

"We should go," I say to Kyle.

At my car, Adair brings me against him. "Call me later, okay?"

A sleek black car rolls up beside us, two men in the front scanning the departing crowd as another opens the back door for Adair.

"You got him to hire executive protection, I see," Kyle says.

"As long as I live here, he'll need them."

———

Kyle's in the kitchen with the refrigerator door open. "Do you ever eat?"

"I stocked up for your last stay, but the grocery store provides more headaches than it's worth, so I haven't shopped much since."

Kyle retrieves a bottle of Guinness. "Glad I didn't drink all of these last time."

We've changed into casual clothes, and I pour a glass of water, saying, "We can go out to eat. I'm hiring a housekeeper who'll come in once a week and also do the grocery shopping."

"You're hiring a housekeeper?" Kyle's at the kitchen table. "Decided to go all in on the new life?"

"Alex advised me to find the positives instead of resenting everything. If a housekeeper does light cleaning and braves the grocery store, those are positives."

Kyle takes a long drink of his beer. "Care to explain what's scary about shopping for groceries?"

"When I've gone to the Suprema Market, I've been stalked for dates, stopped a fight between two soda tycoons, customers swarmed me over the Adair magazine cover, and I got flashed. So scared's not the right term."

"I thought perhaps side effects from the head injury gave you an irrational fear, but those are valid reasons to hesitate. Now, let's talk about Adair."

"Why?"

"It was interesting to meet the man who brought paparazzi and reporters into your life and who you took two bullets to the chest to save."

"What did you think of him?"

"What *you* think is more important."

"Will you at least give me your impression?"

Kyle sits forward, dangling the beer bottle near his thigh. "He's smart, perceptive, funny, kind, hiding some part of him I can't yet figure out, and madly in love with you."

"You think he is? For real?"

Kyle nods. "What puzzles me is why. Is it because he's grateful you saved him, or does he like being with a woman like you without understanding the downside?"

"He's nearly died twice because of me, so he's lived the downside. But you're blowing your lines, Kyle. You should say he likes me for my beauty and charm."

"That goes without saying."

"Anything else?"

"Will Adair wait if you return to your team? I doubt it since people notice him the second he enters a space and would even if he weren't rich and famous. He must have women throwing themselves at him twenty-four-seven."

Once more, the thought of other women pursuing Adair makes me feel disquiet. "He claims I'm the first committed relationship he's wanted, but I'm unsure if he's being real."

"He's convinced you're what he wants, at least right now. Boy's got guts; I could tell the way he didn't drop eye contact with me."

"He did the same with Warden, not backing down at all."

"When did they meet?"

"At a gala when I first moved here and again at the Ladies' League fashion show."

"What about Warden? Didn't he want to attend the funeral?"

"He's on a mission, but he opened up and admitted it's killing him not to have me with him."

"If a high-level operative like him admitted that, he must love you, too." Kyle finishes the bottle and stands. "You've got some important decisions to make."

The doorbell chimes, and José is outside, still in his suit. When he comes in, we tell Kyle about the immigrants forced into slave labor and the three missing housekeepers.

José says, "Emilio thinks the restaurant in question is Château Rouge."

"Château Rouge? The prices are astronomical, and the place is always packed. Is he sure?" I say.

"He sent some of his employees to try and get more information. A few people talked and confirmed the situation."

"We should go out for dinner after all," Kyle says.

———

Sarah, the hostess at Château Rouge, says. "Did you have reservations?"

Adair's smile is sheepish. "No, I've been busy today, so it's my fault, but I wanted my out-of-town guest to enjoy the best food in Rancho Suprema while he's here."

Sarah consults her seating chart. "No worries, Mr. Monroe. Right this way."

"And there's another reason to date him," Sherilyn whispers.

After a planning session with José and Kyle, I called Adair and Sherilyn to give them an overview of our ideas.

"Make sure you wear a sexier-than-usual outfit," Adair said.

"Because?"

"If my name doesn't impress the chef, I doubt he'll turn down compliments from a beautiful woman."

His suggestion is why I selected a red velvet mini dress made of viscose, which exposes an uncomfortable amount of cleavage and unveils my thigh scar to the public for the first time. Upon seeing me in the dress, Adair's initial reaction was to bite his lip, perhaps without realizing it. His obvious yearning caused me to blush to a shade that rivaled the red of the dress.

Sarah seats us in a comfy booth, and Kyle turns to Adair. "How do you tune that out?"

"Tune what out?"

"The star-struck people and excited murmurs. I wouldn't go out in public if I were you."

Adair's face clears. "Oh, that? I pretend the attention's for someone right behind me."

A server approaches our table, and Kyle says, "I guess Guinness is out, so red wine's fine with me."

When Sherilyn and I agree, Adair orders a bottle.

"Perhaps José will be able to find someone to talk to and get word we want to help them," Sherilyn says.

"Too bad Montoya couldn't join us, but he has more legal constraints engaging with staff than we do," I say.

"He caught another homicide, which surprises me since he's still working on Bob's, but he says multiple cases happen," Sherilyn says. "Dating a detective is new territory for me, but I won't complain.

A server pours the wine and takes our orders. Women sneak photos of Adair with their phones, and he moves his hand atop mine while he talks to Kyle about golf. The gesture is absent-minded, but his touch is like taking a tranquilizer.

The conversation turns general when our meals arrive, and we share stories. Kyle tells us about having some food bloggers tour his farm to educate people on where wheat comes from. "They liked riding in the combine best because it was hot, and the cab was air-conditioned."

Sherilyn relays a story about turning down a job because the man wanted to decorate all the rooms in his mansion with the stuffed heads and taxidermied bodies of exotic animals he killed on safaris. "I mean, his vision was gross beyond belief. He wanted me to bring in illegal skin rugs and ivory for accents. When I refused to work with him, he threatened to badmouth me within Rancho and ensure I didn't get any more work. I told him my parents are lawyers, and I documented everything, so if he wanted to go down in flames, try me. You should've seen his face! He's one of those high-and-mighty plutocrats used to getting his way but internally a complete coward."

"What is it with rich people and exotic animals?" I say. "Some people at the Huntly-Hart's party said they smuggled a cheetah into the country. When domestic cats go on a rampage, they can shred you. Think about what a cheetah could do."

"People without common sense still surprise me, although they shouldn't," Kyle says. "What about you, Adair? I'm sure you've got stories."

"Here's one on the animal theme. I attended a party where the hosts had teacup-sized pigs, savannah cats, and peacocks freely wandering about. The cats began to view the pigs and peacocks as potential prey, and it got chaotic fast. The cats sprang into action, ricocheting off people while the pigs and birds scurried underfoot, trying to evade them. In the ensuing pandemonium, guests dropped their drinks and food, but distressed peacocks outdid even the loudest screams of the attendees."

We all laugh, and Kyle says, "The more I learn about living with the rich, the more I intend to stick with farming."

Adair signals to a server. "My girl and I would love to tell the chef how much we enjoyed our meals. Would it be okay to pop into the kitchen for a moment? Tell him it's Adair Monroe. Also, he might know my chef, Alain Simmonet."

"Of course, Mr. Monroe." The man hurries off and returns moments later. "Chef Paul says to please come back."

Adair assists me out of the booth, and I straighten my minuscule dress.

"You've got great legs," Adair says, and I blush.

"*Monsieur* Monroe," a dark-haired man in a chef's uniform greets as we enter the kitchen. "*Et qui est cette jolie femme?*" This translates to "Who is this beautiful woman?"

"*Je suis* Davia Glenn." I smile at him.

"*Tu parles francais!*" The chef's delighted I'm fluent in French.

"Perhaps we should switch to English so I can compliment your staff. Or do they speak Spanish?" I inquire.

Chef Paul says, "Spanish. My sous chef, Jules, has a basic vocabulary, and we get by."

"I'm good at conversational Spanish," I say. "May I?"

Adair engages the chef in conversation while I slip past the cooks on the line and those involved in plating, making for a nineteen or early twenties woman cutting vegetables near the rear of the kitchen.

"*Buenos noches,*" I greet and lean down to appear as if inspecting the vegetables. In Spanish, I tell her to nod if she's not being paid and needs help. She doesn't look away from her duties but dips her head. I ask how many people need assistance, and she widens all fingers on both hands.

"*Gracias,*" I say and move back to Adair. "We should let the chef return to work."

When we leave the kitchen, Adair takes my hand. "Let's give them something to talk about. Did you find out anything? And smile up at me so you look happy and not so intense."

Our faces are close, the customers' regard upon us, and I say, "Yes, ten people need help. Have I told you that you have the most beautiful eyes?"

Adair's gait falters at my words. "I want to kiss you right now."

"Do I seem less intense?"

He laughs. "I'm not sure."

When we retake our seats, we tell Kyle and Sherilyn we confirmed the information from José's cousin.

"Who owns this place?" Kyle says.

"Maybe Sarah will have the information," Sherilyn says.

After dessert and Adair insisting he be allowed to pay, we return to the lobby.

"Did you have a nice evening?" Sarah inquires.

Kyle pats his stomach. "I'll never get a meal like that where I'm from."

"I have a question," Adair says. "Who owns this restaurant?"

"It's owned by ACMW, LLC," she says.

Outside, Sherilyn types a search into her phone. "The service agent is some lawyer here in Rancho Suprema, but I'm going to do a deeper dive and see if I can find any articles from when Château Rouge opened."

While we wait, Adair puts his arm around my shoulders. "You'd make a great secret agent."

Kyle says, "You're a smart guy."

"I found an article from the Suprema Gazette." Sherilyn turns her phone toward us.

Posed before the entrance to Château Rouge are Henry Adams, Kenneth Clayton, Mike McMillan, and Josh Whittaker.

Twenty-Two

"Wise of you to think of including Adair," Kyle says when we're home.

"His name opens doors, and although I appreciate his advice on my wardrobe, I would've preferred to skip that part."

"Poor little rich girl," Kyle teases.

"You try wearing this getup next time and tell me how you feel."

He holds up his hands. "I surrender. Did you tell José we're back?"

"I texted him, and he'll be here in a few."

When José joins us, I update him on what we learned. "The question now is, who decided to hire them? Are the owners directly involved, or was this at a lower management level?"

"The two men who would talk to me said they've only dealt with a manager. Not sure who supplied the work visas, though. They were unhappy telling me much, completely scared."

"Scared of what?" I ask. "At worst, they go back to their country, right?'

"Without proof of being here legally, the feds might tag them with unauthorized entry. Also, one said he borrowed a lot of money to enter and will have no way to pay it off if he leaves. I got the impression most of them did the same, and they'd be consigned to lives of poverty."

"I hadn't considered that," I admit. "I should have, though."

"Wonder who we should report this to," Kyle says. "If we call the feds, there might be other unknown ramifications."

"True. I'll see if Jason McCall might be able to find out more," I say.

"You think he'd do you any favors? The last time I was here, he was more inclined to put a bullet in your skull," Kyle says.

"I think he still feels the same way. He and Adair aren't getting along right now either."

"That's a surprise," Kyle says.

"It is. I'm unsure what their tiff is about, and neither will enlighten me. Did you learn anything else, José?"

"The workforce has been here for about three months and is provided housing and transported by van daily to Château Rouge. They work long hours and aren't allowed to take breaks, but they sneak out for a few minutes when it's hectic."

Kyle yawns. "I say we don't do anything until we find out more."

"Agreed," José says. "I'm off."

After he leaves, Kyle says, "What about the owners?"

I tell him about my date with Kenneth Clayton. "He won't want anything to do with me."

"Can't blame him. Do you know the others?"

"I've been to parties with them twice, and Henry Adams serves with me on the Ladies' League board. Adair says they're in the world heavyweight wealth class, but I can't say much except they bicker with each other."

"Why would they bring in slave labor if they've got all that money?"

"Maybe they're penny pinchers? Maybe they have everything except morals? Hard to say."

Kyle gets up. "Each time I'm here, I'm at a loss. I'm going to turn in. You?"

I nod and hug him. He places his hands on my shoulders, saying, "The more I get to know Adair, the more I like him."

"He seems to have that effect on people."

———

The vibration of my phone at three a.m. wakes me. I bring it onto the bed and mutter a sleepy "Hello?"

"Hey, babe. We're back."

"Warden?"

"Didn't think a video call at this time of night would work." His tone is ebullient.

"Wasn't expecting you back so soon."

"One of those unforeseen changes. Can you come to Colorado?"

"When?"

"How about tomorrow?"

"Tomorrow? Kyle's here because of Bob's funeral, and...."

"Sorry, I forgot. When is it? I could fly out, and then we could go to Boulder together."

"It was yesterday."

Warden exhales. "Wish I could've gone with you, but I'm stoked we got released."

"How long should I plan for? I have to be back before the Home and Garden Tour, which is coming up."

"If you get to Colorado tomorrow, I can fly back to Rancho with you. I've worked non-stop, and Colonel Streeter approved me to be gone for two to three weeks, maybe a month if I'm lucky."

"Okay. Boulder, right?"

"You'll have to fly into Denver, but I'll be there by early afternoon and pick up a rental car. God, I can't wait to kiss you."

―――――

Kyle lowers his coffee mug. "You're going where?"

"Colorado. The team got withdrawn, and I have enough time to spend a few days with Warden, and then he'll come here. I hate to leave you, but—"

"Don't apologize. My flight's in a few days, but I don't mind having this place to myself. Maybe I'll play golf with your other guy if he has extra clubs. Be sure to consider Adair's golf invitation when you decide between him and Warden."

"You're so funny."

"Are you packed?"

"Threw stuff in a carry-on case after making a plane reservation. You can take the Rover and leave it in long-term parking at the airport. I can make the arrangements if you need me to."

"I'll handle them," Kyle says. "I'm not a complete dinosaur."

"Right. You're not extinct."

"Ha! Still sensitive about my dress comment?"

"Nah. Can't resist a chance to give you grief while you're here."

Kyle smiles. "Make up your mind about your future so I can decide whether to sell the farm and move into your guest house or bunk at Adair's. I bet his place is bigger."

"You think? I'll see if he can persuade Jason to find out more about the Château Rouge situation."

"Be sure and ask before you tell him you're jetting off to see Warden. Or maybe leave that part out."

———

"Hello, beautiful," Adair says when I call.

I catch him up on what José learned and the issues we discussed regarding who did the hiring and made arrangements for work visas.

"I'll have Jason do some digging. Now I'm reluctant to buddy up with the men who were at Henry Adam's. You, on the other hand, are a different story. Last night I dreamed about you in that red dress."

"Oh?"

"The best part was when I got you out of it."

His words cause memories of his lips against my throat and his hands on my skin to surface, and my body suffuses with heat.

"Davia?" he says when I remain quiet.

"I-I'm going to Colorado to see Warden," I say in a rush, like tearing off a bandage.

"When?"

"Today. I'm leaving—"

"Don't go."

"Adair, I've been upfront with you; I need time."

"I already know how this will end."

"You do?"

"You'll see him and wonder why you don't connect like you once did. You'll attempt to justify your change of feelings because of your time apart, but you'll realize you've changed and don't want that life anymore. Whether you want to admit it or not, you love me."

"That's not, that's not true—I'm not in love with you. I'm not sure I can trust you."

"Trust? Where's that coming from?"

"I was told you have a reputation as a heartbreaker."

Adair laughs. "And whose heart did I break, exactly?"

"I've never stalked you online or pried into your past."

"You should. If I made a mess of my personal life, the media would have a field day. You saw how they put us on that magazine cover and wrote an article about you being my latest without verification. If I acted that way, a quick Google search would tell you. Remember, don't judge me without facts."

"You're right; I'm sorry."

"Davia, you're the piece I need to complete my life's puzzle. When you're back, come tell me how much you love me."

TWENTY-THREE

I text Sherilyn before boarding: *I'm heading to Colorado for a few days to vacation with Warden. Kyle's still at the house, so stop by if you have time.*

Sherilyn: (Wide-eyed emoji) *Did you tell Adair?*

Me: *Yes.*

I picture my friend banging her head against a wall.

Sherilyn: *Ok. I'll go by tomorrow. Busy today.*

Me: TY (Heart emoji)

A flight attendant announces it's time to board, and I wheel my case toward the correct line. Due to my last-minute booking, I'm in the back, wedged in a corner. I shove my case in a bin and sit, staring out the window.

Come tell me how much you love me.

Did I love Adair? My self-control doesn't hold up around him, but surely this was a normal reaction to his supermodel looks and adorable British accent.

I like him, I decide.

Like.

Warden relaxes against a wall. The moment he sees me, a broad smile transforms him, and he has me in his arms. I put my hand behind his head, fingers tracing the edge of his military-style haircut as he claims my lips.

"I can't believe we made this happen." He takes my luggage and wraps his fingers around one of my hands.

"Are you in plaid because you're a lumberjack?" I tease, pinching a piece of his dark green-and-black flannel sleeve.

"I thought an easy-to-unbutton shirt would be best."

We go to a structure where Warden has a Jeep SUV.

"Sorry, but a Ferrari won't work in the mountains." He stores my bag in the back. "I got us a cabin in Estes Park, which is about an hour and a half, depending on traffic. Want to eat before we go?"

"I'm good."

When we're on the road, Warden takes my hand. "This doesn't feel real, being on vacation with you."

"It doesn't. What are we going to do?"

He smiles again. "Do you have to ask?"

"Besides that."

"Want to plan some outdoor activities?"

"As long as they're limited," I say.

The cityscape soon disappears, replaced by winding roads and pine trees.

"I got us a cabin by the river. A friend from high school handles the bookings, so I used a favor to get one last minute. Let's stop in town and eat before we check in, plus pick up some groceries."

"Planning on burning some calories, are you?"

"What do you think?"

After a meal and shopping, we get the key to our cabin and unload the car.

A patio overlooks a small river, the air is crisp and fresh, and several elk amble past, unafraid.

Warden shuts the curtain and takes my hand. "Come here."

The whole world disappears as his lips meet mine. He lifts me off the floor and carries me to the bedroom. I slip my hands under his shirt to feel his muscled torso and run my fingers along the scar on his side. We kiss each other with all the desire we stored away since the last time we were together. He lays me on the bed, and his unleashed passion almost overwhelms me, but then it's as if someone has found a dial in his brain and twisted it from out of control to the lowest setting. He draws back and says, "I warned myself not to act like some...."

"Oversexed shadow warrior?"

His eyes narrow. "That's it." His hands find my waist and the button of my jeans.

And then the world disappears again, becoming only Warden and his body's hard, familiar planes against mine.

———

I pick up a laminated placard on the kitchen counter. "Did you seriously book the Lovers Lane Cabin for us?"

Warden piles wood into the fireplace in the main room. "When my buddy found out we'd be the only occupants, he chose it."

I'm in his plaid shirt, the tail falling below my knees, and I bring him a beer. He pushes up one side and touches the wide scar on my upper left thigh.

"How's your injury?"

"I managed to wear high heels yesterday without too much trouble."

"Why were you in heels?" Warden prepares to light the fire.

I recall Adair's reaction when he first saw me in the red dress.

The best part was when I got you out of it.

Warden doesn't strike the match in his hand. "Where did you go right then?"

"I was thinking about those people at the restaurant and whether we can help them."

Warden lights the fire. "Did Kyle like playing undercover agent with you? Bet he misses operating."

"He said he's had more action in Rancho than since he left Delta. Would you miss it?"

Warden sinks onto the couch, and I sit beside him. He stares into the fireplace, where the flames flicker, take hold, and burn more steadily.

"Can't imagine a life without the team. I thought not operating would turn you inside out."

"It does, but you know what happened when I got an adrenaline pump at the murder scene last month."

"You almost died. And for that Brit."

"Let's not fight."

"I haven't wanted to bring it up, but what's your relationship with him?"

I look from the fireplace to the ceiling, then back at Warden, who won't make eye contact.

He loves me and wants me all to himself.

"We aren't in a relationship," I say.

Warden focuses on me now. "You're doing it again."

"What?"

"Telling me facts, but not telling me the truth."

"I am."

"You're leaving out how you feel about him."

Whether you want to admit it or not, you're in love with me.

"I'm going to get a glass of water."

Warden puts his hand on my arm. "I'm not dropping this, Davia."

I hesitate, then say, "Okay, Warden, I like him."

"Like him? What do you mean?"

"He's a good person."

"In what way?"

"I need to put this in context. You're in the same place and element with the team. Rancho Suprema is like being dropped into a war, but without the parameters we use. I can't take on the enemy with weapons, only words. The rules of engagement are protocols I have no clue about, and rooms of rich people are more daunting than anything else in my life. When Adair's with me, he's a buffer. He makes sure I get through it all. And, since Bob died, he's been—"

"Your shoulder to cry on?"

"I've cried more since moving to Rancho than all other times in my life added together."

Warden makes a frustrated noise. "You didn't answer my question again. Have you slept with him?"

Define "slept with."

"No."

"I'm going to ignore the delay and give you the benefit of the doubt."

My nails bite into my palms.

Warden's face is stoney. "Let's not fight. I'll change the subject. Have you decided what you'll do when the year's up?"

"How can I? Will Colonel Streeter let me work with you?"

"We're professionals. We worked together without issues when we were attracted to each other."

"He caught us in a rather compromised position."

"Yes, well, he values us together more."

"You think?"

"He gave me the word unofficially that he does." He takes my hand. "Please come back, Davia. I find myself running in the morning, waiting to do my usual speed burst to annoy you, or donning a gas mask, waiting for you to try to beat me doing a drag and carry through a course, or... a million things. "

"Say I recover and get a place back on the team, then what? How long will we work black ops?"

Warden shrugs. "For as long as we can."

"And during our time off?"

"Besides being together, waking up in the same place, making love... what do you mean?"

"Have you thought about having a family?"

Warden blinks. "Have you?"

"Warden, I'm on the short end of this. Women only have so much time, whereas men get more. If you want kids...."

"Kids? More than one?"

"Any."

"Is this why you like the other guy?"

"Oh my god, I'm talking about *our* future, not him."

Warden says, "I'm gonna get another beer. Want anything?"

I decline, bend my knees and wrap my arms around them.

The tension's gone when he returns. "You must be cold."

He puts down the beer, grabs a soft blanket from a corner of the couch, and tucks it around me, nestling me against him. "Davia, I haven't mapped out a future because it's all I can do to get through the now. I'm so tired most days with the training and my responsibilities I can't think."

"I'm sorry to have been so abrupt."

"It's okay. I can't expect you to wait for me if I haven't considered our future. All I've had is a big ache from not being with you."

And he kisses me in a way that makes me reevaluate everything.

———

"You up for a hike?" Warden says the next morning. We're on the front deck, him drinking coffee and me drinking in his features.

"We didn't get much sleep," I say. "You have any gas left in your tank?"

He leans back in his chair, shuts his eyes, and his lips raise in a contented smile. "We could take the Glacier Gorge trail to Sky Pond, the most difficult hike from here, and I'd still have more left over for you."

"Are we testing your brag?"

"Nah. I'm beginning to enjoy time off from all physical activity except one. Want to head over to my parents' place or wait until tomorrow?"

The mention of his parents jangles my nerves, but I say, "Whatever you think."

"Let's wait another day, then. Why don't we go to the Stanley Hotel for lunch? See if we find any ghosts."

"Ghosts?"

"It's where Stephen King wrote *The Shining, and* Kubrick filmed the movie."

"Sounds good, but if you see a ghost, don't hide behind me," I say.

Warden halts his mug midway to taking another drink. "You know what happens when you're a smart ass."

"You'll have to catch me first." I'm up and past before he can react. Scampering through the cabin's sliding door, I call, "This counts as another loss for you."

Before my words are out, he barrels into me and lifts me into his arms.

"I'm happy to pay the penalty," he says as he carries me through the bedroom door.

———

We make it to the Stanley in time to enjoy a late breakfast and spend several hours being tourists, browsing the shops in downtown Estes Park. Warden purchases an item, then comes to me and says, "Turn around and lift your hair."

He clasps a necklace with a square silver pendant containing a blue stone around my neck.

"It's beautiful, Warden. Is it turquoise?"

"They said larimar. Do you like it?"

I kiss him, one hand covering the pendant. "I love it."

Back at the cabin, Warden throws himself onto the couch and turns on the flatscreen TV, but muted.

"Get you anything?" I say.

"No. I need to relax, and then we can get to round...uh, what round are we on again?"

"Are we keeping track?" I pour a glass of water and go toward him but pause. His body language has changed, and he sits upright, back rigid.

On the TV screen is a male entertainment anchor next to a photograph of me in the red dress smiling at Adair, taken when I said he had beautiful eyes.

The caption reads "Adair Monroe's True Love."

Twenty-Four

When I near the couch, Warden says, "Care to explain this?"

"I already told you I've been in Adair's company. He's a high-profile person, and the media—"

"Media engagement isn't the issue," Warden interrupts. "Well, it's *an* issue, but not the main one."

"Then what is?"

He lifts his chin at the paused coverage. "What do you see?"

"Me with Adair?"

"What about how you're looking at each other?"

Smile up at me so you look happy and not so intense.

"There's a reason."

"A reason? First, I never thought you'd wear a revealing dress in his company. Next, that Brit's heart is in his eyes, and you—"

"He helped me get into Château Rouge's kitchen. We needed to appear casual when we returned to our table, but I was mission-focused, so he told me to smile. People often take photos of him, and someone must have sold one to the press."

Warden's face is pale as he comes to where I am. "I can read the nuances of each team member and how they feel at a glance. You're in love with him."

Ignoring his desolate countenance, I poke a finger into his broad chest. "I am, am I? Then why am I here with *you*? Though Kyle's a guest in my home, why did I fly here to see *you*? And how have we spent most of our time since my arrival? If I were in love with Adair—"

"What's in your eyes can't be faked."

"You're basing all these conclusions on a photo, Warden, not my actions. I'm here, though you haven't told me you love me—"

"What? You know I do. You want me to judge you by your actions, but what about mine? I brought the whole team to California to support you when you modeled. Do you think I moved mountains to attend a stupid fashion show because I only *like* you?"

"No, I—"

"Wait. Has that guy said he's in love with you?"

I take in the pine trees and blue skies out the window. "Yes, he has."

"And you didn't think you should tell me?"

"Can you see why I didn't?"

"So, someone took this photo at the restaurant you told me you went to with Kyle and Sherilyn, omitting Adair's presence?"

"Yes, because I foresaw you not understanding."

"Lying by omission, even better. And this outing was after our last conversation when I was gone?"

"Yes, but it was—"

"Stop, Davia. You still haven't figured out why you spend time with a man who isn't me."

He walks out the front door.

———

"So unfair, he is so unfair." I pace up and down, unsure what to do.

Could I have gained access to the kitchen without Adair? Maybe, but his presence guaranteed my entry and was a means to an end, nothing more.

Finding the remote, I start to press the button to resume programming but assess the stilled image first. The way Adair and I hold each other's eyes, we do appear to be in love. I click off the pause button, and another story plays. "Social Media Influencer Children Missing" is the banner beside a photo of Evie and Emily Huntly-Hart.

I turn on the volume.

"The youngest members of family influencer icons, the Huntly-Harts, were kidnapped yesterday. Their parents, Christopher and Samantha, have made an impassioned plea for their return," the anchor narrates before the screen cuts to another video.

Samantha stands behind a bank of microphones, eyes downcast. "Evie and Emily, we love you so much. Please care for each other because we'll be here waiting for you." As she wipes her face, Christopher tightens his arm around her shoulders, listening.

The screen cuts back to compilation videos and photos of the Huntly-Hart family, the newsperson saying, "The Huntly-Harts have a strong family influencer following of over six million people on social media, and their children regularly perform under the name Bedazzled Beaus and Beauties. We pray for the safe return of Evie and Emily. If you have information, please call....."

When the story ends, I switch off the tv and renew my pacing. Who would take the twins? My phone pulses on the kitchen table where I left it, the screen displaying Kyle's name.

"Davia, I hate to be abrupt, but we have a situation out here."

I'm still thinking of the twins. "What's going on?"

"I went out today for the promised round of golf with Adair. Left in the morning and had lunch with him at the club. When I got home, Sherilyn's car was in the driveway, but José and I couldn't find her."

"Maybe she left her car, and someone picked her up?"

Kyle says, "I didn't want to tell you, but I found traces of blood near the gate leading into the backyard. Might be nothing. Maybe a coyote got in here and snagged a rabbit, but...."

"Tell me what your gut says."

"What my gut says isn't good."

"Did you check the security cameras?"

"Next on my list."

"Let me. I can do it remotely on my phone. Hang on." I scroll up my home's security footage and click through. Sherilyn drives up around 11 a.m. and heads for a side gate. Two men with their faces concealed beneath black bandanas lie near the trees beside the guest parking spaces, rush forward, and grab her. She reacts instantly with hits and kicks, but the men overpower her, one landing a hard blow to her face. The men thrust a dark pillowcase over her head and drag her away, out of the camera's sight.

"Kyle, some men managed to bypass my security measures and kidnapped her. One of them struck her, likely the cause of the blood you saw."

"Why would anyone kidnap her?"

"No idea. You need to call Montoya. I'll message you his number and then arrange to be on the first plane back."

"I'll call him and delay my flight home."

We disconnect, me texting him Montoya's information and then scheduling a flight with enough time to reach Denver's airport. Hurrying to the door, I go outside.

The Jeep is gone.

I ring Warden's number, but it goes straight to voicemail. After trying him several more times, I text why I'm leaving. After ten minutes without a response, I rent a car for a one-way trip back to Denver and throw my belongings into my carry-all.

TWENTY-FIVE

It's after midnight when I enter my home. Kyle and Montoya are at the kitchen table, mugs of coffee before them.

"Any news?" I leave my case near the door and join them.

"Nothing," Kyle says.

"Is this because of you?" Montoya questions. The circles beneath his eyes are deep and dark, his face drawn.

"Could be, but I'm unsure." The whole flight home, I replayed the security images in my mind, gauging the skill level of the two men. They got past all my advanced measures, indicating expertise. A broad daylight attack was a risk, but they hadn't appeared bothered.

Kyle says, "The event makes more sense through a prism of your life. Maybe they thought Sherilyn was you?"

"Could be. Maybe it was Badger's people."

"Badger? Who's Badger?" Montoya questions.

"A terrorist," I say. "I can't give you specifics, except I'm on his hit list."

"Does Sherilyn understand who you are?"

"Yes. She disabled one of the assassins he sent after me."

"She what?" Montoya is incredulous.

"Don't be fooled by her. She's trained in self-defense and, coupled with her brain power, is formidable," I say.

Montoya puts his hands on top of his head. "I'm so angry at you right now. Ever since you moved here, there's been a crime wave."

You don't know the half of it.

"Catch me up on what you've done."

"Brought forensics here, gave the media the kidnappers' images and appealed for help from the public. Two kidnappings in Rancho Suprema, The Huntly-Hart twins and Sherilyn, have brought attention from national levels," he says. "Maybe someone who's not a nut job will call in with a tip. The parents offered a big reward to get the twins back, and the FBI entered their info into NCIC."

"NCIC is?" Kyle says.

"National Crime Information Center," Montoya says. "Sheriff's Homicide is responsible for child abductions, so we're also involved. The current sheriff appeared, but I think it was for the camera time."

"Where's Sherilyn's kidnapping in all this?" I say.

"Detectives with Major Crimes have it," he says. "My team's on the Huntly-Hart case, but I told the sarge I needed time because Sherilyn's my girlfriend. He's unhappy, but I need to ensure this investigation doesn't get off track because of the other, more high profile, kidnapping."

"What about Bob's murder? Anything?" I say.

Kyle and Montoya shake their heads, and the detective stands. "I'm out. I was hoping for some direction, but I can't do anything if it's secret squirrel terrorism-related."

"Badger's locked away, and his network's been quiet. Doubt he's the culprit, but I have no idea who another candidate might be."

After Montoya leaves, I tell Kyle, "I'll call Colonel Streeter's office tomorrow and see if anything's going on, but I don't think it's Badger."

"I agree with you. Where's Warden, by the way? Thought both of you would come through the door."

I tell him about the Adair photo, Warden leaving, and his radio silence. Kyle looks at his watch and says, "I think any tantrum should be over by now. You leave him any details?"

"By voicemail and text. He acted more hurt than angry before he left."

"Before he saw the photo, how was he?"

I finger the pendant at my neck. "Happy, relaxed."

"He has more reason to be upset with you than he realizes," Kyle says.

"Does he? Odd way to prove I prefer Adair, flying out of state to be with another man, don't you think?"

"It doesn't take a photo for me to tell how you feel about Adair," Kyle says. "I think you do love him."

I check for teasing humor in his eyes but find none. When he remains silent, anger fills me, and I get up. "I'm not fighting with you about this, too."

Kyle takes the two mugs to the sink, rinses them, and stows them in the dishwasher. I wheel my suitcase to my bedroom without saying anything more.

Once unpacked and showered, I pick up my phone and take it to the chair-and-a-half Sherilyn found, one I can sprawl into for reading.

"Isn't this perfect, Davia?" she'd said. "You can cozy up with Warden. Wait, Adair would fit better because he's not as large. Or—"

"A book will fit best," I said, stopping her from continuing. "I do love the chair, though."

I redial Warden, but his phone goes straight to voicemail. What was he doing? Was he in Boulder with his parents or taking a brutal hike somewhere to work through his feelings?

Slipping on some tennis shoes with my sweats, I go to where the attack on Sherilyn occurred. I retrace events to where they grabbed her, thinking about the security measures they avoided.

They must be pros, expensive, and confident.

Kyle appears at my shoulder. "They wouldn't have been successful if they tried to grab you."

"A two-bit crook got the jump on me near Bryce's."

"No matter how hard you train, the saying about beginner's luck is a thing for a reason."

I give a mirthless laugh. "How do we find Sherilyn? I'm happy to go in guns blazing, but where? And those twins...."

"Remember, do what you can, when you can, wherever you are. Waiting's the hardest part."

I think of the Hanged Man and how it signifies a time to reflect, not take action, but Sherilyn's fate pushes at me. "What can I do, Kyle?"

"First, get some rest. I'm sure you've taken the Warden situation and locked it away somewhere, but you've been through a lot today. And I'm sorry I said what I did about your feelings for Adair. I'm sure my careless words didn't help."

"I waited for you to say you were kidding."

"I'm not, but now's not the time to discuss it. Go to bed."

———

Checking my phone at four a.m., I find no messages from Warden. Unable to sleep, I decide to go for a run. Dressing, I go down my driveway and jog up the road at a slow pace. The sun won't be up for some time, and the streets are quiet. Getting into my old rhythms is easy, but I don't push, monitoring for pulses of pain.

In a short time, downtown Rancho Suprema lies ahead, and I'm happy the roads are empty, so cars don't careen around the curves and come into my path. I make a circle past the shops and businesses, but the only activity is at a local bakery where two people work to make muffins, cakes, and other pastries for the day.

A car drives up beside me. "Ms. Glenn?"

I stop. "Officer Sterling."

"Please call me David. The other's too formal."

"Only if you'll call me Davia. Why are you out?"

"With Bob's murder, the home invasion, commercial burglaries, and two kidnappings, this town's in turmoil. The residents have demanded increased security."

Noting his bowed shoulders and tired eyes, I say, "Have you gotten any sleep?"

"Only on a cot in the office. With all this going on, you shouldn't be out alone."

"I live by situational awareness," I say

"Weren't you injured by those thieves who broke into Bryce's Boutique?"

"I doubt lightning will strike twice."

"Still, you need to be careful. Okay, I must resume my rounds."

"Wait, I have a question."

"What?"

I point at Château Rouge. "Do you know the owners?"

His face brightens. "Sure."

"Who hires the staff? I want to compliment them."

"The manager's Nathan Campbell. He's usually around during the day and evening."

"Has Château Rouge had any problems?"

"Like what?"

"With the staff."

"The staff? No, the only complaints I get are people driving drunk or getting into fistfights. Is there an issue?"

"None at all," I say, unsure if I can trust him. "I'll let you get back to patrol."

"Be careful, please. I don't want another kidnapping victim or any kind for that matter."

———

The sky lightens, and my mood improves from not having any after-effects of pain. Will I be one hundred percent fit sooner than expected and able to rejoin my team?

Please come back, Davia.

An image of Warden's beseeching eyes and words make me recheck my phone, but he hasn't messaged. Sticking it in my back jeans pocket, I go to the kitchen.

"You're up early." Kyle waits beside the espresso machine for his morning fix.

"Couldn't sleep, so I ran, lifted weights, showered..." I go to the fridge and pour myself some iced tea.

"How do you feel?"

"Good, at least so far."

"You don't want to delay your recovery."

"I'm careful. I'm calling Streeter," I say and go onto the back patio.

"Colonel Streeter's office."

"Hi, Luke," I say to aide Luke Upton, waiting for and getting his familiar grunt of dislike when he recognizes my voice.

"What do you want? You've got nine more months of leave."

"I need to talk to Streeter."

Luke pauses, then says, "Fine. I'll transfer you."

"Colonel Streeter," says a gruff voice. I picture the no-nonsense Colonel at his desk. He has bushy eyebrows, salt-and-pepper hair, and the energy of a much younger man.

"Colonel, this is Davia," I say.

"What can I do for you?" He's straight to business, as always.

I disclose Sherilyn's kidnapping and my concerns about Badger in vague terms.

"Rule it out as Badger-related," he says. "His network remains disorganized, and we haven't detected any activity in the states. How's your recovery going?"

"Ran for the first time today and haven't had any issues."

"I'm keeping your place on the team for when your leave is over."

He disconnects.

Turning toward the door to go inside, I receive a text.

Call me.

Warden has surfaced.

TWENTY-SIX

When the number connects, Warden says, "You back in Rancho?"

"Didn't you listen to my voicemails or read my texts?"

"Yes. Any word on Sherilyn?"

I fill him in while pondering his all-business tone. "I spoke with Streeter, who agrees this isn't Badger."

"Maybe someone saw the photo of you with that billionaire, thought you'd make a good ransom target, but got Sherilyn instead."

You with that billionaire. This again?

"I haven't had any communication from Adair, and he would've called if someone tried to ransom me to him. Where have you been?"

"Thinking."

"About?"

"Our future."

"Isn't this a topic we should discuss in person like we did before..." I almost say, 'Before you bailed on me,' but don't.

"Before I saw the photo of you with your true love?"

"Oh my gods," I groan. "What is wrong with you?"

"Wrong with *me*? You're the one who hasn't been upfront."

"You're right; I wasn't, but for this exact reason, you big lunk."

"Seeing you with someone else is worse than taking a round."

"Didn't you listen to anything I said? Adair helped me get more information, nothing more. I need to find out who took Sherilyn and focus on what's right in front of me, Warden, not soothe your bruised ego."

Silence is his response.

"I love you, Davia," he says at last. "I want us to be together, but until you sort your reasons for spending any time with, with, well, you know, I think we should stop seeing each other."

"Stop seeing each other? I expected you to say, 'How can I help?' You spent time with Sherilyn, and I thought you'd be concerned."

"I am, but what can I do? Come to your place and sit around? Isn't local law handling it?"

"You and I are better than most law enforcement agencies."

"On missions, yes. On what we're trained to do, yes. A kidnapping? We can't play hero on other people's turf."

"Two pros took her. We're more capable of dealing with those types than anyone here."

Another long pause, then he says, "Tell you what, I'll run this through back channels and see if anything pops up."

"But you're not going to come in person?"

"I'll be there if you find definitive evidence and need backup. Until then, I meant what I said. Sort your reasons for hanging out with that Brit. We're done."

"Now we've gone from a break to *done*?" I say, astonished. "All right, if that's how you want to play it. I appreciate your offer of limited assistance, but the rest is a major overreaction. Oh, I also took your shirt. If you want it back, you know where I am."

———

When I go inside, Kyle says, "Find out anything?"

"Streeter says it's not Badger, and Warden and I spoke. He's acting like a—"

I search for the correct word.

"Brokenhearted alpha male?" Kyle supplies.

"I can't believe him; I can't. He won't fly here because he says there's nothing to do. He's using sources to get a line on the men who took Sherilyn but offered nothing else."

"What? He's an action guy."

"His action today was to break up with me."

"Do you blame him? He's had Adair thrown in his face twice. First with the magazine, now this new coverage."

"I don't—"

Kyle swats the air, waving away my words. "Stop lying to yourself, Davia."

"I'm not. I went to Colorado to be with Warden and would still be there but for Sherilyn's kidnapping."

"You don't understand men. We're physically tough but also vulnerable. An ultra-alpha like Warden is proud, so his actions are understandable in the context of what occurred. I'm sure he already feels inadequate, caused by the money differential. Enduring more public photos of you and Adair, coupled with you not telling him the complete truth, had to sting."

"Why are you taking his side on this?"

"Side? I'm pointing out facts. Last time I was here, finding and retrieving Adair consumed you. Now I've seen you together, it's plain he's important to you."

I open my mouth, but he says, "And don't you 'whatever' me, young lady."

"I wasn't."

"Uh-huh." Kyle looks at me over the rim of his coffee cup.

"I'm done talking about this. I need to find Sherilyn, but because I have no course of action, I'm going out for lunch."

"Lunch?"

"Inaction's making me lose my mind, but I have some insight into the situation at Château Rouge. I intend to speak with the manager and find out more."

"Do you want company?"

"I'll go with José. Maybe I'll encourage patrons to photograph us together and urge them to send the pictures to a news outlet. If that happens, someone might leak another fake rumor like the one about me being in love with Adair."

As I head toward my bedroom, Kyle says, "It's not fake."

Whatever.

———

Hostess Sarah smiles when I enter Château Rouge, gaze going to José and past. "Adair's not with you?"

"He's busy," I say, "but we did have a wonderful evening, and I want to compliment your manager."

"Nathan's on an errand, but I'll let him know when he returns." She picks up two menus, auburn hair spilling over her arm. "Would you like to sit inside or out?"

"It's a beautiful day, so out."

She seats us near a burbling fountain with water cascading into a Talavera tiled basin. It's not crowded, and a server takes our drink order and hurries away.

"How was your trip to Colorado?" José says.

"Wonderful, horrible, mixed?"

"What happened?"

"Someone took a picture of me with Adair the night we were here, and Warden saw it featured on a TV entertainment program."

José makes a strangled sound. "I guess that's the horrible part?"

"Sherilyn's kidnapping is worse, of course, but the timing of the Adair publicity is bad."

"Is that why Warden's not here?"

I nod.

José says, "With all the dating app horror stories and social media videos about disastrous relationships, I'm beginning to conclude being with someone can be rough."

"Gotta agree with you."

We order, then José says, "I can't believe Sherilyn got abducted. I've tried to find a reasonable explanation but came up with nothing."

"They could've mistaken her for me, are trying to get to me through my friends, or her abduction is unrelated. The who and why is the issue, of course," I say.

A man in his forties with thinning brown hair approaches our table. "I'm Nathan Campbell," he says. "Sarah said you wanted to see me?"

I put out a hand. "I'm Davia Glenn, and this is my friend José Valenzuela Macias."

"You're Adair Monroe's girlfriend," Nathan says, and I don't correct him.

"We spoke with Chef Paul and some of your kitchen staff to compliment them on the delicious food," I say. "Did you hire them? You're so discerning if you did."

"Who exactly are you referring to? The owners hired the chef, but not the day-to-day crews."

"So you brought in the others?"

"Kitchen staff is transitory. The employees you reference aren't here any longer."

I frown. "Why?"

"They must've found better opportunities. The restaurant business is like that." His tone is dismissive. "We hope you and Mr. Monroe will dine with us again soon."

When he goes back inside, José says, "They're not here anymore? Where did they go?"

"Seems pretty odd."

"I'll find out if my cousin learned anything."

"Adair said he'd have Jason do a background on the company, and I'll check if he's uncovered anything relevant."

"Another mystery to solve," José says. "It's like the Sherilyn situation. Until we get a lead, we can't act."

I tap my finger on the table, mulling what to do next.

Whether I want to or not, I need to call Adair.

Twenty-Seven

After lunch, José goes toward his cousin's restaurant, and I go to my car and dial.

"Davia, are you back?" Adair says.

"I flew home when I learned about Sherilyn's kidnapping."

"I've been wanting to talk to you, but you were with, uh—"

"Why can't either of you use names?" I snap. "Warden, I was with Warden."

"Okay...Warden." He says the name with a hint of disgust. "Have you found out anything about who took Sherilyn?"

"Detective Montoya's doing all he can to find her, and Warden's checking with sources, but so far, nothing."

"Is, uh, Warden here with you?"

"No, he split with me."

"He did?" Adair aims for nonchalant and fails.

"Did you see the recent photo of you and me taken at Château Rouge?"

"No, but I've been occupied with other matters."

"Someone photographed us, and it got displayed on a television entertainment program. The image gives the impression we're in love."

"Impression?"

"I don't want to talk about this. I'm calling because I went to Château Rouge today for lunch with José to learn more about the situation, but the manager said all the employees left."

"Left?"

"The hostess backed up the story."

"I've had more unexpected problems with the merger. Jason's been assisting me, so I'm unsure how much time he's devoted to delving into the LLC."

"Can you find out?"

"Of course. Davia?"

"Yes?"

"When can I see you?"

"I need to find Sherilyn. Evie and Emily also being kidnapped tears me up."

"Me, too. No matter how busy I've been, Sherilyn and those sweet girls have been at the back of my mind."

"Call me if Jason learned anything."

"I know I already asked, but when can I see you? I miss you."

When I don't have the overwhelming urge to find comfort in your arms.

"I want to be available if I get a lead on anything and keep my head in the game."

"Do I distract you?"

"Do you distr—yes, Adair, you do. When I'm around you, my willpower shuts off."

"That's because—"

"I spent time in Colorado with Warden, and we didn't only talk. We did adult things."

Adair gulps. "Okay, I get the picture. But he split with you over a photo?"

"Not only a photo. The magazine cover, your competition to take me away from him... Warden says I need to figure out why I haven't cut ties with you."

"You know why."

I ignore his statement. "Why would you want a woman who's disloyal?"

"Disloyal is the opposite of who you are. What we're talking about are our feelings for each other."

"I can't do this right now."

Adair hesitates, then says, "If Jason learns anything, I'll let you know."

———

Kyle is on the patio reading a book. "Picked this out of your library for a distraction. Learn anything?"

"The manager said the people Adair and I saw left due to the transitory nature of the industry."

"Did you believe him?"

"I believe they weren't working, but I didn't interrogate him. Corroborated the story with Sarah, the hostess."

"Maybe we spooked them."

"Spooked who? Management? The employees?"

"Both? Where would they go?"

"Back to Mexico? I wonder if someone overheard me in the kitchen?"

"Maybe they talked between themselves later, and someone listened in. Hard to say. Did you talk to Adair?"

"Yes, but he and Jason have been dealing with a business issue."

Kyle picks up his book again. "So we wait."

———

Adair contacts me several hours later.

"Jason's a pro at finding information and said the corporation brought the immigrants into the country on temporary work visas. He said this is a common practice by companies and individuals within the U.S. If they try to leave, their employers threaten to report their status to immigration authorities. He discovered Château Rouge has engaged in this practice since it opened, hiring at least thirty people, maybe more, in the fifteen years it's been in business."

"I regret ever eating there," I say.

"Same, scratching it off my list now."

"Anything else?"

"Odd thing, previous staff also disappeared. There's no record of where they went or if they returned to their home countries. He couldn't find any official reports, investigations, or formal complaints against the corporation."

"Other people have disappeared, and I don't believe in coincidences. I wonder if they're connected?"

"Exploited laborers are much different than Sherilyn and the twins."

"And three housekeepers from this area," I add.

"Didn't know about that," Adair says. "Davia, I want to see you and—"

"Please give me some time, Adair. It's unrealistic for you to expect me to throw myself into your arms when Warden only split from me yesterday. With Sherilyn and everything else going on, I haven't had time to sort through my feelings."

"I only want to see you so we can talk; no throwing yourself at me required."

"I'll think about it."

"I'll be here whenever you need me. Hang on, Jason is saying something." After a few moments, Adair says, "Jason said to tell you to scope out the Kensingtons, too."

"The Kensingtons? For what?"

"He has some intel he can't share in detail, but he investigated the disappearances of some underage women in England, and the trail pointed in their direction. Nothing ever came of it, but he doesn't like coincidences either."

I'm about to disconnect when Adair says, "Please be careful. Remember, I love you."

TWENTY-EIGHT

The burly guard finishes his car search with the same efficiency as when I first visited Hazelton Manor.

He hands back my license. "Where's your friend?".

"Murdered."

"That so?" His empty eyes don't flicker.

When the gates open, I don't drive fast, working to appear interested in the manicured grounds instead of attempting to spot security measures I might have missed.

If I have to break into this fortress, will I succeed?

Two men in suits with earpieces flank me from my car to the front door. Inside, Linda Riley waits with her ever-present tablet.

"Ms. Glenn, good to see you again, and my sympathies about Mr. Brooks."

"Thank you. I appreciate you making time for a final pre-tour inspection."

Linda says. "Shall we?"

As I shadow her through the building, I wonder if Bob's spirit is beside me, skipping along without his cane and ready to laugh over any new, crazy-expensive feature Linda might point out.

"Brant Kensington requested we serve refreshments," she says, "so they'll be available in the formal dining space."

"Will you give me a complete exterior tour?"

"I'll show you." Bradford Kensington says, and I work not to jump.

How did he sneak up on us? I try to spot a secret door, but nothing's obvious.

"Are you sure, Mr. Kensington?"

"Who would be more familiar with Hazelton's features than me?" His tone is imperious, and Linda shrinks back.

"No one," she says, eyes on the floor.

I force a smile. "I can't wait to learn more about the property."

Like where you might stash some kidnapped people.

His returned smile is devoid of warmth as we approach a line of golf carts. Men in suits rush forward, leaving their posts beside buildings, but Bradford puts up a hand, and they stop.

"You've increased security since I was last here," I comment as I get into the cart Bradford selects.

"You've got an eye for detail. They're here in preparation for the upcoming event. We have many priceless items, and I'm a cautious man."

"Smart," I say. "Because a person's wealthy, it doesn't mean they have a conscience."

"True enough."

He takes us past sculptures, flowers, fountains, and more. "I'm sure Linda mentioned the formal gardens and orangery."

"She did, but she didn't tell me what those buildings are for." I point back at some structures behind the primary residence.

Bradford stops the cart, turning his head. "She didn't? One houses our art collection."

"I wasn't sure of the museum's location."

"I'll give you a tour." He reverses and heads back up the path.

"How much is your art worth again? I apologize, but I can't come up with the number."

"Four, five hundred million," Bradford says.

What's a hundred million between friends?

We halt beside a building with ornate architecture similar to the main house. Bradford climbs the stairs, but instead of taking a key out of a pocket, he clicks a screen, and it scans his face. The door unlocks.

"More cutting-edge security?" I observe.

"We make sure to upgrade each time technology improves, especially with all these home invasions."

"Did you layout your home like Bruce Wayne's? Secret panels, hidden corridors, tunnels, and a bat cave?"

Bradford stops, hand on the door. "We have tunnels and some inner corridors to get to our panic rooms."

"Panic rooms?"

"Our two rooms can withstand nuclear blasts and have enough food and water to last generations, but the décor is as luxurious as the common spaces. In addition to the backup generators, water filtration, air purification systems, emergency communications, and bulletproof windows, each is a Faraday cage to repel electromagnetic attacks."

And a partridge in a pear tree.

"Won't you get bored?"

He enters the room, and automatic lights switch on. "Of course not. We have theaters, gyms, spas, and other amenities in each. We also have a gas system built into the main residence, which can produce a dense fog to confuse intruders."

Unable to halt my movie-themed commentary, I say, "Quite James Bond."

"I suppose. What do you think?" Bradford gestures to painted high ceilings, walls hung with priceless paintings whose artists I'm sure not to recognize, and graceful sculptures.

"This is incredible. Reminds me of the Palace at Versailles."

"We wanted a hall of mirrors to simulate Versailles, which is why we used these gold framed mirrors between each piece of art."

"Why didn't you move the Versailles wing here instead?"

Bradford's smile is wry. "Did Linda send you details of the collection? We have audio tour headsets, but not enough for a hundred people. Maybe fifty, not sure. We use them when we host charity events."

"I'm unsure what Beatrice Gibbs, the Ladies' League President, will wish to focus on. We only have several hours, and your estate would take days to appreciate. We slated your car collection. How many cars do you own?"

"I feel like you're testing my knowledge of my material possessions."

"Not intentionally."

"One hundred or so, I think. Want to see the other rooms in here?"

"No, this is enough for today. Does Hazelton have a private airstrip further back on the property?"

"I wish, but there's not enough room," Bradford says. "I have two eight-seat helicopters and helipads."

We go back outside, and he secures the door.

"And these buildings are?" I indicate some other structures.

"One is my gun collection, and the others are for storage." Bradford is dismissive. "Takes loads of equipment to keep this place in order, and we have to put it somewhere."

"Linda told me you have an extensive firearm collection but said she needed your permission to open the building."

Bradford stops the cart. "Do you know anything about guns?"

"I grew up shooting, so yes."

"I take great pride in what I've put together but am unsure if others would be so keen. The gun ownership issue and the second amendment are controversial topics. I'd let you see them now, but I'm due at another appointment soon."

"Whatever you decide is fine. Where's Brant?"

"Since he's an adult, he doesn't always share his schedule," Bradford says, looping around and returning to our starting point. Inside, Linda waits right where we left her.

"Linda, please be prepared to accommodate a tour of our museum," Bradford says.

"Yes, sir."

"Davia, wonderful to see you. Are you coming to Henry's tomorrow night?"

"Uh, he hasn't reached out."

"Perhaps I've confused the dates."

When Bradford leaves me with Linda, we go to her office, but my mind is on the extensive security, tunnels, and barriers. If I needed to rescue anyone here, the mission was near impossible.

———

"One of my cousin's chefs saw the employees at Château Rouge getting into a van escorted by two dark SUVs," José tells me when I arrive home. "Said the norm was for them to arrive and depart work in a van, but without what seemed to be extra security."

"Maybe they got spooked or, as Jason McCall learned, perhaps they rotate crews after a prescribed time. I wonder where they went?"

"Trafficked on to other people, maybe?"

"I'm not sure. I doubt Jason will stop his inquiries, so maybe we'll learn more."

"I keep forgetting, but did Ana Sanchez pass her background?"

I scroll through the emails on my phone, find a file, and log in to read the results. "Hm, no issues, but with those goons grabbing Sherilyn, I'm reluctant to have anyone here."

"Maybe push back her start date?"

"Smart idea."

Would any regular person in my orbit be safe?

José picks up a rake. "I'm going to do some clean-up and stop trying to solve what happened to Sherilyn. I keep expecting her to return and tell you where to find the bodies of the men who took her."

"Yeah, me, too."

Before I go inside, a text from Detective Robbie Rodríguez comes through.

Did you forget about coming in to view the CCTV footage?

Me: *Been out of state. What's a good time?*

Rodríguez: *Are you available today?*

Me: *Be with you in thirty.*

I find Kyle, tell him what José learned, and my destination. "If you're bored, you can tag along."

"I'm going to call Adair and see if I can meet Jason McCall. You know that old maxim; two heads are better than one. The inaction is getting to me."

"I hear you. This shouldn't take long, but text if you learn anything new."

———

"Did you get a pet turkey yet?" I ask Rodríguez when he retrieves me.

"Cute." He brings me back to the elevator. "You realize my laughter at the turkey's demise is how I react to most dark events, so I meant no disrespect."

"Coping by using humor isn't unhealthy," I say, not wishing to be a hypocrite.

"We're in here." We enter an equipment-filled room with a powered-on computer. "I had a tech get this ready. Go ahead, sit."

He touches the play button, and night vision black and white footage from a business across a street from Bryce's begins. A tree bends and sways, partially obstructing the scene, and heavy rain blurs the images. A sizable van drives by and positions itself so no one can read the license plates.

"The van's a Mercedes-Benz Sprinter, an expensive vehicle for low-level crooks," he says. "We're trying to trace sales of the model, but, like anything, getting the data takes time."

A man in dark clothing, his identity obscured by a mask and ballcap, drags the van's side door back, and other men spill out. One carries a pipe. Leaning forward, squinting in a futile attempt to bring the image into focus, a hint of recognition surfaces.

Rodríguez pauses the feed. "Did you remember something?"

"No, but," I study the man. "he seems familiar."

"Why?"

I lift my shoulders. "Dunno. Maybe he resembles someone with a similar build, not sure."

He presses play again. A thief busts through Bryce's door, and the others extract garments and load them in the van. I come into a far corner of the screen, hunched against the wind and rain. The man with the pipe leaps out of a shadow, and I disable him with a kick to his knee, causing two other men to rush me. One goes down, and the other bends over, but how I took them out is unclear from the angle.

Two more men run at me, but the pipe-wielding man bounds up, strikes a glancing blow to my head, and I fall. He jumps over me and assists another man. The thieves resume looting Bryce's store, but several are unsteady from my attack. When the van speeds away, I lie face down on the sidewalk.

"You took out three men in short order," Rodríguez says.

"The pipe wielder overcame my strike to his knee, so I failed."

"You're trained in martial arts?"

"I'm an only child, so my parents wanted me to be safe. Had a few taekwondo classes as a kid."

"Ric, I mean Detective Montoya, said there's more to you than meets the eye. Is he right?"

"I don't know what he means."

Rodríguez crosses his arms. "You were lucky the blow didn't kill you."

"Agreed." I continue to study the footage until Alex Gordon appears. His body obscures the CCTV from recording him scooping up my gun and replacing it in my bag. "Say, did Montoya bring you in on Bob Brook's murder? Officer Sterling said someone ransacked the house, and I thought the theft might link to the home invasions you're investigating."

"You saw Stacey Templeton's place, the thorough clean out of valuables. The Brooks scene was different. They took some expensive items but left a Picasso, designer bags, and valuable jewelry in a safe."

I think of the abstract painting above the living room sofa. "No one was there when I arrived, no fleeing cars or people, so I didn't interrupt anything."

"I exchanged information with other law enforcement specialists working the home invasion cases, and this one doesn't fit their pattern. Too amateur. Heard the victim was your friend, so my condolences. Montoya's working overtime to solve the case."

"With his girlfriend taken, I don't think his mind's on Bob's murder right now."

"True." Rodríguez's sigh is weary. "He's burning it hard, and I'm afraid he'll give out."

"He's made of tough stuff." Unable to say I'm also working to find her, I review the film again, but nothing clicks. "I'm not a lot of help."

"Maybe it'll come back to you."

"Doubtful. It's been over a week, and nothing's surfaced."

———

I text Kyle to report I'm clear, and he responds, *Do you have time to swing by Adair's?*

Me: *Because?*

Kyle: *Your honey misses you. Kidding. Jason wants to talk.*

When did Jason ever want to talk to me?

Driving, I attempt to identify the man with the pipe, but his identity remains a mystery, and my thoughts return to Sherilyn. Was she kidnapped because of me? Was she the true target? Why couldn't I find a lead and save her? Realizing I clench the steering wheel so hard my fingers ache, I loosen my grip but can't rid myself of the concern and disappointment that permeates me.

Adair's security gates are open, and I want to scold his bodyguards about their lackadaisical attitude toward his safety. What if home invaders got in?

When I approach the front door, Adair steps out before I knock and, without a word, embraces me.

Come tell me how much you love me.

"Did you pay Kyle to lure me here by text?"

"I promised to give him all my money if he would."

"Liar."

"All right, I only promised him half. I mean, I do have obligations." He takes my hand." Jason ordered me to bring you to his office so he can act important."

Further down the hall, Adair stops to press an elevator button with his free hand. Inside, he seems more intent, and I expect his mouth and hands to be on me, but he inhales enough for his chest to expand.

"Practicing breathing exercises?"

He exhales. "It helps me to remember to control myself around you."

We go to an office with numerous computers, cubicles, and people I don't recognize.

"This is Jason's office and staff." Adair doesn't move from the doorway.

"Are you a vampire and need permission to enter?"

"I like your explanation better than the real reason. Jason's been throwing stuff and shouting the past few weeks, and I like to be careful in case he decides to chuck a trashcan at me. Helluva way to show he's relieved I survived."

"I thought he'd be thrilled to get you back."

"He relishes adopting an overbearing parental role because he's been in my life since I was barely out of nappies. The mood I was in after the kidnapping, grateful to be alive yet gutted, put us in an unhealthy headspace."

Kyle and Jason are in a sitting area, coffee cups on a table. Jason waves for us to join them, and I ignore his staff staring at me, imagining them thinking: *She's the demon spawn who makes our boss lose his mind and sweep objects off tables like a villain.*

"How'd it go with the video?" Kyle says.

"The guy who attacked me's familiar, but I can't put a name to him. The images weren't clear because of the storm and a thrashing tree. Detective Rodríguez said he thinks amateurs committed the home invasion where Bob died."

Adair sits beside me on a short couch. Jason's cast isn't off yet, and his crutches balance against his chair. Has Kyle shared about his prosthetic leg to remind Jason he's lucky?

"Wish you'd told me sooner Kyle was your trainer," Jason says. "We crossed paths back in the day, put it together when we got a look at each other."

"Oh?" It made sense as they're of similar age and occupation, although they served different countries.

Adair says in a quiet voice, "Our minders are friends, and I'm not sure if that's good or bad."

"You know our ears work, right?" Kyle says.

Jason addresses me. "You went to Hazelton? Any sign of the twins?"

"No, but they've increased their security tenfold, saying it's for the tour. Once you get past the external protection and heavy gates, their internal security is extensive. Bradford said they have secret corridors, underground tunnels, and the like. They use the latest biometrics for entrances and have two panic rooms able to withstand nuclear blasts. Didn't spot a weakness."

"Are you sure the twins are there?" Adair says.

"Only a guess," Jason says. "My other suspects are the Huntly-Harts. When I saw their press statement, their body language was off. They're involved somehow."

"I saw a clip of their statement," I say., "but had other things on my mind."

"Jenny, would you bring me the Huntly-Hart video, please?" Jason says to a trim woman in her late thirties who appears as buttoned up and efficient as him.

"Yes, Mr. McCall." She taps a laptop and places it on the table.

I pay attention to Christopher and Samantha's body language this time. They avert their eyes from the cameras, Samantha wiping invisible tears while Christopher has his arm around her, his hand gripping her left shoulder. A reporter inquires about who might have the children, and Samantha looks up. "We have no idea who might have done such a thing."

Kyle says, "Her blink rate is through the roof, and she's rubbing her hand over the one Christopher has on her arm like she'll grind a hole in it."

"An adapter to stress," I say, "which makes some sense, but she didn't lose control until the question about who might have the girls."

"A pair of liars was my conclusion," Jason says.

"Why did you tie this to the Kensingtons besides their previous history?" I say.

"They came into town, and somebody took those twins. Kyle says the girls ran past them at Bob Brooks' funeral, so maybe that put them on their radar."

"This is minimal evidence at best. Where does Sherilyn come into this?" I say.

"No idea," Jason admits.

"I see two courses of action," I say. "We can attempt to get to the Huntly-Harts and interrogate them, but from what I learned last month when the Myles murder case went national, the media was in a frenzy, so accessing them will be near impossible. Or we confirm Bradford's statement that Henry Adams is having a gathering tomorrow night and try for an invite and pressure the Kensingtons."

Adair sits up straighter. "I'll call Henry for advice about a hedge fund strategy, then attempt to wrangle an invitation by mentioning how much we enjoyed his last get-together."

"Who wouldn't love to boast you graced their home twice?" Jason says, but his tone is teasing, and I'm pleased their friendship is back on even footing.

Adair excuses himself to make the call, and Jason tells me, "If you destroy my boy's heart, you and I will have issues."

"When don't we? Off-topic, but you have security problems. The main gates to the property were open when I arrived."

"I bet Adair opened them for you," Jason says. "He's back to living life on a whim, and his protection detail can't control him."

"Kyle, you should open an executive protection service," I suggest. "You'll make better money than wheat farming."

"The clients would be more of a pain than the hard work, weather, and drops in market prices."

Adair returns, saying, "Bradford was right, Henry's having a get-together, but he only wants me to attend. Says it's a boys-only night."

I relay what Hannah said about all the men cheating on their wives. "I think Josh Whittaker's oblique reference to after-dinner entertainment might have meant they bring in women."

"Wouldn't doubt it," Adair says. "I won't pretend I'm an angel, and I've been on the billionaire circuit a few times. Excess is the norm."

An image of Adair draped with nubile young women causes a burning sensation in the pit of my stomach.

"You're being naïve," Jason scolds. "From what I learned about those men, altruism isn't in their vocabulary. I suspect they plan to put you in a compromising position. Maybe record you, have a girl accuse you of rape—get leverage over you."

"That's plausible," Kyle says. "They're out of your wealth class yet exploit labor, so blackmail isn't a stretch."

"Makes sense," Adair says. "What should we do?"

"You should go, Adair," I say. "But you'll need protection."

"Rather rude, don't you think, showing up to someone's private home with bodyguards?" Adair says, and Jason gives me an 'I told you so' look.

"I'll go," Kyle says.

"But—" Adair begins.

"I'll go as your unofficial bodyguard," Kyle clarifies. "If this becomes anything, you'll need someone like me."

"They saw you with us at Bob's funeral, but no one introduced you to them. It might work," I say.

"And I'll assemble a team if we need more than force," Jason says. "Perhaps we'll find evidence of their wrongdoing on computers."

"But won't taking Kyle make them suspicious? I mean..." Adair persists, but I take him by the forearm. "I need to talk to you."

I lead him out of the room and to the end of the corridor.

"If you want to be alone with me, I'm willing," he says, smiling.

"Adair, you're not taking your security seriously again. Kyle needs to go with you."

"Why? Those middle-aged billionaires will hire sex workers and complain about their marriages."

"If you don't promise me you'll take Kyle and do what your protection detail says from now on, I won't speak to you again."

"You won't—why are you giving me a death glare?"

"I went through hell to bring you back when you got kidnapped. You were..." My voice becomes shaky at the memory of him shuffling, eyes downcast, and spirit broken. "The condition you were in, I wanted to die."

Adair's face falls, and he places his hands on my shoulders. "God, Davia, I'm sorry. I didn't realize finding me in that condition upset you. You almost died to save me, but you were all business, no reaction."

"My training holds me together, but you've pierced my mental defenses. Only you."

Come tell me how much you love me.

"I don't realize a lot because I'm still a mess, not thinking about anyone but myself," he says. "I want to live with the freedom I had before the kidnapping and torture, so I pretend the event never happened."

"You can't, Adair. You have to stay safe, if not for you, for me."

"I promise I'll be careful from here out."

"You swear?"

"I do."

"Besides having Kyle go to Henry Adams' home with you, I'll be on the periphery as backup."

"Having you there will help me stay composed," Adair says. "I'm not sure how I'll react after what I went through, but I'll work to be level-headed."

"Are you still having problems?"

"Mainly nightmares. Haven't slept well since you lay beside me, so perhaps you should be my nighttime protector."

His words whisk me back to our nap, my cheek on his bare skin and the feel of him. Adair cups my face as Kyle and Jason leave the office.

"You two lovebirds done?" Kyle says.

Adair gives me a swift kiss. "Did he call us *love*birds?"

"Don't push it," I say, but can't stop my slight smile.

"I think Kyle likes me."

"He's only using you as a golf buddy."

On our way out, I say, "Wait, Adair. I'll text you and Jason one of the housekeepers' photos. Her name's Olivia and she's around fifteen. Maybe she'll be at Henry's."

Adair studies the image on his phone. "She's familiar. Do you think she was one of the women putting out food the last time?"

"I was too nervous about the occasion to focus," I confess.

Kyle glowers at me. "You're going to get a situational awareness lecture when we get home."

I brace myself for another well-deserved reproof from my mentor. The anxiety brought on by parties might be the death of me yet.

Back at my property, an unfamiliar car sits beside Sherilyn's white Mercedes. We park in the garage, and Kyle says, "Whose car is that?"

"Not sure. Maybe José has company."

When we go in, Warden's in the kitchen drinking a can of soda. When he sees me, he says, "I came to get my shirt."

TWENTY-NINE

"Explain who you are and what you're doing here." Kyle's hand is near the .22 he carries in his waistband

Warden's persona changes to lethal, and the two men dead-eye each other.

I touch Kyle's arm. "This is James Warden."

Neither relaxes, so I mouth "Stop" to Kyle, and he drops his hand.

"You should've messaged me you'd be here," I say. "This is my Delta Force mentor, Kyle Kavanagh."

Recognition dawns. "Kyle Kavanagh?"

Noting Warden's buff physique, Kyle says, "Me calling you Captain America wasn't too far off."

Warden makes an amused sound, but a mix of emotions fills his eyes.

Kyle says, "I'm going to change." He nods to Warden and heads toward his bedroom.

When he's gone, Warden says, "I'm sorry, Davia, I have no excuse for my behavior."

"That's right; you don't. To say I'm confused by your presence is an understatement." Pressure from my back molars pressing together makes me conscious of how tense I am. "You said we were over."

Warden looks down. "I shouldn't have."

"Damn right, you shouldn't have," Kyle says as he returns to the kitchen. "Forgot to grab a Guinness."

My heart warms at his excuse to ensure I'm okay. After retrieving his beer, Kyle tells Warden, "If you can fix this, I'll believe pigs can fly," then leaves again.

Color leaves Warden's face. "What did he mean?"

"Kyle didn't have to be a trained operator to figure out I was irritated when I got home from Colorado. I also spoke to him right after you called to say we're no longer an item. I don't think he likes you much right now."

"But what about you, Davia? Do you still like me?"

"I like you, Warden, but your actions are a different story. You left instead of talking to me."

"I needed time to process how I felt about you falling in love with that Brit."

An exasperated noise escapes me. "I'm not defending myself again. Let me get your shirt so you can leave."

As I go past him, he takes my arm. "Don't do this, Dav."

Facing him, I notice the pronounced lines at the corners of his eyes, but my temper doesn't diminish. "Don't do what? You said you were here for your shirt."

"I used it as an excuse to see you, to apologize."

I shake off his grip. "I get you don't like Adair, but you made matters worse when you didn't go all-in on helping me find Sherilyn."

"I said I'd help you get her back if you found her location, and I sent the kidnappers' photos to my sources, though their disguises obscure their ID."

"You should've been my emotional support in this."

"Emotional support?" He scratches the back of his head. "How on earth have you gone from being a badass during our dangerous assignments to needing me to babysit you?"

"You're one to ignore nuances, aren't you? With the team, our lives go from waiting around bored to 150% adrenaline overload in seconds, but not here."

"Sure, but what's made you so different?"

"I don't have to bottle up my emotions 24/7."

"So, you're not coming back to the team?"

"When did I say that? Are you listening?

"Yes, I—"

"Then how did you go from me not compartmentalizing my feelings to me not returning? Sherilyn's my first real female friend, and I refuse to pretend I'm okay when inaction and hopelessness are turning me inside out. What if someone on the team got taken."

"I'd do anything I could to find them and bring them back, not wallow in, whatever this is."

"Wallow?" I snap. "I've stayed busy trying to find the smallest clue about Sherilyn and worked on other matters. Detective Montoya's dating Sherilyn, so he's doing all he can to find her and work the twins' disappearance. Bob Brooks' murder remains unsolved, and though I saw footage of the Bryce burglary, I still have no memories."

Warden lets out a low whistle. "Anything else?"

"Adair's going to Henry Adams' home tomorrow night for a get-together. Adam's one of the men who owns Château Rouge. The other owners will attend and might use the housekeepers or some restaurant workers for entertainment, and people we suspect might have the twins will also be there. Kyle's going with him, and I'm back up."

"I'll help you."

"You do realize I'm there for Adair, to protect Adair."

Warden's full lips press flat, but he catches himself and blanks out his face. "Fine."

"You're good with protecting Adair?"

He folds his arms. "I guess."

"You need to say 'Yes.' I have enough going on without monitoring a pissing contest between you two."

"Yes," he manages.

"Do you have any luggage?"

"It's in the car."

"Go get it, and I'll unlock the guest house."

"The guest—"

"If you don't like it, leave."

"Fine." He goes to his car.

———

Kyle lounges on a chair under an umbrella, reading the same book as before. "Is Warden still alive?" he says when I approach.

"For the moment. He'll bunk out here."

"His choice or yours?"

"Mine."

"Now I've seen him; I'm impressed you beat him."

"A testament to your training."

"He's more handsome than I expected; even that jagged scar through his eyebrow doesn't detract. Maybe his looks add to his cocksure attitude."

"He doesn't need to add to his attitude." I unlock the guest house and open some of the windows. When I near the door, Kyle and Warden talk outside.

"My advice," Kyle's saying, "is stop viewing Davia through your team leader lens. Have you considered what might happen if she can't recover from her injury?"

"Of course."

"What's she going to do? Star in *Real Housewives of Special Operations* while you're on missions?"

"No." Warden's voice is steely.

"You understand why she likes Adair, don't you?"

"Enlighten me."

"He doesn't have her boxed in by expectations."

Warden makes a derisive sound. "He can do anything because he's so rich."

"You think how he treats her is due to his bank account? No, he loves her without placing parameters."

"You've met him?"

"Yes, and I like him."

"Why?"

"I like any man who makes Davia happy. At the moment, that's not you."

At this, I step outside and approach Warden, who holds a duffel bag. "Here's the key."

———

Unable to sleep, I stare upward. When life was rough, I memorized spots, slight flaws, or paint chips in the ceilings of whatever room housed me at the time. It's after midnight. I decide to get up just as Warden knocks on my patio door.

Opening it, I say, "Did you learn anything?"

Warden's tossed on a worn top with sweats, but that's all. No matter how displeased I am, his presence makes thinking about anything but him difficult.

"You weren't asleep?" He rubs the inside corner of an eye and yawns.

"No. What's up?"

"Got a message about the identities of the kidnappers."

"Come in." I indicate my sitting area.

Warden plops down in a chair. "Two men came into the country from Italy about three or four days ago, some high-priced muscle. We spotted them by searching for pros coming into Southern California."

"Who hired them?"

Warden yawns again. "We don't have an identity, but whoever did has a lot of money because these two aren't cheap."

"They got here after Bob Brooks' funeral. All the potential suspects attended and could have seen Sherilyn then hired these men to snatch her."

"If they were after her and not you."

"True. Do you have their photos?"

Warden fishes his phone out of a pants pocket. "I'll text them to you."

Going to my nightstand, I retrieve my phone and study the faces. "Never seen them."

Warden rises. "Sorry, it's a dead end."

"Worth a shot, and I appreciate it."

I go with him to the door. Warden's long-lashed green eyes grow hooded as he looks at my lips and into my eyes. Only a few days before, I would've stepped into his arms. Now, I only watch as he returns to the guest house.

THIRTY

We sit in my Rover across the street from Henry Adams' home, grateful the adjacent property is under construction and we can back in behind some fencing. Warden's in the driver's side and fiddles with the walkie-talkies tuned to Kyle's frequency. Adair and Kyle won't arrive for another hour, but we're here early to scope out a vantage point and prepare. José's positioned further down the street in case more backup is necessary.

Warden doesn't look at me. Instead, he checks his weapon and the position of his gear like we're about to engage a platoon.

"You look tired," I say rather than telling him how much I wanted to crawl into bed beside him the previous night.

"Didn't sleep much after we spoke."

"Me either."

At last, he faces me. "I don't know how to fix what's gone wrong between us, Davia, but right now, we both need to get our heads in the game rather than dwell on our problems."

"Agreed."

We lapse back into silence.

Soon, people begin to arrive. Josh Whittaker turns into the address in a Bentley. He emerges smoking a cigar. Mike McMillan roars up in a red Ferrari, the men greeting each other with backslaps and broad smiles. They enter Henry's house without bothering to knock.

"Mid-life compensation?" Warden says.

"Most people around here drive flashy cars, so I can't say for sure."

Next is Kenneth Clayton in the million-dollar Bugatti he drove on our date. Kenneth pushes dull brown hair from his mustachioed face, his gold Rolex studded with diamonds flashing in the light.

"He's the guy I had to go on a date with when I first got here," I say.

"If he were the only type of man you dated, I'd never worry."

When Kenneth goes inside, Adair and Kyle arrive. Kyle drives a black car from Adair's collection. It looks like a moving panther, and Warden can't disguise his envy. "Nice wheels," he says.

"That's a Bugatti La Voiture Noire, but it's more expensive than the one Kenneth Clayton drove. Kenneth's cost a million, but this one's nearly nineteen million. I learned that when Jason McCall emailed me the details on Adair's supercar collection in preparation for the Ladies' League tour."

Warden appears more unhappy. "Lucky guy."

Kyle backs in, angling for an easy escape, then checks the surroundings before opening the passenger door. When Adair stands, Warden says, "Much as I hate him, he's one beautiful bastard."

Adair has a new fade haircut, a lock falling across his forehead, and his casual black t-shirt and jeans still make him look like he's stepped off a runway.

"Let's stay focused on the mission," I tell Warden, as much to remind myself as him.

Once the men go in, Warden says, "Might be an uneventful night."

"Might be. Adair says billionaires often bring in sex workers."

"They get to choose from supermodels and high-end hookers? Predictable. Do you think your boy toy indulges in that behavior?"

"Adair's admitted he's not an angel, so maybe?"

"He did, huh? I can't believe he'd say anything to ruin his perfect image."

"Warden, we need to—"

"Focus on the mission."

A walkie crackles and Kyle says in a low voice, "They're waiting for someone, but your knight's socializing with the four men, and the only danger I see is they'll drink too much at the open patio bar."

"Your knight?" Warden questions.

"Long story."

Another car turns in, and Bradford Kensington disembarks from an understated Mercedes in his trademark cardigan and black-framed glasses.

"He's the richest guy here tonight," I say.

"Richer than your Brit?"

"All these men are wealthier than Adair."

"Seriously?"

"He's a small fish in comparison."

When Bradford's inside, time stretches, night falls, and we receive periodic messages from Kyle that all is "business and b.s."

"I realize this is more comfortable than a Humvee, but I wish I could stretch my legs," Warden says.

After nothing happens for several hours, we give in and take turns getting out to stretch, grateful we blacked out the interior lights to secrete our movement.

Warden fidgets in his seat. "My ass feels like cement."

"Better than lying flat on a roof for hours waiting for a snipe and making the shot despite a windstorm," I say.

"Or not being able to drink the water because we might get cholera."

"How about hitting a house, and it's nothing like the source informed us? We get separated because we're dealing with different threats and come face-to-face with a guy with an AK-47."

"Or having an eight-year-old waving a piece of paper and saying he has information, but he has on a suicide vest, and we have to take him out."

We grow quiet, remembering the moment, then lock the scene away again.

Before continuing our reminiscences, a van turns into the driveway, flanked by two dark SUVs. Men in suits pour out of the leading and trailing vehicles, look in both directions on the street, and then wave for another man to open the van's door.

Seven women huddle together, some with tears streaming. The

white phosphor binoculars I utilize provide a clear picture, and I recognize Olivia from her aunt's photo and also the woman from the Château Rouge kitchen. Before I can radio Kyle, a black Lamborghini roars into the driveway.

The person who steps out is Hannah McMillan.

———

"Who's that?" Warden puts down his binoculars while I work to reconcile the phone-obsessed Hannah with the enraged person who marches toward the women and slaps one hard across the face.

"Rancho Suprema's Ghislaine Maxwell." I reference the woman who recruited and groomed underage women for Jeffrey Epstein,

Warden lets Kyle know he has company, seven friendlies, and five hostiles.

"I'm outnumbered." Kyle sounds entertained.

"The incoming blonde female is the daughter of one of the men inside. On our way," I say.

Warden and I exit the Rover but stop when a fast-moving vehicle approaches. It's a Rancho Private Security SUV. Has trouble at this location been reported?

The two men charged with maintaining perimeter security step out of the way and wave the car in. Officer David Sterling saunters toward the house.

WTF?

Warden sends me a questioning look, and I shrug. That Sterling's face brightened when he spoke about the owners of Château Rouge makes sense if he enjoys the benefits of these boys-only nights.

"Do you know the uniform?" Kyle's voice is soft in my earpiece.

I push away my disappointment. "Yes. Not on our side."

"The only woman I've seen is blonde and around your age. Not sure where they stashed the others," Kyle says. "She came to the room to say the entertainment arrived and then left."

"Roger," I say, then signal to Warden.

We blend into the shadows in our black outfits and ballcaps. Thick bamboo, trees, and plants front the property, and we get into position across from our targets. The two men left as lookouts talk to each other and don't observe their surroundings. Why would they? I doubt they encountered any trained operatives in this ritzy community.

Warden uses hand signals to count down to zero, and we rush forward, guns out and in their faces. We put gloved hands on their mouths, disable their communication equipment, and order them into one of the SUVs. We zip-tie their hands to interior grab bars.

"Two down," Warden says for Kyle's benefit.

"No shooting, remember?" Kyle says.

The only sound is our soft, rhythmic breathing as we go through a gate leading to the residence's rear. I think of how often my team approached a target with no one the wiser until Ned, our most skilled breacher, set a well-placed charge, clicked the initiator, and exploded a door. Then came gunfire, screams, more explosions, and the acrid smell of gunpowder.

We pause near a door, going to opposite sides. Warden tries the handle, and it's unlocked. I glide in with my gun raised, and he's right behind me. As we check each room, I stop myself from calling "Clear."

The rooms off the vast, unlit hall are a gym, a movie theater, and a barbershop/beauty salon. At an intersection, I pause and peek around the corner. Stationed before four rooms are four men, all armed and alert.

Footsteps and voices drift toward us, getting louder, and we melt back into the shadows. A calm covers me in my familiar role, trained to stay quiet until it's no longer an option. Warden is silent beside me, but his presence brings me strength and a certainty that we can impose our will on whatever's thrown our way.

The men draw near, and I recognize Henry Adams' voice as he says, "We have some virgin territory tonight, perfect for you, Adair."

"Bet you haven't had one of those in a while, right?" says Josh Whittaker.

"Uh, no," Adair manages.

"Because it's your first time, you can have your pick," Henry says. "Good thing your protection stayed where he was. He might have wanted in on the action."

The men laugh, not realizing Kyle remained behind so we wouldn't fight on two fronts. They draw within feet of our position.

As they do, a figure throws open the outside door so hard it bangs against the wall. The hall brightens with illumination as Hannah McMillan bellows, "We have intruders!"

THIRTY-ONE

Face contorted, Hannah points at Warden and me. We lift our firearms, ready for anything, and Henry and Josh turn ashen.

An armed guard dashes out of the hall right in front of the men, and Adair reacts instantly. He seizes his arm and propels him into a wall. The unexpected action causes the man to drop his gun, and Adair scoops it up while another henchman charges forward. I order him to freeze as Warden grabs a third thug's collar and shoves his gun in the man's face. A fourth gunman appears, and Warden throws the man he holds into him. The collision causes the man's finger to jerk on his trigger.

A bullet smashes into the wall inches from Adair.

"You need to get out of here!" I shout, my emotions a whirlwind. Adair gives me a quick head shake and forces his prisoner to sit.

While I'm distracted, Hannah smashes into me with so much force I stumble into Warden, who's bent over, securing his two combatants. I turn to engage Hannah, and the man I controlled flees toward the rooms with the captive women. Henry Adams and Josh Whittaker see their chance and bolt back the way they came.

Hannah claws at my face with long acrylic nails. "You've ruined everything!" Twisting, I slam my elbow into her midsection, and she doubles over.

Before she recovers, I latch onto one of her arms and wrench it behind her to thread a zip tie around one wrist. When she struggles, I kick the back of a knee to cause her to drop to the floor and I secure the other arm.

"Stay on your stomach and don't move, or you won't move again," I warn.

Warden secures his assailants back-to-back and tosses Adair a zip tie for his prisoner.

"Go," Warden tells me, motioning toward the rooms with the captive women.

I raise my knee off Hannah's back, but Officer Sterling and the guard reappear before I can move. Both have guns pressed to the temples of women they use as shields. One of them is Olivia, Ana Sanchez's niece.

———

"Let them go." Warden's voice rings with the expectation of immediate compliance.

"Or what?" Sterling taunts.

Does Sterling see certain death in the nothingness of our eyes, or does he underestimate our capabilities?

"Let them go," Warden repeats. His voice is milder now but filled with promises of annihilation if the men don't do as he says.

Hannah struggles, and I place a boot between her shoulder blades. "Don't move," I order. Adair's face is pale as he grips his confiscated gun, its muzzle pointed at the floor.

Can he shoot someone if needed, or will the stress make him crack?

"You won't win," Sterling says. "We have videos of prominent officials getting up to naughty behavior with minors. Trust me when I say we own them."

"We?" I question.

"You've chosen to go against the wrong people," he jeers. "You're foolish if you believe anyone will help you with an investigation or prosecution. Think about all the people who took the Lolita Express to Epstein Island. Other than Ghislaine Maxwell, how many are doing time? None. You need to give up now and beg forgiveness."

At his words, Olivia begins hyperventilating and jerks away from her guard, desperate. He lifts his weapon and aims it at her.

Bang!

The guard falls, and Olivia rushes past me and through the still-open door to the outside. Blood spreads across the tiled floor as the wounded man drops his gun to clutch the injury with both hands.

Adair lowers his weapon.

Eyes wild, Officer Sterling drags his prisoner backward. Warden takes the fallen man's gun and tucks it into his waistband.

"Watch them," I tell Adair, and he says okay, although he's paler than before. "José, Ana's niece is coming your way."

José says. "I'll pick her up in my truck."

"Anyone down?" comes Kyle's worried voice in my earpiece.

"One hostile," Warden says.

Sterling enters the nearest room, hostage in tow, and the lock clicks.

We take positions on both sides of the entry.

"What now?" I ask Warden.

At my words, a volley of gunfire blasts through the door, and we twist away, putting up arms to deflect flying splinters of wood.

When the barrage ends, Warden places a finger on his lips. How can we gain access without Sterling shooting a hostage or us? We don't have explosives to breach the barrier, and no alternative entry points are apparent. If we shoot the doorknob, will it shatter and allow us immediate access, or will the knob jam? Will the round ricochet?

"The natives are getting restless," Kyle says.

We don't need words.

Warden shoots the knob. When he kicks the door, I go in fast and low.

"Get down, get down!" I warn the hostages as my shoulder rams into Sterling's body and knocks him backward while I seize his gun arm and throw it up.

Warden's right behind me and wrenches Sterling's gun away.

"You'll pay for this," Sterling snarls, "like Bob Brooks."

I blink. "What did you say?"

Warden hauls Sterling to his feet while three women cower in the corner of the bedroom. Facing me, Sterling says, "You'll go out like Bob Brooks. He got too nosy."

"You killed him?"

"He shouldn't have trusted me."

I step nearer, and Sterling spits in my face.

Warden's arm draws back to ram a fist down his throat, but I say, "Don't."

A corner of Sterling's mouth lifts, smug. "You can't touch me."

"Really?" I head-butt him in the face.

His hands fly to his broken and bleeding nose while I wipe his saliva off with my sleeve. I snap on his zip ties and tighten them so hard they slice into his wrists.

"Clear," Warden says to Kyle through the headpiece. "Be with you in two mikes."

Instructing the hostages to come with me, I open the other bedrooms, tell the women in Spanish to stay in one room and lock the door from the inside until I give a specific knock, which I demonstrate.

"Let's go," I tell Warden, and we march Sterling out. Adair's body is rigid from tension, but the situation remains static. I quickly assess the man Adair shot, determine it's a superficial wound, and bind him.

"Get up," I instruct, nudging him with my foot.

"He shot me!" the man says.

"You heard her, get up," Warden says, and the man complies. "All right, all of you, let's go."

Hannah and Sterling gravitate toward each other while the three hired thugs assist their wounded companion.

Adair comes to my side, and I touch his arm. "You doing all right?"

"Better than expected." He puts the gun in his waistband. "You?"

Right now, I feel nothing. The mission isn't over.

"I'm—" I pause.

"Fine," he finishes.

The word is barely out when the two men we secured in the van enter through the exterior door, their guns aimed at us.

THIRTY-TWO

"Shoot them!" Hannah shrieks.

Chaos erupts. The prisoners run in different directions. Hannah shouts at Officer Sterling to do something, and he knocks me backward.

"What are you waiting for?" Hannah roars at the new arrivals, and they point their muzzles at Adair, the closest target.

"No!" I attempt to shove Sterling off, horror flooding me.

Warden steps in front of Adair.

Gunfire rings in the space, the noise deafening as multiple rounds slam into Warden, and he falls backward.

"Sitrep," Kyle demands in my earpiece.

"Warden's down." Unable to process, I step into the whizzing bullets, uncaring. My training takes over, and I center my weapon on the man on the right, taking him down with two quick rounds to his center mass. The other man aims for me, but my bullets hit his torso.

Furious, I rush forward and remove their firearms. They're bleeding, but I almost administer kill shots for what they've done. Shoving the guns in my waistband, I stalk toward Hannah and Sterling. "Sit the hell down! If you move, you're dead. Got it?"

They comply.

Adair crouches beside Warden, saying something in low, urgent tones. My heart leaps with relief when Warden moves.

"Where?" I kneel in his blood.

He coughs. "Three to the vest and one to my gun arm, I think."

Peeling back his sleeve, I observe an abrasion on his bicep extending to his shoulder, but the bullet hasn't penetrated. Blood seeps from his right thigh, and I retrieve the knife worn on my hip and slit his pants leg.

Warden coughs again. "How bad?"

"It'll hurt like a bitch, but—" I begin.

"It's a long way from my heart?" He tries to smile but grimaces instead.

Adair removes a handkerchief from a pocket, hands it to me, and I wipe away the blood, assessing.

"It's your lucky day," I say. "This one's a deep groove, but nothing major, although you won't compete in marathons anytime soon. Adair, press there, please,"

"This will be the only time you can beat me at running," Warden jokes, but his words are forced as pain covers his face.

"Did you hear everything?" I say to Kyle.

"Affirmative. ETA?"

"Four mikes. I'm going to get those goons who ran away like little girls, be right back." I say.

"You do remember you're a girl, right?" Warden chokes out.

As I stand, Adair turns his head.

One of the men I shot is now on an elbow aiming a gun at me.

Adair launches forward to shield me, and we crash to the floor.

Gunfire rings out.

"Clear." Warden's voice radiates anger as he lowers his weapon.

The weight of Adair's body presses me down, unmoving. "Adair, are you hit? Oh god, Adair."

He raises himself. "They missed me. Are you okay?"

"In one piece because of you."

When we untangle and stand, Adair hugs me against him and says, "I can't lose you."

Warden watches, inscrutable.

"You won't," I say, "Let's try this again."

The men huddle in a bedroom, attempting to undo each other's bindings. The moment I go in, gun raised, they stop. None make eye contact, and all obey my orders.

"Still bleeding?" I ask Adair, who's back at Warden's side. He raises the blood-soaked handkerchief.

"Not as much, but the flow is steady."

"Give me your hand," Warden says to Adair, who hauls him to his feet. He tests putting weight on his leg.

"Want to lean on me?" Adair offers.

"I want you to get your gun out," Warden growls. "I'm not taking any more bullets for you."

———

Kyle relaxes when we enter the room, lowering his firearm to his side, but I recognize he's a coiled snake.

Hannah and Sterling go to two empty chairs while I order the other prisoners to sit against a wall. The man Adair wounded leaves a trail of blood on the plush carpet.

Adair and Warden stop a few feet from Kyle.

Kyle catches sight of Warden's injuries. "You good?"

Warden nods. "They beat me to the trigger."

Henry Adams, Kenneth Clayton, Josh Whittaker, Mike McMillan, and Bradford Kensington slump on two couches. Henry, Kenneth, and Josh study the floor. Mike's face is red, his eyes bulging as he glares at us, while Bradford takes in the scene with one side of his mouth lifted in a contemptuous smile. Officer Sterling's uniform is blood-splattered, his nose misshapen and swollen from where I broke it. Hannah struggles against her ties, a volcano of rage.

Bradford says, "You need to let us go."

I struggle to keep my voice level. "Your hired muscle almost killed two people I care about, so you aren't going anywhere."

"Your parents' names are Mary and Russell Glenn, right?" Bradford's conversational with no trace of stress.

My stomach lurches, and the desire to empty my remaining rounds into him almost overcomes me, but I keep my face blank.

Kyle takes a step forward. "I suggest you forget those names, or I guarantee you won't live to repeat them."

Bradford recognizes the promise of absolute destruction underscoring Kyle's soft words. He regroups, then says, "How about you, Adair? Your mom, Kate, and your sister, Adalyn? I'm sure you wouldn't want anything to happen to them."

The other men become emboldened by Bradford, contributing vigorous nods and muttering, "You tell them." Kenneth Clayton's the only one who remains silent, eyes fixed on the floor.

Henry Adams says, "We can destroy your lives with a phone call."

Adair unfolds from where he leaned against a wall. "Not going to happen."

Bradford's lip curls. "It's not? How will you stop us?"

Adair's cold countenance is new to me, his beautiful eyes hard and hostile. "We have the videos. You know, the ones you recorded to use as blackmail, which I'm sure contain you as well, as you're the type of people who love replaying their conquests."

Bradford sneers. "You're bluffing."

Adair's cell phone rings. When he disconnects, he tells us, "That was confirmation."

Mike McMillan hurdles to his feet, pushing a beefy hand through his blond hair. "You can't do this!"

I concentrate on his tall build and scroll up the image from the footage of Bryce's burglary.

Kyle observes me. "What is it?"

"He's the crook who cracked my head with a pipe."

Warden's hulking frame rotates toward Mike, eyes narrowed. Mike freezes, then stammers, "She had a gun! I mean, it was all a lark, wasn't it?"

Henry and Josh motion for him to stop talking, but he continues. "The stores had insurance. It wasn't a loss, and if Hannah hadn't come across the TikTok video we—"

Hannah bares her teeth. "Shut up, Dad!"

"It was your idea, and you convinced the rest of us," Mike protests.

"I said to shut it!"

In the face of his daughter's rage, Mike collapses on the couch, silent.

"Getting back to the files," Adair says. "If you think you can stop us, you're wrong. You're not the only people with inside sources. My team will expose the corrupt officials and ensure they're prosecuted, along with you."

"And you for murder," I say to Sterling.

His face creases with scorn, but the movement makes him flinch with pain and brace his injured nose. "You don't have any proof."

"You confessed," I tell him.

"A confession without physical evidence never flies," he says. "Besides, what confession? My word against yours."

"You're right," I say. "I'm confused, though. Bob was your friend."

"Sure, I liked him."

"Liked?"

Sterling's eyes grow contemplative. "We were good buddies for a long time, but—"

I don't say anything, waiting.

"Bob saw Hannah talking to some young girls and giving them large amounts of cash, but when she slapped one, he became concerned."

"Let me guess," I say to Hannah. "You lured them by saying some rich men would help their lives, give them gifts, the typical promise of a better future?"

Hannah makes a disgusted noise. "They'll do anything for money and a few trinkets."

"And you decided eliminating Bob was the best option?" I say to Sterling.

"I could've lied, but he never let stuff slide. He would've bugged me until I gave him answers and, if I said I found them, wanted to help give them a better life. His interference would've caused no end of trouble. So I promised him I'd look into it. He told me about the open house, and I went over when no one was around. A few whacks with my Maglite, and he was done."

I glance at Adair, and he nods. We wear recording devices that Jason monitors.

Distant sirens grow louder, and the assembled people twist in their seats.

"Don't move," Warden orders, projecting extreme danger though his wounds continue to bleed. Kyle straightens, and I take a defensive posture, prepared for anything.

"I'll let them in," Adair says.

———

Detectives Rodríguez and Montoya enter with a contingent of uniformed deputies.

"Got your message," Montoya says.

"He's Bob Brooks' killer," I point to Sterling, and Montoya's face darkens.

"She's lying," Sterling says. "Bob was my friend, and I have no motive whatsoever. You should arrest the people with guns. They came in here and held us hostage."

Montoya sends me a questioning look.

"We taped his confession." I leave off further explanation.

Sterling's head snaps up, eyes widening. "You what? That's illegal."

"You made the statement in a group setting with no expectation of privacy," I say, having discussed legalities with Jason at our planning stage.

Sterling struggles to his feet. "I'm a respected police officer, and the community won't stand for this."

"Let's test your theory," Montoya says, and a uniformed officer escorts Sterling out.

I tap Rodríguez and indicate Mike McMillan. "He's the one who attacked me near Bryce's."

"You had a gun," he protests. "She could've killed Henry, Kenneth, or Josh."

Henry sputters. "We only had crowbars and pipes, but a gun? That's assault."

Rodríguez sighs. "Arrest them, please," he tells more uniforms who take the men away. "Officers are getting statements from the young women, but this will take a while to sort."

Hannah begins to cry, gulping in air like a toddler having a tantrum, but there's no wetness on her cheeks.

"She's the ringleader," I say to Rodríguez and Montoya. "Get a search warrant for her phone, and I'm sure you'll find all kinds of incriminating evidence. She groomed the young women and encouraged her dad and his friends to commit burglaries for fun."

Hannah's faux-terrified façade drops away. "I bet you think Adair will shield you from what's to come, but he doesn't have our connections. We'll destroy you all,"

"You only got a taste of what we're able to give back," I say.

Hannah smirks. "You have no idea how deep this goes."

"We'll find out," I say, and Rodríguez tells the deputy to take her away.

Another sheriff has Bradford Kensington, but he pauses in front of me. "I need to talk to you."

"Why? Want to threaten me some more?"

"I'll get out of these charges. I didn't plan any of this, and you won't find me on the recordings. I'll claim these clowns planned to blackmail me tonight. Given my reputation and no prior criminal history, I won't have any charges leveled against me."

"Why are you telling me this?"

"Because I know where your friend is."

THIRTY-THREE

"You know where Sherilyn is?" I question, and Montoya is beside me in an instant.

"Ah, Detective, I suppose you want her back, too?" Bradford says.

At his words, Montoya's fists clench.

"Let's listen to what he has to say," I caution.

"Unless you guarantee I'm released, I won't say another word." Bradford holds out his handcuffed hands, studying his fingernails, bored, while Montoya tenses.

"I need to talk to you," I tell Montoya, but he doesn't move or acknowledge me. I put a hand on his arm, but he yanks it away, so I place both hands on his shoulders. "The first step forward is to come with me."

After a mutinous moment, he relents. We leave Bradford with the uniform, move a distance away, and drop our voices.

"Adair needs to call Jason to see if Bradford's in the video files," I say. "If he's lying, we've got him."

"Who's Jason?"

"Adair's right-hand man."

Warden's on a couch, and Adair hands him a clean hand towel he retrieved to staunch the continued bleeding. Montoya's gaze goes between the two men.

"What?" I say, and he glances at the ceiling in disbelief.

I fill in Adair, and he excuses himself to make the call. While he's gone, a deputy comes into the room and whispers to Montoya, who says, "Why are there dead men in the back?"

Warden gestures to his blood-stained clothing. "They shot me."

"Who are 'they' exactly?" Montoya asks.

"Some men who guarded the trafficked women," I say.

Adair returns. "Nothing's come up with Bradford so far. Jason will call me back."

"Did you see what happened to Warden?" Montoya says.

"Two men aimed at me, but Warden took the bullets instead," Adair says. "Davia shot them, but one came up with a second gun, and Warden took him out."

"Ballistics and bloodstain pattern analysis will verify your statements, right?" Montoya asks.

"It's the truth," I say.

A team of paramedics enters with a stretcher and equipment, and Montoya puts up a hand. "Over here, if it's not obvious already."

They set their gear around Warden, and one inserts an IV, saying, "We'll need to transport you and replace some of the blood you lost."

Warden stands, glaring down at them. "I'm not dizzy, and I'm not going to a hospital."

The older of the two paramedics remove the blood-soaked handkerchief and towel. "You're not a superhero."

"He'll dispute your assessment," I say.

Warden sits again. "Treat me here, okay?"

The younger paramedic takes Warden's vitals. "He's in the normal range but needs a doctor to clear any residue and double-check."

"You can do that, right, Dav?" Warden says.

"I'm not Hodge, and we're not in a war zone. You're going in."

Warden's face is mulish, and Kyle, listening nearby, approaches. "No need to reinforce my original assessment that you're a dumbass."

"My medical insurance won't cover..." Warden protests, but Adair says, "I'm pretty sure I can handle the bills. I owe you."

Kyle says. "You're going, no excuses."

Warden's internal war is plain on his troubled face. I'm sure he wants Kyle to like him by doing what he requests but resents Adair even more.

"Give me the key to the Rover, and I'll follow and report," Kyle says.

"I've got them." Warden hands him the key.

Adair puts out his hand. "Thank you again."

Ignoring him, Warden says, "Stay mission-focused, and I'll be back to help."

"Keep him civil with the doctors," I instruct Kyle and kiss Warden on his cheek.

———

Adair's phone rings. When the call concludes, he says, "Jason's team discovered someone categorized the files by name, and Bradford's not among them. Detective, a file implicates a sheriff named Detective Sgt. Leo Hurst."

Montoya tips his head to the side. "Are you sure?"

"Yes, and I have other news. All the men you arrested are in the videos, and so is Hannah. She liked to watch her dad, so that's a balls-up situation."

"But Bradford Kensington's not in them?" I press.

"No, and neither is Brant, which surprises me," Adair says. "Several years ago, we pursued the same girl in Spain until I learned she was fifteen but appeared older due to makeup and styling. I backed out, but Brant didn't."

"Brant said you prevailed over him."

"He would. He's the type to cause trouble."

Montoya vibrates with impatience. "Let's find out about Sherilyn."

Bradford's chest is puffed out, and his shoulders squared while he waits, sure he'll be released.

"Where's Sherilyn?" Montoya says without preamble.

Bradford raises his handcuffed wrists again. "Let me go."

"Not happening until you tell us where she is and we verify. You think you'll get out of the charges, but the process can be as quick or slow as I dictate."

"My son paid some Italian talent, and they took her."

"What?" I say. "Why?"

"I think he had different plans." Bradford looks toward Adair. "He doesn't care for Adair's happiness with you, so you were the target. When he learned you were gone, I overheard the men describing Sherilyn to him, and he said to take her instead. After meeting Sherilyn at the funeral, he mentioned her to me, letting me in on a few things he'd like to do with her."

Montoya steps forward. "If he did anything...."

Bradford shrugs. "He might have."

I put myself in front of Montoya.

"Where is she?" I say to Bradford.

"I'm not sure."

"You said you knew where she was," Montoya says.

"Brant has her. Where exactly? No idea."

"You've lied already, so this isn't giving me much confidence," Montoya says. "You say you've done nothing wrong, but then give up your son. To me, that means you're hiding something."

"I'm not lying," Bradford protests.

"Without more specifics, I can't get a warrant, even with a judge who'd sign off on anything." Montoya's distress makes him pace.

"The Ladies' League Home and Garden Tour is tomorrow. Do you think she's at Hazelton?" I ask Bradford.

"Maybe. Brant mentioned he's leaving right after the tour, though. Knowing him, he'll dispose of her before his departure."

"Then you need to allow me unrestricted access and get me around all the security," I say.

Bradford's amber eyes turn cold behind his thick black glasses. "I'm not cooperating with you."

"Your choice. I'll get her back and bring Brant to join you in a cell."

"Most people in this community have no idea who you are, do they?" Bradford says.

"They do. I'm Adair Monroe's girl."

THIRTY-FOUR

The morning of the tour, Kyle and Warden are in the kitchen drinking coffee when I join them.

Warden takes in my navy linen pants, fitted tank, and embroidered sweater I paired with gold jewelry. "How in the world will you rescue Sherilyn in that outfit?"

Kyle backhands him in his wounded arm. "What you mean to say is, 'Davia, you look beautiful.'"

Warden puts a hand on his injury. "Uh, yes, you do."

"Think of it as Rancho camouflage," I say.

As I pass Kyle, he tugs my ponytail. "You'll fit right in."

"Why does your statement disturb me? You ready?"

"We'll be ready way ahead of you," Warden says.

The men plan to take high-ground positions with a panorama of the Kensington property, Warden with a sniper rifle and Kyle spotting. They scouted the area and found a location the previous night.

"Hopefully, you won't have to shoot anyone. I think we've used our 'Get out of Jail Free' card," I say. "Montoya presented the dead men as justifiable homicide."

"It *was* justified," Warden says. "Those thugs had it coming."

"I agree. Montoya played the video of Detective Sgt. Hurst having sex with a minor for the Sheriff and gave her the names of the other men. It smoothed things out, and Montoya gained a lot of clout," I say. "Now, we need to find Sherilyn. I'd better roll."

"Wish I was going with you instead of that—Adair," Warden says, sullen.

"You can lend him your rifle and see what happens," I say. "Remember, we stick with our strengths."

Warden lifts an eyebrow. "Since when are society functions your strength?"

"Fake it til..." Kyle inserts. "And stop being so sulky, Captain America. "

Warden turns his head, but not before I register the hurt in his eyes.

"Be right back." I replace my jewelry with the necklace Warden gave me in Colorado. Will he understand the message that he'll be with me in my heart if not in person?

When I return, Warden's keen gaze goes to my neckline, where the pendant catches the light, and his face fills with hope.

———

At the Ladies' League building, members sign in the paid attendees. Luxury coach buses idle on the street, and an air of anticipation hovers as people converse.

"Davia, I expected you to be here sooner," Beatrice Gibbs says.

"My committee members have it under control, right, Francis?"

Francis smiles. "Yes, this has been so easy."

Amelia Meadows joins us and says, "Nicole Wolf texted me to say she couldn't make it, and Jennifer and Hannah aren't here."

"Henry and Minerva Adams aren't either. Wonder what happened," Francis says.

Everything's a-okay, but not on their end.

Beatrice says, "It's time to depart. Make the announcement, please."

Francis does the honors, somehow able to project a strong voice over the din, and people begin to load the buses.

I take my Rover, saying I must ensure all is ready before everyone arrives.

———

When I park at Stacey Templeton's and open my door, a white male turkey with a red head greets me. A royal blue fascinator, a jumble of blue fabric flowers beneath a flat circular brim, provides him a festive look.

Stacey opens her door, wearing a matching hat. "Davia, this is Triple T5!"

"Hello, T5," I say, and the turkey totters toward Stacey. Did it give me a little nod, or was I imagining things?

"T4 now tops my sculpture, memorialized and soaring forever before us." Stacey indicates a new bronze turkey with wings spread flying above the others.

"I'm sure he's honored."

The buses drive in, and Stacey and T5 greet the participants, who consult their programs and then spread out to see the estate. Stacey's a changed woman, back to her vibrant self with T5 beside her, laughing and talking, which lifts my spirits.

The expansive closet overflows with designer bags, clothes, and shoes once more, and the hat wall is replete with new wonders.

"Who wants champagne?" A server at the closet bar inquires, and people surge forward to partake.

When the time to leave arrives, Stacey throws her arms around me in an exuberant hug. "I appreciate all you've done for me, Davia. I never would've made it through what happened without you. Even If they never catch who broke in, I'll choose to keep only good memories of T4."

———

Upon reaching Adair's residence, he emerges from the home, and I think of Jason saying, "All you'll need to succeed here is for His Gorgeousness to appear." When he nears, his hands cradle both sides of my face, and his lips meet mine with an intensity rivaling the day he dragged me into a bedroom. My restraint slips away, and I reciprocate.

"You might want to redo your lipstick." He wipes his mouth with a thumb. "Or perhaps not, as I intend a repeat performance. If the Sherilyn rescue goes wrong, I don't want to die without taking advantage of my time with you."

"I won't let you die."

"Nor me, you," he says as we enter the house.

"She only wants you for your library, Mr. Monroe," Jason says from where he waits inside the foyer.

Adair shoots me a crooked grin. "It's yours. We can spend our free time there. I've got some Ovid poetry I can read you, or maybe I'll stick with my countryman Lord Byron's prose."

"Remember the rescue," I remind him, not wanting my thoughts diverted from what's to come.

Six men and women in dark suits with earpieces wait further away. They focus on me, as they should, recognizing the most significant threat.

The buses arrive, and Jason nods to the security detail. They move toward pre-designated positions, and Adair and I greet the people streaming into his home, reinforcing the fake rumor that I love him.

"It's not fake." I hear Kyle say, and I assess the now, where Adair's beside me, chatting to the arrivals. He winks at me, and I feel...what?

Happy. My mind's on the upcoming rescue, yet my soul's lighter when I'm with Adair. Is this love?

When people go off in different directions to enjoy the estate, he says, "Want to make out with me for the next hour?"

"You're incorrigible."

"I thought you'd say irresistible."

Adair kisses me again as some women enter the hall.

"Sorry," Adair says to them, trying to sound guilty but failing.

When they hurry on, he says, "We need to seclude ourselves."

"Only until lunch. Your appearance is mandatory."

We take an elevator to Adair's suite. Picture windows cast a soft light on an elegant but comfortable décor.

"This is beautiful," I say.

"More beautiful because you're here." Adair takes me into his arms.

"Adair—"

"Don't. He's not here. It's you and me."

"He might not be, but—"

Adair looks down at me. "He saved my life, and I'm grateful, but you need to admit the truth. We've all been together, and I know who you love, and that's me."

"You? Why do you say that?"

"He took multiple rounds, and you were all business. You thought that guard shot me, and I heard the terror in your voice when you called my name. Warden knows, too."

I disengage from him. "Do you think that's the first time someone injured Warden when we were together? Or me in front of him? No. Even if he were dead, I'd deal with the immediate threat and let the emotions hit later. We're soldiers."

"Your emotions came right out for me, Davia."

"You didn't have a vest. From the angle, it might have been game over."

"My willingness to sacrifice myself for you should be viewed as a positive."

"A positive? We move in different worlds. Have you thought about what being with you is like for me? I don't want to spend my life as 'Adair Monroe's girl.' Having paparazzi dogging me, wondering when I'll be on the news with you—"

Adair laughs. "The future's much simpler. You and I get married, have some kids, and this bachelor is off the market and of no more interest to the press. I'm not a Hollywood celebrity, nor important enough to stay in the limelight forever."

"Married? Adair—"

"It's happening."

His sureness is unnerving and not what I need before the upcoming rescue.

"We have important business at Hazelton today, finding and saving Sherilyn, not this fantasy of yours. I'm going back downstairs," I say.

THIRTY-FIVE

"Be sure and pay attention to the security protocols at the Kensington property," I tell Adair as we drive there in the Rover.

"You're the expert, not me."

"I don't want—"

"Anything to happen to me," Adair finishes.

We go through the security check, and two men escort us to where Linda Riley waits near the front door.

"Mr. Kensington texted me and said he won't be here," she apologizes. "He's tied up."

Locked up is more like it.

I feign ignorance. "Do you mean Bradford?"

"Yes, I saw Brant earlier when I supervised the caterers."

"Oh? Where is he? We know each other, and I'd love to say hello," Adair says.

'I'm not sure, but he'll be out to greet the visitors."

"Do you mind if I do a quick walkthrough?" I say. "The buses should be here in fifteen."

Linda bristles. "I made sure everything's ready."

"Think of Davia as a Type A personality," Adair says. "She's thorough."

"I need to meet the caterer for the refreshments right now," Linda says.

"I've got the map, and it won't take long. I'm doing this because the president of the Ladies' League can be demanding," I say.

Linda makes a face. "That Beatrice Gibbs woman? She's called me daily because she's convinced you don't comprehend how important Hazelton is as a property. I assured her you've been here several times, but she keeps calling."

"Then you realize why I need to do this," I say.

"Yes, all right. If you need anything, text me." She bustles away while Adair and I pretend to examine one of the vaunted gold door knobs.

"This place is a tad overdone," he says.

"Do you know how many sculptures and paintings you own?"

"Touché."

We hustle to a staircase cordoned off with a rope, jump over, and make for the second floor. I expect to encounter security, but the hall is empty, and we enter one of the bedroom suites. Inside, we stop, astonished.

We take in gold and crystal chandeliers, gold filigreed ceiling trim, a humongous bed on a raised platform separated from the rest of the room by pillars, and a low wall decorated with more gold. All the furniture is in the style of Louis XIV, and an intricate gold screen is before a sizable marble fireplace.

"Now, will you concede the 'overdone' comment?" Adair says.

"Can't wait to see the bathroom."

I focus on locating any jib doors hidden in the walls. Jason found the blueprints for the property, and we discussed the layout, deciding there had to be an entrance from the master into tunnels or other corridors.

Adair takes one side of the opulent room, pressing and feeling his way while I take the other.

"Got it," Adair says, faster than expected, indicating an opening near the bed. "Thought Bradford would want an escape route near where he sleeps."

"Smart. Let's go."

We move through the opening, and the hall beyond is more spacious than expected. As the door slides shut behind us, the area illuminates. After a short distance, we reach an intersection with multiple corridors.

"Now what?" Adair says.

"Let's hope Linda's forgotten about us and hasn't sent security. If Beatrice and the buses have arrived, she'll have her hands full. Here." I hand Adair a small flashlight from my bag. "If I find anything, I'll text."

"Same." Adair goes to his right while I consider my choices. I visualize the layout and recall to the left are guest wings, drawing rooms, etc.

I plunge straight ahead, fighting off my concern for Adair. If he runs into security, would they injure him? If only Detective Montoya could be here rather than waiting on the perimeter for my call.

A mix of voices ahead causes me to stop.

"I appreciate you flying us in for this, Brant," a man says. "but scheduling the auction at the same time as a property tour is either a gutsy or foolhardy move."

Brant sniggers. "I thought about canceling the whole thing, but why? I have so many delicious treats to offer."

Laughter explodes.

"What ages are we talking about?" a man says, voice tinged with anticipation.

"An assortment, the oldest's fourteen. Plus one pretty blonde adult, petite but fiery."

Sherilyn and...kids? Were Evie and Emily here?

"Once you pay up, you can spend a few hours in a guest room or take them," Brant says. "If they don't survive, I have a clean-up crew ready to harvest organs."

Fighting the urge to confront them, I slow my breathing.

"Listen, I need to go greet people upstairs," Brant says. "I've got a buffet and booze for your enjoyment in the anteroom to the auditorium where we'll have the auction. Be back in an hour."

Excited conversation between the men grows less distinct as they move away.

Creeping forward, I come to a door and look into the recently vacated room. White pieces of paper line a wall, each with a photo below a number. Among them is a picture of Sherilyn with a bruised and battered face, and the final two images are of Emily and Evie.

If I had a weapon, would I find the men enjoying Brant's buffet and execute them?

With the clock ticking down the hour until the auction, I need firepower and know exactly where to get it.

———

Adair's at the bottom of the stairs leading to the bedrooms, our agreed rendezvous.

"Let's go somewhere we can talk," I say, a previous text providing him with details of what I found.

He takes my hand, bending nearer. "This is another one of those times I need to remind you to lighten up. Right now, you'd terrify a serial killer with a chainsaw."

I fake-smile at him. "I'm—"

"Fine."

As we pass the room with refreshments, a familiar face pours a drink for an attendee. José dips his head in acknowledgment. He received my group text, as did Montoya, Warden, and Kyle.

Brittany and Kennedy come toward us, accompanied by Alex Gordon.

"Ooh, you two are so striking together," Kennedy coos to Adair and me.

"We are, aren't we?" Adair's arm goes around my waist.

Alex gives me a quizzical look and says, "I have something important to tell you, LT."

"If it's about my investments," I begin, but he says, "I would never discuss business here. It'll only take a sec."

Adair releases me, and Brittany and Kennedy immediately inundate him with questions about what he's been doing. Alex and I move a distance away.

"What's going on?" he says.

"What do you mean?"

"Don't b.s. a b.s.-er. Reading people is one of my skills, and something bad has happened despite the lovey-dovey front with your pretty boy."

Can I trust Alex Gordon? What did my gut say?

"I'm on my way to Bradford Kensington's armory."

Alex scrutinizes me. "Leave the British babe magnet where he is, and let me go with you."

I glance back to where Adair listens to Brittany's babbling, but his eyes are on me.

"I'll be back, Adair," I say. "Alex needs my help."

His brow furrows. "Are you sure?"

Alex moves the fingers of his right hand near his waist to mimic a gun. Adair's gaze travels from Alex to me, and I say, "Never let them see you coming."

A tight line replaces the relaxed curve of Adair's mouth, but he nods his understanding.

THIRTY-SIX

"What's happened?" Alex keeps his voice quiet.

"Sherilyn and the twins are about to be auctioned off to some men in a room below us, but I'm unsure of their exact location. I couldn't bring any firepower, but Bradford Kensington has a gun collection I need to get into."

"You do realize there's like forty armed enforcers, right?"

"Is that all?"

I receive a text from Montoya: *Do you have eyes on her or the kids?*

Me: *No verification. Off to arm up.*

Montoya: *Exigent circumstances are calling my name.*

José: *Tell me where to meet you when you find them.*

Warden: *Overwatch ready.*

Adair: *Please be safe.*

We pass enthralled guests in a state of high excitement over Hazelton's amenities and grandeur, in contrast to security in black suits and mirrored sunglasses standing like watchful sentinels of death. The saltwater pool's movie screen plays *Taken,* starring Liam Neeson.

"Gotta love the irony," Alex says. "Intentional?"

"I'm sure Brant thinks showing a movie with human trafficking scenes is hysterical."

As I say this, Brant comes into view. He's surrounded by women, waving his hand like 'Aw, shucks. So nice of you to compliment my incredible estate.'

"Let's sync up with him when he's free," I say.

"How do you want to play this?"

"He hates Adair. Ready to be my new boyfriend?"

"Thought you'd never ask."

————

Brant has an abashed look as he touches one of the women on the arm, giving the appearance of a regretful goodbye. When he's a distance away, the act fades, and he's bright-eyed, his pace brisk as he heads toward the rear of the home.

Before he turns a corner, Alex says, "Hey, Brant. Got a second?"

He faces us, and I sense his displeasure before his mask falls into place.

"I'm in a bit of a hurry."

Alex throws his arm around my shoulders when we're within a few feet of Brant. "Davia and I appreciate you hosting this event. Isn't that right, baby?"

Brant does a double-take. "What happened to Adair?"

"He was a real snooze in bed," I say. "but Alex is, well—"

"A reformed player," Alex cuts in. "I only belong to Davia and grant all her wishes."

"You do? I guess you're a lucky lady," Brant says, tone leering.

"I am. And Alex is teaching me how to shoot. Your dad mentioned his gun collection but didn't have time to show me due to an appointment. Now I'm super interested."

Brant glances at his watch. "I also have an appointment I can't miss—"

"We don't want to keep you, but a peek won't take long, will it?' Alex presses. "If you have to leave, some of your not-inconspicuous regiment can ensure we don't misbehave."

Brant musters an insincere smile. "Okay, I'll go open the vault."

Bingo.

———

Alex holds my hand as we trail Brant toward a distant building, and four guards accompany us. Brant deactivates the entry door by presenting his face for a scan.

"Think of it as a present for you ditching Adair. After you." He rechecks his watch.

"Your advice about him at Amelia's stuck," I say. "I don't want to be another trophy."

"Is there bad blood between you and Adair?" Alex says.

"He loves the appearance of taking the high road when, in truth, he's no better than the rest of us."

"A guy with integrity? How tedious," Alex comments.

"Right? Hang on." Brant goes to an imposing door, inputs a code into an electric pad, and spins the wheel. When open, I notice the door has a series of military-style locking bars of imposing thickness. Inside, Brant touches a switch, and the glass-front wall displays light up.

"Wow," Alex says, not faking his awe.

Pistols, rifles, and shotguns from various eras fill the room's length.

"This is incredible," I say, impressed. "Do you have ammunition for these, too?"

"Of course, a whole room. One of the Holland & Holland Nitro Express game shotguns requires rounds costing $140 or more." Brant says.

"$140 for one round?" I imagine loading one and firing it right through Brant.

"I'll show you," Brant says and pauses at the door to a large ammo pantry organized and labeled with enough to hold off another country for five years.

"Amazing," Alex says. "You've inspired me to invest in a similar collection."

Brant looks down his aquiline nose at Alex. "Do you have that kind of money?"

"No," Alex concedes, "but I'll do my best."

"I've got to leave, but feel free to take your time. If you have questions, find me later."

"This is such a treat," I say, deciding which weapons to choose.

"Anything for a woman wise enough to dump Adair Monroe."

Alex and Brant shake hands, and then Brant departs without a backward glance while two men take positions on either side of the vault door.

Alex bends his head. "Figured out a plan?"

"I'm ready to do some World War II reenactment. You?"

"World War II?"

"I'm taking the M1 Carbine and German Luger. Plus, a pocketful of these V-40 grenades is a nod to modern times. You?"

"I like the Springfield 1911."

"Solid choice. Ready for a skirmish?"

"I am. I have some skills, so don't be surprised. Of course, I'm saving my most impressive talents for when you and I are alone."

"Is that so?"

"There's the hard-as-diamonds glare I was waiting for."

———

"What did you think, baby?" Alex says to me.

"Do you have this much firepower?" I caress one of his biceps, sending him an adoring look through my lashes.

"I do, and much, much more," he promises.

The guards look away from us, embarrassed.

I deliver a hard punch to one's solar plexus, and he drops. Alex is as efficient, and the other man goes down. He removes the handcuffs suspended from his man's belt, and I do the same.

"Surprised you again, didn't I?" he says as we secure our prisoners to a display case table cemented into the floor.

"Gotta admit, you did."

Alex and I put on their communication gear. "These will come in handy," I say.

"Do you think more hired men wait outside?"

"I doubt it. Unlike Bradford, who was suspicious of me, Brant's only focused on his pleasures."

"Where's Bradford?"

"In custody. Long story."

"Surprised Brant didn't say anything about his absence."

"Bradford said they often go their separate ways."

Conscious of time slipping away, I hurry to remove the M1 from its display rack, pleased an original canvas pouch attached to the stock contains two more fifteen-round magazines. The Luger holds eight rounds, and after locating ammo, I load them and put two V40 grenades in my crossbody bag.

"Any ideas on a way out?" Alex says.

Putting the carbine's canvas sling over my shoulders, I say, "Hazelton has tunnels all over this place, so I bet they built a secret door some-where. Since there's not a lot of unused wall space, it shouldn't be too tricky to find."

As we begin our search, Alex says, "So, how long will our relation-ship last?"

"Warden's on overwatch with a sniper rifle, so I suggest remaining appropriate in open areas. As for Adair, I predict pistols at dawn."

Alex laughs. "Why do I agree?"

A panel slides open. "Got it," I say.

"What about them?" He indicates the handcuffed men.

"Let's shut the vault door and leave them."

———

The passage isn't as luxurious as the ones in the main house. Wood beams support dirt walls and the air's musty and cool like a mine shaft.

Alex halts at an intersection. "Got any idea which way we should go?"

"I have a keen sense of direction; the main home is to the left. "

The tunnel becomes better built and broader the further we go, and we pause to listen. Running footsteps come in our direction, someone at speed but stumbling instead of steady. The steps grow louder and louder, and we take positions on opposite sides of the wall. I raise my rifle and Alex his automatic, waiting.

Sherilyn bursts into view.

THIRTY-SEVEN

"Davia?" Sherilyn's face is bruised and swollen, and she drags a foot. "Oh, thank heavens."

Lowering my weapon, I say, "How badly are you hurt?"

"The time here's been rough, but you have to save those kids."

"Where are they?"

"They were in a cell next to me, but guards came and got them a little while ago. When one came for me, I took him down and ran. Where are we?"

"Beneath the Kensington property. Montoya's at the gates with backup, waiting. I'll text him I found you."

His message back is instant. *Is she okay?*

Yes. I'm sending her out of the tunnels with Alex Gordon.

Montoya: *Tell her I'm coming.*

I relay his message and say to Alex, "Here, take my phone. I've turned off the lock, and it has all the numbers. Keep Montoya updated on your position."

"But you can't go in alone," Alex protests.

"I can help you, too," Sherilyn says but sways.

"I've got this. Go back two passages and head right," I say. "It will take you to a door into Bradford Kensington's master suite."

"You got it, LT," Alex says.

"Promise me you'll get them out," Sherilyn says.

I hug her. "Promise. Now, go."

Sherilyn leans on Alex for support, and I continue. A series of rooms with heavy prison cell doors is a short distance ahead. A man lies on the floor of one, unconscious and bloody.

Kudos, Sherilyn.

Going in, I retrieve keys from his still form and lock the door as I leave. Footsteps come toward me, and I plunge into an empty room.

Two Kensington minions troop past, then halt beside the door to Sherilyn's room.

The communication device in my ear crackles, and an urgent voice says, "We have an escaped prisoner, a blonde in her twenties, and one of our men is down. Red alert status."

The men unlock the door to enter, and I sneak in behind them. Lifting the rifle, I raise it with both hands above my right shoulder and bring it full force into one man's head. He goes down. The other turns, and I kick his legs out from underneath him and slam the butt stock into his face. After removing their keys, I slip back out, lock the door and continue.

Raucous laughter draws me to an entry, and I ease my head around the opening. An auditorium lies below me, and eight men sit at the front with Brant standing before them. One says, "I hope you let us test the merchandise before our final purchases."

"The price goes up, but if that's what you want, I'm fine with 'try before you buy," Brant says.

Sentries are positioned on opposite sides of a stage, hands on weapons. Bright spotlights shine on the auction's items: eight naked children in a line. Clasping hands at the center, eyes downcast, and faces streaked with tears are Evie and Emily.

———

The odds are bad—two armed men and eight unpredictable buyers with Brant.

My internal clock tells me it's been less than five minutes since I parted from Sherilyn and Alex. Will Montoya be able to enter the property without pushback? Will reinforcements be able to find me?

Backing out, I ponder the potential of an explosive diversion to cause instability in the tunnel. A room across from me contains a stack of tables, some empty barrels, and cleaning supplies.

Improvise and adapt, buy time.

Yanking the pin on a grenade, I toss it in.

Four seconds later, the door to the supply room blows. The guards leave their stage positions and rush up the stairs as I enter the auditorium and make for the kids.

The men in the audience are on their feet, necks swiveling. Brant makes placating gestures but catches sight of me, and comprehension dawns. He spins, shouting to one of the security who isn't yet out the door, "Shoot her!"

The guard's muzzle moves toward me, and I fire the carbine.

He falls.

I position myself before the children to shield them and center my weapon on Brant. The eight children on stage are a mix of boys and girls, eyes wide. The oldest is a teenager, and my sorrow at their plight is held at bay by the immediate situation.

"Don't any of you move," I warn.

"Lucky shot," Brant drawls, his lip curling like his father's had before his arrest at Henry Adams' home.

"Feel free to test me," I say.

"Alex Gordon—"

"Isn't my first trainer," I interrupt. "Would a newbie shooter pick a lightweight, practical rifle out of your arsenal? Most would pick up a Glock."

"Perhaps," Brant says. "Or you're bluffing."

"Like I said, feel free to test my marksmanship."

Three guards appear in a doorway, observe their fallen comrade, and draw their firearms.

"Have them put down their guns and leave," I say.

"Do it," Brant says, and they back away, but the chatter in my ear relays they're updating reinforcements.

I nudge the teenage girl beside me. Her frightened eyes peer up at me through a curtain of long, dark hair. "I know you're scared, but you need to take the other children, get off this stage, and wait nearby, okay? I don't want you caught in any potential cross-fire."

"I-I understand." She shepherds the others away.

Brant says. "Has dating Adair Monroe made you think you're important? People like you can't stop people like me."

"Funny, but your dad said something similar."

"My dad?"

"He gave you up; said you had Sherilyn."

"You're lying."

It's been ten minutes since Alex and Sherilyn left to find more help, so I keep the conversation going. "Am I?"

Brant hesitates, his eyes shifting to the side, then his nose wrinkles. "My dad's not sentimental, so you might be right. His brutality's surprised me a few times."

"And you auction kids off to, what's the new term, minor-attracted persons?" My gaze goes to the men beyond Brant. They're a variety of ages and appearances, all with a common core of evil. "I'll stick with pedophiles. Does Bradford get involved in this, too?"

"Dad prefers to destroy businesses and people who get in his way. I can't wait to see what he'll do to you."

"He's already threatened me. How did you get the twins?"

Brant makes a scoffing sound. "Their parents sold them to me."

"Why would they do that?"

"They're like anyone else, money and prestige are a priority in their lives, and I can offer them both. Those kids are adopted, like the rest. Christopher and Samantha have a talent for taking in aesthetically pleasing kids, putting them on their subscription channels, with special content of them bathing and other stuff on their private feeds for subscribers. A couple of my regulars saw them and wanted a more personal experience, so I facilitated the exchange."

Seething feelings surge through me, and my finger moves toward the trigger.

"I want to kill you," I say to Brant, and the coldness of my voice causes him to freeze. Chatter increases in my security earpiece, and there's the sharp sound of repeated gunfire. What was happening and where?

Brant regains some composure. "No wonder you ditched Adair for Alex Gordon. He lives more on the edge than Monroe ever will."

"Why do you hate Adair so much?"

"Adair was in the same circles as me. He realized my preference for underage girls when he saw me with them. Suddenly MI6 was up in my business for a second time. About five years before, they gave me problems, but we bought them off. Since Adair's babysitter's former MI6, it doesn't take a genius to make the connection. Of course, they had no proof and backed off. That, and another load of cash sent to the right people. You were smart to get away from him."

"Does this mean our relationship's over, Davia?"

Adair stands in the doorway.

———

Brant says, "Come to beg Davia to return to you, Monroe? You don't stand a chance against Alex Gordon."

"Then I wonder why Alex handed me this .45 and wished me luck?" Adair moves down the aisle to Brant's right and toward the stage. "You remain firmly in the 'scum of the earth' category, Brant, which is no surprise."

"Your self-righteousness got old eons ago," Brant responds.

"Where's Montoya?" I ask.

"Having trouble with security. Brant's people have no problem shooting at deputy sheriffs or tour attendees. Gun battles have broken out across the property, but a sniper keeps preventing a massacre."

The seated men begin to babble to each other at Adair's words, panicking anew.

"Adair, there's some scared kids off stage to my right, and you need to get them out of here. A couple of little ones will be happy to see you."

Adair inhales at my words, his attention moving to where the naked children huddle together in the wings. He hustles onto the stage and past me toward them.

As he does, footsteps come from the hall, and six men in dark suits stream into the auditorium.

All have their guns out and aimed at me.

Thirty-Eight

I point my muzzle square at Brant's chest, and he raises his hands. The guards stay in position at the top of the auditorium steps but don't lower their weapons.

"You're outnumbered," Brant says.

"What else is new? Have them put their weapons on the ground."

"Or what?" he taunts. "If you shoot me, your stalemate ends in a hail of gunfire."

"At least you and some of these stains on humanity will be dead."

A plump man in the front row leaps to his feet, shouting, "I didn't sign up for this!" He crashes into Brant in his haste to escape. The two men topple, and the guards' fingers move toward triggers as I pivot and run.

Brant yells, "Get her!" Bullets rip into the wooden floor of the stage. I spray suppressing fire, making Brant's shooters flinch and miss as I throw myself down and skid into the wings.

Getting up, I dash toward where I last saw Adair and the kids. A door opens into another tunnel, and Adair's distant voice says, "You're all brave, but we need to keep going. Davia's got our backs, okay?"

I hurry to catch them, checking behind me as I go. When I reach the group, blankets wrap some children, while others are in a mismatch of tops and jackets. The twins stop when they catch sight of me, but I say, "Evie, Emily, I'm happy to see you, but keep going."

Adair falls back beside me. "What happened to Brant?"

"I was too busy dodging bullets to check. We need to shelter somewhere until this battle plays out."

A figure appears before us, and I train my weapon before I realize it's José. He picks up a small child, saying, "I know the way out."

Adair lifts a twin in each arm. The dark-haired teen urges the others forward, and we continue our journey. I walk backward, weapon trained on our rear.

There's a whirring sound and a soft hiss.

A sleek, unassuming aluminum-cased module on the hall's wall transforms from a modern decoration to a mechanical sentinel poised to safeguard its surroundings. Down the hall, at regular intervals, more mechanisms trigger.

Billowing fog pours into the corridor.

———

"Fog blasters," I say as the hall becomes engulfed in an ever-thickening miasma. Within seconds, visibility is zero. "Everyone put a hand on the wall and hold the person beside you."

"I'm setting you down," Adair says to the twins. He clicks on the flashlight I gave him while I deploy another. The bright beams cast a light glow in a small bubble but reduce the fog's density by only a fraction.

"Is everyone in position?" I ask, and José reports he's at the front, and frightened voices affirm they've done as requested.

"I know this will be a challenge, but we need to keep going as fast as we can." I keep my shoulder against Adair. "Can you remember the way back, José?"

"It's not far, but there are twists and turns. This place is a labyrinth."

We inch along, the tendrils of fog expanding and surrounding us like the coils of ghostly serpents. The hall descends into an impenetrable veil of white nothingness.

"Stop," José's disembodied voice says. "I need a second to recall my course from the house to here because there's a door to my left. Let me think."

The muffled sound of distant, heavy footsteps echoes.

"Make a decision fast," I warn. "I think we have company."

"We'll go through here. Hang together," José says, and the line moves again. I grasp Adair's arm. "I'm staying. I'll find you."

In the stillness, his tension radiates. He covers my hand with his and says, "I'll be waiting."

———

Minutes tick past, and footsteps grow louder. Do they have infrared goggles? Making my way to the door, I step through. Reaching into my bag for the remaining grenade, I crouch. Will a detonation destabilize the tunnel and block my path? I cradle the compact metal device in my palm, weighing my options.

When the footsteps draw near, I pull the pin, the clang muted by the thick air. I launch the V40 into the mist, the tiny grenade an unseen specter.

A thunderous roar turns the once-silent tunnel into a storm of shock and fury. The confined space amplifies the blast, a shockwave rocking the hallway and shaking loose a shower of dust and debris in a violent crescendo. The intense heat clears away the fog. A wall and part of the roofline have collapsed, and three men lie prone. Two others stagger back, hands to their ears, disoriented. Lifting my rifle, I shoot them. My cartridge clicks empty, and I reload.

As I do, pounding footsteps run toward me. A figure looms, gun in hand. Twisting, I slam the rifle's butt into his knee. His gun drops, and I kick it away. Another man seizes my rifle and tosses it. I reach for the Luger, but he swings at my hand, knocking the gun down the corridor as I recognize the pair as Sherilyn's kidnappers.

Thug One and Thug Two.

Before the first man regains his footing, his ally lifts his gun.

A bullet tears past, grazing my neck.

A brief touch comes away with blood, but I can't waste time. Thug One rises, and I drive my shoulder into him, which makes him slam into his pal. Another round discharges, careening into the floor. Thug Two recovers and raises the gun again. In a move I practiced so often with Kyle, it's like breathing; I turn his wrist and flick the weapon away. As it spins past, I kick his groin, and he bends over. I deliver an elbow strike to his chin, his head snaps back, and he falls.

The other man crashes into me, his face a mask of predatory intensity. He puts a huge hand around my throat, but I thrust it away and rotate to smash my elbow into his face. While he's stunned, I run forward to retrieve Thug Two's gun from where it landed. Surprisingly, Thug One shakes off the pain and rushes to tackle me. We hit the floor with my fingertips inches from my goal.

Although blood spills from his nose, my opponent's twice my size. His face twists with concentration as he pounds repeated blows into my kidneys and drops his substantial weight onto me. Ignoring the pain, I tense my muscles and gather my power. In an explosion of movement, I arch my back with enough force to throw him off balance.

Rolling onto my side, I dodge another blow as we stand. We trade punches, grunting, swearing, and not giving an inch. A fist connects with the side of my head, and it takes everything to focus as the room begins to spin. Disoriented, I lose my balance. My assailant comes up with a knife and lunges forward.

Stepping aside, I grab his wrist as his momentum propels him. Slamming my hand into his shoulder, I force him flat onto his face with his knife arm extended straight out by his side. Placing my foot on his wrist, I recover the knife and shove it into Thug One's carotid.

Thug Two is up and lurching toward his dead buddy's gun. I use my remaining strength to pick up the other fallen weapon, lift my arm, and kill him.

THIRTY-NINE

I put my back against a wall, bent over in pain. The fog has dissipated enough to make the pathways clear. Carrying the dead man's gun, my recovered rifle, and the Luger, I go after the kids. After five minutes of forcing myself to lumber along, clutching my sides, I hear Adair say, "Do you think this is an exit?"

When I come into view, he rushes to me.

"Davia, what happened?"

Putting a hand to my temple, I say, "Took another blow to the head."

Adair tilts my face up, and his eyebrows draw together. "Your neck's bleeding."

"But how's my outfit?"

José says, "Found it," and activates another jib door.

"Do you need me to help you walk?" Adair says.

"Uh, took some punches to the kidneys, so that's not the best idea right now."

José and the children enter a cavernous wine cellar. Adair pauses inside the door, taking in the thousands of bottles. "José, how'd you get past the security for this room when you came to find us?"

"What security?"

"Now I feel like a complete spendthrift," Adair says.

"This will get us to the servants' quarters and a chef's kitchen. We can take shelter in one of the bedrooms," José says.

I say, "They have security cameras, and if they have men monitoring the house, they'll know your location immediately."

Shouts and gunfire continue to ring in my earpiece, but I keep my face neutral not to frighten the children any more than they already are. José places the child he carries on the floor, saying, "I'll check for any cameras. This uniform lets me blend, be right back."

Adair sets down the twins, but they cling to him, and I give them a reassuring smile.

José returns. "All clear, let's go."

"I'm going to help Montoya," I say.

"The stairs to the main floors are that way," José says.

"Wait." Adair hands me my phone, removes the .45 Alex gave him from his waistband, says, "I love you," and goes after the others. I allow myself to watch his broad-shouldered back until he disappears around a corner.

———

As I ascend the stairs, I unsling the rifle from around my neck and place it behind a decorative plant, then take out the Luger and the gun I took from the dead men. Deciding to keep them both, I situate one in the front of my waistband, the other in the back. I find myself near the room with refreshments. When I enter, thirty alarmed faces turn toward me.

"Davia, what's going on?" Beatrice Gibbs demands. "Why is all this gunfire happening? The police are shooting at the Kensingtons' security!"

"They are? I've been at the art museum at the rear of the property, so I wasn't aware."

A fashionable woman wrinkles her nose. "You look rather disheveled and dusty. And—are you bleeding?"

"My job as Ladies' League Vice President is important, so I've been cleaning areas the servants missed."

"It's impossible to find good help these days," the woman says, and some of the others chime their approval of this sentiment.

"I suggest you stay here and lock the door from the inside when I go. Stay low, maybe beneath these tables, and don't come out until you get clearance from the sheriffs, okay?"

The women stare at the carpeted floor like I've asked them to crawl through shattered glass. At last, they drop to their knees, lift corners of floor-length tablecloths, and go underneath.

"Beatrice, lock this, okay?" I say.

"Where are you going?"

"I have Ladies' League responsibilities."

———

On the patio, a deputy sheriff trades gunfire with a Kensington guard. Bullets have shattered the movie screen by the pool, and a man lies face down nearby. Taking out my phone, I text Montoya. *Kids are safe. Where are you?*

Montoya: *Back of property. Two pilots ran for helicopters.*

Be right there.

Slipping out the door, I keep near the building and away from the ongoing gun battle, hurrying to its corner. As I turn it, I come face-to-face with a guard. My hand moves for my gun as his finger moves toward the trigger.

The man's chest explodes, and he drops.

My phone vibrates with a text notification.

Warden: *You're welcome.*

I give a thumbs up to the unseen Kyle and Warden, then get in an abandoned golf cart and zip off. Montoya waves at me from the art museum's door, and I stop and join him. Alex and Sherilyn are inside.

Sherilyn says, "Did you save the children?"

"They're with Adair and José in the servant's quarters, but I couldn't stop Brant and his cronies."

"I think they're going to fly out of here," Alex says.

"We need to catch them," I say.

Alex looks at Montoya. "So, detective, how do you feel about arson?"

———

Montoya gives him an uncomprehending look. "What are you talking about?"

"This is where my investment knowledge comes in handy. While we waited, I looked around. The 'no expense spared' image the Kensington's gave when they built Hazelton is false as there isn't a sprinkler system in here. Maybe they thought their insurance was enough. I opened a back room marked private containing a store of priceless paintings."

"Your point is?" I'm impatient to stop the helicopters from leaving.

"I'm knowledgeable about the art scene and recognized much of what's back there is stolen, so uninsured," he says. "Want to make around $200 million go up in smoke?"

"Do you think a fire will cause Brant to go off track?" I say.

Alex shrugs. "Even if he doesn't bat an eye, I feel a burning desire to inflict some pain in that guy's life."

"You shouldn't be involved in this," I say to Montoya.

"But I carry a lighter." He removes one from a pants pocket.

"Ric—" Sherilyn's hand is on his arm.

"They kidnapped and hurt you," Montoya says. "My original idea was to kill Brant Kensington, so I won't mind damaging his bottom line."

"As long as you're sure, I'm good with this," Sherilyn says, "because I wanted to kill him, too."

"I need to stop their ability to leave," I say.

"I'll go with you." Montoya tosses his lighter to Alex. "Have fun."

FORTY

The thunderous sound of spinning rotors on two Sikorsky helicopters reaches us. With Montoya beside me, I'm confident his deputies won't view me as an enemy, so I take out the Luger. He sends me a curious look.

"Raided their armory."

The two copters sit beyond the three storage buildings that Bradford showed me on our golf cart tour. The men from the auditorium stream out of the main building's wing and make for the nearest bird. Two security guards hurry after them, one carrying an infant, the other dragging a toddler by his arm.

"I thought you rescued all of the kids," Montoya says, his tone sharp.

"It was a rabbit warren down there."

He barks into his radio for immediate backup.

Smoke begins to pour from the art museum. Sherilyn and Alex appear in its doorway, and Sherilyn fixes her attention on the ruffians with their tiny hostages. She strides after us as fast as her injured foot allows, with Alex right behind.

To slow the fleeing creeps, I fire rounds into the ground before them. The men spin and crouch in confusion, one squeezing his eyes shut, another clapping his hands to the sides of his head.

The goon carrying the baby hands the bundled infant to his partner, takes out his automatic and aims it at me. There's no clear shot without injuring one of the hostages, so I throw myself to the unforgiving ground, ignoring the searing pain that courses through my body from my recent injuries. Montoya drops to his knees, and we wait for incoming rounds.

The gunman's body jolts, blood sprays from his chest, and he falls.

Montoya's head swivels.

"Warden," I say, renewing my chase as the other guard makes for the helicopter.

Montoya runs beside me. "Where is he?"

"He's off property with a rifle. Kyle's spotting."

"Pays to have friends in high places."

We go past the outbuildings when the rear door of one opens, and Brant appears. Due to our position, Warden won't be able to help, so I point my gun at him and order, "Stop right there."

Another four-person security team in dark suits spills out and surrounds Brant.

"Backup's almost here," Montoya says as their bullets zip past us.

"We can't let those kids get away."

"I've called in air support, but they're on another matter and can't be here for at least an hour."

Brant's about to make for one of the helicopters when a man hurtles out of the building, wraps an arm around his throat, and puts a gun to his head.

It's Adair.

———

Brant's elbow connects with Adair's midsection, and he bends over as Brant slams a fist into his face. Adair's gun topples to the ground. The pair tumble back through the door into the building, and my attention splits between the fight and the hostages about to board the helicopter.

Montoya and I fire simultaneously, taking down Brant's guards. As they collapse, I race to where the line of perverts claw and fight to enter the helicopter. The hired gun with the children waits behind them, the toddler's face red from crying.

"Stay where you are," I command, gun pointed. "I mean it."

Sherilyn limps up and wrenches the baby from the man's arms. Alex picks up the boy, and they retreat toward Montoya. The detective focuses on where Adair and Brant are locked in a brutal fistfight. Brant's bleeding from his nose, and both men exchange relentless blows to each other's faces and upper bodies.

I secure the guard with his handcuffs, instructing him to sit. In the time it takes to bind him, the helicopter door shuts. Unable to access its interior, I shoot at the engine above the passenger cabin but can't acquire my target. The Lugar clicks empty. The pilot ascends and flies away.

The second helicopter's primary pilot waits for Brant; his head turned to watch the ongoing brawl. I reach for my other piece and make for the open stairs of the craft. Inside, I speed past the plush leather seats to the open cockpit door. Aiming at the pilots, I say, "Get out right now!"

They raise their hands, rush back through the cabin, and jump to the ground. The moment they're out, I close the door. Strapping in, I bring my mind to the task at hand. As I increase the rotor speed, the chopper lifts, and I maintain a steady but accelerated rate of climb. The other helicopter isn't far ahead, not yet at the edge of the Kensington property, its pace sedate. Pushing limits, I race after it, mirroring its movements.

"You're not getting away," I promise.

Climbing to a higher altitude, I speed above the helicopter and descend in front of it. My craft's blades create a powerful and chaotic force of air backwash, the current's disturbance an invisible menace.

The other Sikorsky begins to buck and sway. The pilots fight to regain control as the torrent twists the delicate equilibrium, and the once steady flight becomes a precarious dance. The helicopter's movements grow more erratic and unpredictable, its altitude fluctuating wildly.

The craft plummets.

Its skids impact the earth, the long tubes of metal twisting and bending. Next, the fuselage rotates onto its side and slams into the ground. The tail boom breaks apart, and the main rotors dig out chunks of earth, spraying dirt.

Got you.

While my attention's on the downed copter, the engine in my craft reacts to the intermingled air. After several sputters, the power cuts off.

I'm going to crash.

FORTY-ONE

I slam down the collective, feeling the bird drop beneath me as it glides in descent, the rotors whipping in the wind, maintaining RPMs. At the last second, I flare, pull up the collective, and let the inertia of the auto-rotated, spinning blades cushion my landing. The craft shudders to an abrupt stop, jolting me in my seat like a rollercoaster ride.

Shaking off the after-effects of the landing and the agony of my battered body, I open the door and sprint toward the crash site about fifty yards behind me. Montoya and a team of sheriff deputies approach from the opposite direction.

"Nice work," he says, then orders the uniforms to evacuate any survivors. In the distance, a fire truck sprays water on the art museum, and an ambulance drives toward us.

"What about Adair?"

"He took a beating but got the best of Brant Kensington. A uniform's with that POS, and more paramedics are helping assess people. You should get looked at, too. Your descent was violent."

"I'm fine."

As the ambulance nears, Adair hops out. He hurries to me, placing his hands on my upper arms. "I saw you crash. Are you all right?"

"The landing wasn't that rough." I touch his bruised cheek and take in his split, bloody lower lip, and swollen eye. "You, however, are an idiot."

"You called me the same after I stopped a gunman from shooting you. Why do you call me names when I help you?"

"The assassin cracked you in the head with his gun, and Brant hurt you. Adair, you're not—"

"Not what? Able to match your skills? Of course not, but I'm not useless either." He droops a little, and I kick myself for my harsh words.

"I'm jealous I didn't get to beat the crap out of Brant myself. You exceeded expectations when you helped me get those children to safety and ensured Brant didn't get away. "

Adair straightens and smiles. "Ouch." He touches his cut lip. "No matter these injuries, it was rather satisfying."

"What happened to the children?"

"José stayed with them in the house when I went to find you, saw Brant, and followed him." Adair takes my hand. "Two little girls think you're a superhero."

"I bet they think you are, too."

"I'm your knight in shining armor, remember? They expect that from me."

"I can't believe the Huntly-Harts sold those sweet kids. I wonder what will happen to the adopted children now."

"They'll likely go into the foster system, but I'll have Jason monitor their situation and ensure they get the right care, counseling, and place- ment with a loving family."

"When I saw all those kids on the stage, exposed—" My words trail off.

"Did you get in touch with some unexpected feelings?"

"Something like that."

Adair grows serious. "It took all my willpower to get everyone out of there rather than unloading all of my ammo into Brant and company."

"So you understand what I mean when I say, 'something like that.'"

"I do." He stops. "On a different subject, I feel a bit of a fool."

"Why?"

"When I took you by helicopter to my yacht last month, I wanted to impress you. I remember asking if you'd ever been in a helicopter and telling you not to be nervous."

"It was sweet."

"It's nice of you to say sweet instead of clueless. I'd kiss you, but I have a cut lip, and Warden has a sniper rifle."

I hug him hard, then step away before I ask him to make it up to me later. We don't break eye contact, and Adair finally says, "I'm going to check on the kids."

In the distance, José and Sherilyn have the rescued hostages at an ambulance. They stand firm before some uninjured Ladies' League members demanding treatment, holding them back until paramedics check the children.

I say, "José and Sherilyn have a core of tenacity sure to beat the over-privileged. I'll be there after I talk to Brant."

"Kick him anywhere I missed, okay?"

———

Brant Kensington's facial injuries are more significant than Adair's, which pleases me. He's in handcuffs, and a grim-faced deputy stays alert nearby.

"I should've listened to my dad," he says when I near.

"About what?"

"He found you troubling, couldn't pinpoint why. He has great instincts."

"Her nickname's Little Troublemaker," Alex says from where he sits on a stack of barrels near Brant. "Rather an understatement."

"You realize no one'll be able to convict me of anything," Brant says as if Alex hasn't spoken.

"Oh? You think?" I say. "Will you mention your connections, say you own everyone, and threaten me and my family's safety?"

"Yes," Brant says.

"Funny, your dad used the same playbook before we arrested him."

"My dad's been arrested?"

"Didn't he call you?"

He frowns. "No."

"Perhaps he doesn't approve of your life choices," I say. "Prefers to keep any potential entanglement with you separate."

Brant lapses into silence, and Alex stands, dusting off the back of his fitted jeans.

"I doubt you'll bother with a medical exam, LT, so where are you headed?"

"I want to find Emily and Evie."

"I'll tag along," Alex says. "Oh, Brant, there was a fire in your art museum. A back room, in particular, got destroyed."

Brant's mouth falls open. "What did you say?"

"Where there's smoke and all," Alex says. "I'm sure your insurance will handle your pedo property losses."

———

Adair and Kyle talk to Emily and Evie, who sit on a bench near a small garden just past the ambulances. When Alex and I approach, they squeal my name and hug me.

"We prayed you and your knight would save us," Evie says.

"I wish I would've found you sooner."

"That lady was so nice to us." Emily points at Sherilyn, who pushes one of the attendees back from where an EMT examines a child. "She was in a separate room but talked to us at night when she heard us crying. She reminded us to stay strong and said help was coming. Does she have a knight?"

"She does. He's a detective who helped catch the bad men today."

Evie's eyes get big, gaze moving past me. "Who's that? He looks like the boss of the knights."

Warden approaches, exuding self-assurance despite his limp. When he draws near, he says, "Fancy flying."

"Fancy shooting. Evie, Emily, this is James Warden."

The girls stare up at him, and Emily says, "Are you the leader of all the knights?"

Warden sends me an uncomprehending look.

"They thought Adair was my prince charming, but I said he's a knight."

"So, Adair's a knight, is he?" Warden kneels with care beside the twins. "Then you're right. I'm totally his boss."

———

I join Beatrice Gibbs and Francis Downs as the shaken attendees board the tour buses.

"Davia, do you know what happened?" Beatrice says.

"I'm not sure, but this event will be the talk of the town, don't you think?"

"This disaster had better not reflect poorly on the Ladies' League, or I'll tell everyone the whole was your fault, " Beatrice promises.

"I wouldn't expect anything less."

"Don't be so hard on her, Beatrice," Francis says, surprising me. "Her bruises and cuts tell you that she tried to make everything work."

Beatrice gives me a once-over. "I'll take that into account."

News helicopters swoop overhead. Fire trucks, paramedics, ambulances, and patrol cars depart while evidence teams and the medical examiner arrive. Kyle and Warden leave in my Maserati, and I retrieve the Rover and drive to where Adair waits.

"Ready to get a lecture from Jason?" I say.

He flips the visor down and studies his face. "Yeah, I'm in for it. At least I'm safe until he has his cast off, but then he'll probably strong-arm me into the trunk of a car and take me somewhere he can lock me away from you."

"Can you blame him?"

When we reach Adair's home, he says, "I would've kissed you back there if I didn't have this busted lip, Warden be damned."

"Do I need to mention you're an idiot again?"

"No, but remember, I'm your idiot."

Forty-Two

Two weeks pass, yet Rancho Suprema remains in turmoil.

"Do you think media outlets flip coins to see which story gets priority coverage?" Sherilyn says. "The Huntly-Harts sell their twins, Château Rouge closes due to their owners indulging in labor trafficking, or rich scions rape and pillage as facilitated by Hannah?"

"Or Brant Kensington and his pedo-buddies get exposed?" I say. "Or Rancho Suprema searches for a new chief for their private security force since Sterling's charged with Bob Brooks' murder?"

We sit near the pool with refreshments. Sherilyn's foot's in a boot, but the bruises on her face are almost gone.

"Ric told me Detective Rodríguez caught the Jenson's Jewelry burglars, who were entirely unrelated to the Bryce's Boutique break-in," Sherilyn says. "I think I need an Excel sheet to keep track of all of this."

"The best part is Beatrice Gibbs refuses to acknowledge my existence."

"Perhaps you can take a break and return to Colorado to finish your vacation with Warden."

"I told him I'm not at a place where I feel comfortable meeting his parents, and he has to return to work soon. We were both unfair to each other, and fixing the problems between us will take some time."

José enters through the side gate. "Thought Ana Sanchez was working today," he says, pouring himself a glass of tea.

"She called to say she's running late," I say. "She has to take Olivia to an appointment with a psychologist, and an immigration attorney's helping her apply for a U-Visa to get a work permit. Most of the undocumented workers from Château Rouge, or the ones the authorities located, are getting assistance."

Sherilyn rises. "It's been nice to have a break from work, but I have an appointment soon."

I stand and hug her. "Thanks for stopping by."

"Let me know how your date with Alex goes," she says.

"Will you stop labeling our trip to the Safari Park a date?"

"I love it when you're unable to hide your dismay," she says. "I must admit, after how Alex acted at Hazelton, he's growing on me."

———

Emily and Evie fight to stand still as green, blue, yellow, and orange feathered Lorikeets perch on their shoulders and arms, wanting some nectar the girls hold in paper cups. Alex came up with the idea to pick up the twins early from Stacey Templeton, their temporary guardian, to make the first round of feedings when the birds would be the most enthusiastic.

"More are incoming, so don't move," Alex warns.

Another bird swoops down to land atop Evie's curls, and she and Emily bubble with excitement but remain calm.

"Look, Uncle Alex. I've got five now!" Evie says.

Alex scrapes a hand through his hair. "That's, uh, great."

"Didn't picture kids in your future so soon?" I say.

"When I first proposed this, I didn't imagine us at the Safari Park with kids in tow," he admits. "Had a whole different scenario in mind."

"What? Did you plan to seduce me by letting me feed apples to the rhinos and carrots to the giraffes?"

He smirks. "You think I give up my secrets that easily? Besides, now I know the big guy's so accurate with a rifle, I'll wait until he kills your pretty boy and is carted off for murder before I try anything. I'm not stupid, you know."

———

The kitchen fills with the delicious odor of one of the casseroles Ana Sanchez left me to reheat for dinner. I have the house's sound system playing a mix of music from BTS to Dua Lipa.

As I pour myself a glass of wine, my phone vibrates on the counter. *Unknown caller.*

A low laugh greets me when I answer. "Enjoying a nice, relaxing evening, Ms. Glenn?"

"Didn't expect to hear from you, Bradford."

I scroll through all the security measures implemented since rescuing the children from Hazelton. Will a sniper test my bulletproof glass? I suspect that's not Bradford's style.

"Told you I wouldn't be charged."

"Thought boasting would be beneath you."

"The personal touch is best when making promises."

"By promises, I assume you mean threats."

"Promises are different than threats."

I don't reply, thinking Bradford shouldn't have warned me he was coming.

The silence stretches between us.

The line disconnects.

THE END

LAVISH AND LETHAL
By

Laura E. Akers

**Read on for the riveting first chapter of
Book Four in the Davia Glenn Series.
Releasing soon on Amazon and through booksellers worldwide**

CHAPTER ONE

"Leave it to you to find matching Shetlands," I say to Adair, who holds the leads to two golden ponies with fluffy, flaxen manes.

"Twin girls, twin ponies, right?" he says to Evie and Emily, who sit tall in their English saddles, their blonde, curly hair peeking out from beneath helmets.

The six-year-olds beam at him.

"Here you go, Davia." Adair hands me the lead to Evie's mount, and I wrap the rope around my saddle horn rather than look into his aquamarine eyes or, worse, at his lips.

Adair tied his Thoroughbred to the trailer he drove to our meeting place. When he goes to mount, I pull my gaze away from his lean physique, emphasized by fitted breeches tucked into knee-high English boots, and ask Evie, "Are you ready to get out on the trails?"

"Yes!" Her voice is high-pitched and excited. "Your knight's instructor gave us lessons."

Is Adair Monroe my knight in shining armor, or a curse?

"Adair told me you're both naturals, so he wanted to surprise you today."

"Ready?" Adair asks me, now on his horse holding Emily's lead.

We start forward on a wide path manicured with mulch. Forty miles

of trails is one of the many perks of living in Rancho Suprema, California. When I moved to this pricy zip code four months ago to fulfill an
inheritance requirement, I viewed everything as a negative, but now I
look for positives.

Split-rail fencing defines the outer trail border, beyond which multi-
colored flowers bloom. Adair and I ride next to each other, the girls on
either side. He grins at me. "I hope you're picturing our future where
you're my wife and these are our kids."

Opening my mouth to retort, I stop. Why ruin a beautiful day?
Instead, I say, "We've been together a long time if our kids are six. Or
perhaps we started a family right away?"

"I'm going to want you all to myself for quite some time, so we've
been married at least ten years."

"That also means my past hasn't caused more problems. Is Jason
happy for us?"

"He smiles at us at least once every two years."

"That often?"

"You're right. Once every five. He likes our kids, though. They bring
out the indulgent side he hid from MI6, and he sneaks them candy
despite our protests."

"This is quite the idyllic fantasy you've got going. Do you write
fiction?"

"Fiction? I play this as a movie in my mind every night before I go to
sleep, although I must admit the details are much more, uh," he lowers
his voice and leans closer. "Erotic."

Before I can respond, thundering hooves strike a resounding beat
behind us, and a man astride a brown Warmblood blows past. Our
horses spook, heads spinning, and the ponies nearly unseat the girls.

Face stormy, Adair steps off his mount. "Is everyone okay?"

I unwrap Evie's lead and toss it to him.

"Davia, what are you—"

"You know what. Back in a few."

I put Ace into a jog, then a gallop. Making a smooching sound to
encourage his pace, I scan the trail ahead and catch sight of a flowing tail
disappearing around a curve. Standing in my stirrups and bending over
Ace's neck, I allow him to fly across the ground at full speed.

When I round the corner, my horse draws level with the other rider, the outside of my leg bumping his. The man turns, eyes widening, as I seize his horse's reins. Ace plants his rear, causing the Warmblood to wheel around and stop, the abrupt movement pitching the rider off. He slams into the ground with ferocious impact, and a cloud of dust billows out to cover his once-pristine jodhpurs and polo shirt. The man staggers to his feet, face red with anger.

"What the hell are you doing?" He grips a scraped and bleeding arm.

"Thinking about how I should have brought a whip today."

"A what?"

"A crop? A switch? Anything to beat some sense into you."

The man bares his perfect teeth. "How dare you—"

"Stop you for a chat?" I pull my black ballcap lower. "Think of this as a public service announcement for those who ignore trail etiquette. When you sped past us back there, my group members might have wound up like you or worse. Two of them are only six years old."

"I, uh, I—"

"Want to tell me you're sorry and won't ever do anything like that again?"

The man remains unapologetic. "How am I supposed to remount without a block? My horse is too tall for me to put my foot in the stirrup."

"Should I care about this?"

"I doubt you do."

"I might have helped if you'd apologized. Enjoy your walk." I gather my reins, wheel Ace around, and ride away.

———

"Did you catch the bad man?" Evie asks when I retake her lead from Adair. The twins' posture is rigid, their faces tense, which makes me want to hunt down the miscreant again and do something much worse.

"Why don't we take this other branch of the trail?" Adair suggests. "I'm afraid if we run into whoever that maniac was, I'll wind up in another fistfight. Jason says I'm only allowed one every decade."

"Good idea."

We turn our horses down a trail leading into a more secluded area. Trees bound a wide dirt path and shade us. Some sunlight filters through the leaves, and a hawk circles high overhead.

"I think this loops around and takes us past a corral where we can leave the horses and get a snack at the Golf Club's outdoor shack. Would you like some ice cream?" Adair asks.

"You'll get us ice cream?" the girls chorus, and when he affirms he will, their delight is palpable. Adair uses this moment to hook his thumb into my belt loop, pull me close and give me a quick kiss on the cheek.

"What was that for?"

"Do I need a reason to kiss the woman I love, especially after she saved me the trouble of another black eye and busted lip?"

"I guess not." I smile at him.

The grove ends, and the trail continues across an open pasture surrounded by sloping hills. The June heat casts idle tranquility over us, with no breeze to stir the untended field of dried grass.

"Evie, Emily, are you up for a trot?" Adair asks.

"You mean a jog," I correct.

"That's western rider terminology and doesn't apply to us, does it, girls?"

"Typical snooty English attitude," I tease.

We cue the horses into a steady pace, with the twins and Adair posting in time to their mount's hoofbeats. Ace has a comfortable gait, so I relax in my saddle, lulled into a feeling of happiness.

A steady hum no louder than the slight wind created by our accelerated movement catches my ear, and I frown. Craning my neck, I scan the sky, squinting into the sun.

Without warning, a metallic speck drops out of the air, and I recognize the tiny object as a military-grade drone. Its intrusive murmur raises the hair on my neck. Why would someone deploy a drone out here?

"Adair, watch out," I call.

The sinister threat veers straight at us, buzzing past the horses like an enraged hornet. The ponies startle, whinnying in terror, as the girls pull back on their reins to keep them under control. The device's unseen pilot causes it to sail past the pony Evie's riding, and it bolts sideways, yanking its lead from Adair's hand. The little steed flees in a blind panic, and Evie shrieks in terror.

"I'll get her," Adair promises and rides after her.

I knot Emily's lead around my saddle horn, dismount, and lift her off her mount. Dropping my reins to the ground, Ace stands unmoving despite the pony whirling at his side.

"Come on." I seize Emily's hand. "Keep your head down." We sprint toward a nearby cluster of trees. After ensuring there are no rattlesnakes, I comb the horizon for the instigator of the attack but observe no one.

The drone circles Adair as he chases after Evie, then returns to swoop around Ace's head, its sinister whine almost a mocking laugh. As a testament to Ace's training, he pins his ears back but doesn't move. After a brief, unrelenting attack, the drone flits away.

"You need to stay here and don't move," I say to Emily, who trembles beside me. "Can you do that?"

She nods, eyes filled with unshed tears. I give her a reassuring squeeze and run for Ace, mount, unwrap the pony's lead and let it fall to the ground. The Shetland's head raises, and the freed animal dashes away.

I follow the disappearing drone off the path and across the untended field, watching for gopher holes. With a sudden burst of acceleration, the gadget zooms off, streaking through the sky and up a steep incline like an arrow released from a bow. Reaching the edge of the field and coming onto a winding road, I dig my heels into my horse's sides, urging him into a furious, heart-pounding run. We race upward, Ace's muscles taut and sweat dripping as we close the distance with our mechanical prey.

When we crest the hill, a distant figure holds a controller near the passenger side of a dark SUV. The operator spies me as the drone folds its propellers and lands in their outstretched hand. Heart sinking, I urge Ace to run harder and faster, but the SUV's passenger door slams shut, and the engine roars to life. Tires spin, and it accelerates away down a rutted dirt road, kicking up a storm of dust that fills my lungs and stings my eyes, adding to the bitter taste of defeat.

Pulling back on the reins, I ease Ace to a halt while the vehicle disappears into a swirling cloud of fine, gritty sand and the shimmering heat haze that rises above the road.

Was that attack intended for Adair or me? The kids?

Coughing, I wipe the dirt from my face and return to where Adair waits beside Evie and her frightened pony. I dismount and motion for Emily to join us, and we give the girls hugs and praise for their horsemanship and keeping cool heads.

"Did you catch them?" Adair asks while the twins retrieve the other pony, which crops some nearby grass.

"No. I can only say it was two people in a dark SUV. The drone operator was too far away for me to tell if it was a man or woman, and dirt obscured the license."

My unexpressed thoughts are a swirling storm of questions, riddled with frustration at not catching the perpetrators. If this is the start of a game or a threat to Adair and the twins, the next move will be mine, and I won't stop until the truth is laid bare.

About the Author

Laura Akers is a former prosecuting attorney who handled high-profile murder, rape, domestic violence, and gang trials.

She's a Clubhouse moderator for the Beta Reader/Writer's Critique Group and the Thriller/Crime Mystery Space, both rooms where writers discuss improving their craft.

Suicide prevention is a cause close to her heart since losing a close attorney friend. She's an ambassador for Mission 22, an organization working to prevent veteran suicide. She also supports Operation Underground Railroad and Veterans For Child Rescue who work against child trafficking.

She loves Korean dramas, photography, and spending time with her cats. Find her at https://www.LauraAkers.com

Acknowledgments

Thank you to all the supportive readers and fans of The Davia Glenn series. Without your reviews and social media posts, I wouldn't have achieved the level of success I have.

For advice on how Alex Gordon would advise Davia, I greatly appreciate the input of Timothy Canty, CPFA Vice President - Investments at Wedbush, a wealth management company.

And thanks to Warren B. and Craig D. for info on firearms and crashing helicopters, JB for advice on homicides & bad supervisors, & Deb V. for socialite info.

For writing input, I can't imagine finishing this novel without the friendship and critiques by Collings MacCrae, Peter Jolt, Anne Lucy-Shanley, and members of the Clubhouse Beta Readers/ Writers Critique Group. Also a shout-out to my amazing ARC team!

Special thanks to cover artist Cherie Foxley and audiobook narrator, Stacey Lind.

www.ingramcontent.com/pod-product-compliance
Lightning Source LLC
Chambersburg PA
CBHW071245300726
48975CB00002B/559